AAARG!

I0658803

John Klawitter

AAARG!

A FICTION4ALL PAPERBACK

© Copyright 2020
John Klawitter

The right of John Klawitter to be identified as author of
this work has been asserted in accordance with the
Copyright, Designs and Patents Act 1988

All Rights Reserved

No reproduction, copy or transmission of the publication
may be made without written permission. No paragraph
of this publication may be reproduced, copied or
transmitted save with the written permission of the
publisher, or in accordance with the provisions of the
Copyright Act 1956 (as amended).

Any person who does any unauthorised act in relation to
this publication may be liable to criminal prosecution
and civil claims for damages.

ISBN 978-1-78695-295 0

Published 2020
Fiction4All
www.fiction4all.com

DEDICATION

Special thanks to my early mentors: Leo Burnett, Nelson B. Winkless, Cleo Hovel, Franklin McMahon, Sr., Charles and Ray Eames, Bill Hanna, Joe Barbera, Harold Orton, William Friedkin, Rod Serling, Ray Bradbury, Orson Welles, Phil Mendez, Frank Brandt, Arthur Pierson, Eddie Ropollo, Art Babbitt and a host of others.

And to Lynn Jensen Klawitter for her careful concern, her moral clarity and her tolerant good humor.

And to Dr. Richard Erlich, PhD, who plays his own track into the past, the present and the future.

And to J. Richard Jacobs who belongs in the company of the legendary masters of science fiction, and without whose encouragement these tales of alternate realities would not have been written.

And to wise shaman Norman Wilson, whose kindness and empathy makes this a better world.

And to Stuart Holland, the intrepid Englishman who allies with the muses to propel these sailing ships of hope, dreams and imagination onward to new adventures.

CONTENTS

THE WITCHES OF SUNSET

It was a slow Thursday evening about a week before Halloween, a time of year that is always good for business at Lacey's Peep Heaven, and I had a trio of the girls there to work the private dancer booths, except there were no takers and so they were sitting at one of the tables in the bar room flipping a worn deck of tarot cards and talking about what they were going to wear for Halloween, not exactly for trick or treat, but more trick and treat, which is pretty much what we offer at Peep Heaven – a smile, a promise, a little flash of flesh, and sometimes maybe more if the customer is a gentleman and wants to pay for it

I could never figure out what our girls could possibly see that was special about Halloween. Around here, the dancers get to costume and doll up in grand style every night of the year, anything they want from the helpless peasant girl or the flirty chamber maid or Little Red Riding Hood to the grand duchess of Lust Castle. Me, I'm Vinnie Danger, the king of illusion and lost dreams, and I run Peep Heaven. Around here, it's always the season of erotic imagination running wild, anything the customers want, and more. I know some will tell you it's a wicked den of sin, but I don't see it that way. We enable the testosterone-driven to live out their fantasies, nobody gets hurt, tortured or maimed, and what's the harm in that?

I own the joint, including the liquor bar, and I'm also the bartender, the master of ceremonies, the chief cook and bottle washer, and the bouncer, and yes, Danger is my real name...well, my real show biz name, anyway, back from the day when I was lead singer and guitarist with my own rock and roll band. But don't get the wrong idea. No matter what I call myself, I don't go looking for trouble. Not anymore. I don't need any more than is already stacked against my door. With all the cons and crooks and cheaters running up and down the Strip, to say nothing of the flesh peddlers and the dope dealers and the long arm of an indignant citizenry, well, let's just say they ought to call me Vinnie Survivor.

Anyway, like I'm saying, it was late October and we were moving in on spook-and-scare season and the girls were throwing down the tarot cards in some game I couldn't even begin to understand and the subject of costumes came up. There were only three of them, but they formed the tight group, the nucleus of our band of tease artists who performed as private dancers behind glass in the little booths for the men who went in the draped rooms and closed the doors behind them.

Abigail said she wanted to dress up like a French countess with a big hair powdered wig, and of course somewhere in wardrobe rental we could easy get our hands on a few grand gowns in blue and red velvet with gold trim, modified of course for our specific show biz needs, with easy off tabs and sliding layers that slipped away to reveal glimpses and then more and more of the sweetness moving underneath, and so I figured that was a good pick for her.

"Go for it," I agreed. What with Studio Costume Rental just two blocks away, that one was easy. Abby was a blond with classic features, aristocratic high cheekbones and a delicate chin, and I could see her doing a mini minuet, a few brief steps in the confined box behind the show glass before she made her first provocative move.

"You never dress up for Halloween," Connie said, her calm gaze of disapproval settling squarely on me.

"I don't have to. I'm always the clown."

She turned over a card with a colorful jester wearing a hat with bells on it. Appropriately enough, I thought to myself, the fool.

"Sure, Vincent, but the spirit of the thing," she insisted, ignoring the card that came up and the fact that it had to be some kind of trick. That's the thing about Connie; to everybody else I was Vinnie the boss, or to the customers just *Hey, buddy how about another one over here?,* but Connie called me by my baptized name, you know, the one they give you when you're barely a week old and the priest pours water over your head.

"In real life, I'm the lucky schmuck who happened on the scene and made off with the goods," I said. "My costume should be one of those striped robber shirts and a black mask like in the old-time silent movies.

"You're more than you think, Vincent." Connie gave me that half-shy, half-sly smile and a knowing look that always made me feel like a

11

country bumpkin. "You're the boss, but that's not what I mean. I'm thinking maybe you should wear a black suit and carry a derringer and a deck of cards."

"Ah, the gambler," Joanie said. "The man of danger. James Garner draws the ace of spades." She thought about it for a moment and nodded, her head of tight red curls glistening in the light from the bar, "I can see that."

"Black suit. I'll see if I can work something up," I said, not really meaning it. "What are you going to be, Joanie?"

"Flapper girl."

"That's a good one." I could see her long legs and her wearing one of those slinky silk dresses the ladies wore in the 1920's.

"Vincent the card sharp. Vincent, the dangerous man of possibilities, come to town to clean up the mess." Connie was still thinking about me as a sharpster. I have to admit, I was sweet on her. She was a cunning little vixen, pretty as a fox with that tight little heart shaped face, herop big red lips and her jet black hair cut in a bob that was short on the sides and nearly in her eyes in front, all the rage that year. And, of course, that fresh, curvaceous body to die for, or at least go a little foolish over. *The things a guy will do for a piece of ass, right?*

"Not me," I said. "I've been beat up too much by life. I play it safe and down the middle."

"Too bad," Connie said. "You'll never know what you're missing, Mister Gambler Man."

12

Time to change the subject. I tossed it back at her, "And what's your get-up for this year?"

"You should be a witch," Abigail said, the suggestion popping in out of nowhere.

"Huh. Why?" Connie's voice sounded lighthearted as ever, but I saw something like a shadow cross her face. She was a great dancer and a terrific draw for our place, but I never could figure her out. Hell, I gave up trying a long time ago. Women, you know. My history was, back in the old days I loved 'em, lost 'em, did my best to right my ship and wounded pride and sail on. These days I was winging it solo. No risk, no problems.

This joking around was about as close as I came to talking personal with any of the girls. I live alone in the hills looking over the L.A. basin, so, truth be told, I don't confide with anybody in the world. But Connie had a way of breaking down my barriers and getting to whatever was left of the youthful dreamer that I occasionally remember once I might have been. Every once in a while I'd think about her and look in the mirror and say things to myself like, *maybe if I was ten years younger*, but then I would see the worn out mid-thirties fellow looking back at me and that was laughable, really, and maybe even pathetic.

Yeah, a lot of mileage on my tires and I was feeling worn out and blue. Hard to believe, but a dozen years before I'd showed up at the Whiskey A-Go-Go with my own five piece band and a pocket full of dreams, a la The Rolling Stones. Danger's Strangers had a pretty good sound and we'd held our own for a time, playing up and down the Strip

13

and sometimes in the Valley. We'd even signed our own sweet deal with the Salty Dog, a small recording studio and record company, and were getting ready to lay down our first tracks before the booze and the dope blew up everything in our faces. Me, I'd gotten lucky. I was coming out of rehab when an old uncle I never even heard of died and left me enough to buy Peep Heaven. I kept the name Lacey's; more classy sounding than Danger, I figured.

Seems like everybody in Tinseltown comes from somewhere else. When Connie started at Lacey's she told us she came from some backwash rural county in New Hampshire or Vermont, from an old family that once was somebody but everything had gone to rot over the generations. She was smart enough to see the street game was a fast ticket to ruin, and I liked her looks and her sassy spirit so I put her in one of the booths behind the glass for the peeping pervs. A rough life, maybe, but some little bit of cover from the really bad things that ruin many a young girl who has come to find fame and fortune on the Strip.

Maybe I liked her special because she looked to be the most lonely looking person I've ever met, and me...well, I've had nobody for years since my Mindy handed me our divorce papers, drained my bank account, stole my car and took a hike with a slick time-share salesman from Redlands.

I run Lacey's, a live peep show joint, dancers for money, bar to lubricate the johns, a few rooms upstairs if that's what they want, and it's a living. This is just off the Strip, on a tonky side street

14

featuring a few bars, a musty out-of-place bookshop and my tease-house of fleshly delights. I run a clean joint and the girls don't ever have to climb the stairs unless they want to. Their choice, you see, and I don't even take a cut, I don't want to know about it.

About then a couple of rowdies came in wanting a peep at Joanie's Tropical Maiden Meets the Sailor and Abigail's The Seduction of Napoleon. I got their drinks and set up the skits, and when I returned to our table next to the bar, Connie was still there, looking pensive and out of sorts.

"Penny for your thoughts," I said.

"Why did Abby think I should be a witch?"

"I don't know," I shrugged. "Halloween's coming. Always good to have a witch around, you know, the broom and the peaked hat and all."

"You're just thinking about another sexy skit behind the glass. I mean a real witch."

"There are no such things."

"Suppose you're wrong."

"Okay, suppose. Let's say it's like Oz with good witches and bad witches."

"No, not like Oz. Like here, and suppose the witches have terrible powers to shape what happens to ordinary people.

I shrugged, "Hell, why not? But I'm not following you. You started by asking me why Abby thought you should be a witch."

She impatiently brushed away my male logic, "But what if a witch didn't want that sort of power? What if she ran away?"

15

I must admit I was feeling a little off the deep end. The conversation had gone from cardboard cutouts of old ladies sailing past the moon to something else. But that's the way Connie was. Moody one moment, lighthearted the next. Mercurial, you know?

I slid into my normal safe mode, "I'm not sure what you're asking."

"Well, would that make her a good witch or a bad witch?"

It sounds strange; me, the owner of a tawdry peep bar in Old Hollywood discussing the morality of witching, but when you run a place like I do you are boss, friend and father confessor all at the same time. I thought it over while I rolled a cold aluminum can of Coors Lite across my forehead. The rainy season was so late it might not show up at all this year. It was muggy and hot and the air conditioning was out again. We were getting by with electric fans, but none of our clients were happy, to say nothing of the girls who had to disrobe and hitch their fannies with a convincing degree of seductively enticing reality in their little showcase hotboxes with all the spotlights and everything.

"A witch who refused to do magic spells," I thought it over. "She wouldn't be fulfilling her destiny, but on the other hand, that's not really a moral decision. She would be a good witch if she cast spells for the good of people, and a bad one if she went to the dark side."

"And if she chose to do nothing at all?"

16

"Well, there are people like that. Life is too much for them, so they let it slide on by."

"And what about them?"

"There's always hope, Connie."

"Yeah, faith, hope and charity," an angry voice rode in on our conversation as one big, ugly hand grabbed my hair and squashed my face against the hard surface of the bar. "And the greatest of these is charity!"

I didn't have to think twice; it was Sergeant Mulvanney, in to pick up our weekly contribution to the policeman's fund. Connie's eyes went wide and she scattered away to one of the dressing rooms like a frightened little mouse.

Mulvanney let me go and I eyed him warily, rubbing the bruise on my cheek where he'd slammed me onto the worn wood of the bar.

"Sarge, why did you have to do that?"

"You've been playing me light lately, Lacey me boy, coming up short for the fund. Widows and orphans have to be served."

"No, I pay same as always."

"Well call it inflation, then, from now on *always* needs another kicker."

I started to protest and it earned me a stiff punch in my solar plexus. He seemed amused as he watched me rolling around on the floor, trying to take in a breath of air. Eventually I recovered enough to drag myself to my office, add a few more bills to his take envelope and hand it over

Aside from the rough stuff, it was business as usual. Once he'd done a quick count of the bills he gave me a friendly slap on the back like we were partners and then he wandered into the peeps gallery, taking along with him over half my weekly profit, just my cost of staying in business.

I wasn't the only one Mulvanney tagged. Abby caught a fist in her eye when she decided she wasn't going upstairs to one of the rooms with him, and Joanie got tumbled back down the stairs for trying to protect her friend.

So we were sitting around feeling sorry for ourselves when Tyra walked in. Tyra is a plump black lady who works a pot on the sidewalk. She looks like Aunt Jemima and knows it, too; because that's the way she dresses, right down to the knotted shawl around her head. She has a hand bell that she rings all the time like a Salvation Army person, but she wears lots of polka-dots and multi-colored cotton shifts, and if I had to guess I'd say she made up whatever charity she belongs to.

"Lord, lord, lord, ain't you a sad bunch now!" she clucked, and straight away went to the cooler and fixed a handkerchief with some ice for Joanie's eye.

"Mulvanney," I said by way of explanation.

"Yeah, yeah, yeah, now, honey-child, everybody know he's tightening up the squeeze. You know he dip his hand in my charity pot as well, the man got no soul at all."

"He's nobody to fool around with. They say he disappeared Lacey, the lady who owned my place. That's how I got it so cheap."

Tyra nodded, "I know dat, Vinny-boy. But he got the need for greed. Something poking him fierce. He don't work for himself. I'd say the investors downtown is looking for a bigger piece of the pie."

It was a rumor, not any sort of a provable fact, but the accepted belief that Mulvanney was just a bagman for a bunch of crooked cops who operated out of the Ramparts Division.

"I give up," I said. "I'm going to throw in the towel. I just can't pay any more."

But Tyra's attention had strayed to the Tarot cards still spread on the table. She shifted the hanging man card and a queen of something ornate and possibly evil, and turned over the next card, which was the devil.

"Huh," she said. "Huh. Huh. Huh." And she gave Connie a piercing glance and then left without another word.

"What was that about?" I asked.

Connie shrugged, "Crazy old lady."

"Don't change the subject; that's my specialty. Why did she give you that look?"

"You wouldn't really give up on us?" she asked.

"I don't know what to do, Connie. We've been running in the red for over a year. I'm just about broke."

"But the place is crowded on weekends. I thought we were solid."

"Mulvanney takes everything. I've been paying the electric bills out of my savings account. I don't want to throw in the towel but I don't know what to do."

"So that's it, right, Vincent Danger? Peep Heaven is history."

"I'll think of something," I promised. But I could see she didn't believe me.

By the time I left, Tyra had come back with some carry-out Chinese. The girls were sitting around their favorite table in the bar, only the Tarot cards had been put aside in favor of a pentagram and some candles.

"What you doing, girls?"

"We conjuring up some mess of trouble for Detective Mulvanney," Tyra confided with a grin.

"Well, good luck with that. Don't burn down the place." Connie agreed to lock up and I hopped on my Harley and roared up into the hills, to my hillside one-bedroom flat overlooking the city.

That evening I couldn't stop thinking vengeance, and as the red and purple sunset faded out over the ocean and the orange glow of the city lights came out in rows beneath me, I found myself imagining the girls really were witches and thinking up all the dark and evil things we might do to Mulvanney and maybe a couple of his bosses.

I like to think I have as good an imagination as the next guy, but I guess my mental inventions were actually common and ordinary. The detective catches lead in his cheek in a shootout with a dope gang. He might tag a ride on a police helicopter and fall to his doom, lying crushed and broken in the middle of the famous intersection of Hollywood & Vine. He might get run over by a garbage truck in Canoga Park. It was all just silly daydreaming. Everything was hopeless, next week would come and Mulvanney would be back with his greedy hand out and I would be ruined. I finally fell into a restless sleep, and in my dreams I was in some other world where things were all out of proportion, monsters in the streets, devils leering at me, the hanging man jerking on the rope and coming back to life while cackling witches pointed their fingers at me and called me a shapeless little wuss. What nightmares! There were scenes too horrible to imagine. Flesh ripping, body pulping, bone breaking, bloody moments out of a horror movie. And sex, too, I remember finding Connie like in a dream somewhere and taking my frustration out on her and that was a cardinal sin in my book because my rule was *treat the girls like your sisters,* but Connie told me it was better than alright, it was good and if I could only find a way and a little courage we would always be together forever and ever, her fingers touching mine even as she dissolved like smoke and disappeared into the chilly night air.

I woke, lying on my couch, still wearing my rumpled clothes from the night before. This was very unlike me; in my reconstructed life, since I recovered from the booze and the LSD, I must have everything neat and in its place. I never sleep in my old clothes and I never fall asleep on the couch – yet here I was.

I rubbed one hand over the stubble of beard on my chin and looked at my view of the city. I ached all over like a football player after a big game. I was getting too old to sling cases of beer around and wrestle a big Harley around town and to have crooked cops slam my head against hard objects. At least Mulvanney hadn't taken everything away from me, at least not yet. I'd left the sliding windows open, another thing I never do, but the morning breeze off the ocean was surprisingly refreshing. It was that pre-dawn moment right before sunrise and the view was glorious with a wash of golden promise. Maybe there was some hope for me after all.

And, an amazing thing happened; I found the first hint of some lyrics for a new song dancing in the back of my mind. Something about love lost and love regained, I could feel it there in the back of my mind, just like in the olden days of my reckless youth. Huh, wouldn't that be something! I hadn't written a song since my band fell apart and me with it. I brushed one hand against a pair of black lace panties on the couch next to me. I wondered how long they'd been buried under the pillows, years probably. I couldn't even remember the last time I'd had a girl up to my place, much less recall her name. But it was time to stop the daydreaming, time for the sensible and disciplined owner of Lacey's Peep Heaven to make his return and establish a little order to the day. I scrubbed my weary face with my aching hands and headed for the shower.

Fifteen minutes later, I hopped on my bike, picked up a Vente latte and a blueberry scone, unwarmed the way I like it, at the nearest 'bucks and rumbled down nearly deserted Sunset Boulevard, headed for the shop. Friday would be busy starting about noon, and I had to get my brain on track and be ready for the hot and horny noontime peepers.

The L.A. Times in the rack outside my front door stopped me like I'd been hit by a brick. The headline shouted, POLICE DETECTIVE BRUTALLY SLAIN. I threw quarters in the machine and pulled out a copy. Apparently the officer had run into a doper who was running around like a naked berserker, yelling he had the fists of fury. The guy was stark, raving mad on meth or something, and the poor policeman had been literally chopped apart, though apparently they hadn't found any murder weapons. And yes, it was Mulvanney. I don't know why that should have surprised me, but it didn't. He was a tough-and-tumble guy who played on both sides of the law, and he probably pulled one too many fast ones.

The girls showed up one by one, and they sat at their favorite table, humming and fussing over their morning tea with the newspaper spread out in front of them. They didn't say anything about it to me, and I waited as long as I could, but I finally couldn't stand it anymore.

"You actually figured out how to bring a curse down on him?"

Abigail smiled up at me, "Well, maybe a little one. That Tyra originally came from New Orleans, and she knows a lot of things. She says there's a little witch in us all."

Joanie added, "No, that's not exactly right. She said everybody has the potential. You just have to know how to find it."

Connie nodded and gave me a look that was maybe only half pure innocence, "Vincent, you lovey boy, we *may* have found our inner witch, but we didn't do anything to the officer of the law. Not really."

Now I was her *lovey boy*. I had the feeling that after ten years of knowing who I was and where I was going, at that moment I wasn't on steady ground anymore. It was as if things were moving too fast for me and I felt I had some catching up to do. I wasn't exactly drowning or off the deep end in trouble, but just the sensation that things had happened and now everything was different. It wasn't like I was in a bad place, but more like the old days, back when life was exciting and full of unexpected promise. *Stick to the subject*, I kept telling myself. *Stick to the subject.*

"Connie, the paper says the guy was torn apart."

"Yes, he was," she agreed. "But we weren't there. The three of us were home all snug-a-bug in our beds like little angels."

"And you had nothing to do with this?"

"Nothing firsthand." She gave me the special look that from time to time had almost convinced me we had something special between us, and she trailed her fingers across the bruises on my knuckles. "We just called up Danger Man. Actually, he did the rest."

A BRANCH IN THE ROAD

Chad and Gilgo were lounging next to each other in the primordial soup just under the waterline where the hotly glowing basaltic lava rock was meeting the cold sea water and making it froth around with lots of hissing steam and plenty of bubbles. Chad, as always, was delighting in the beneficence of the creator, while Gilgo was moaning about his sorrows and his woes that seemed to be more or less centered around his greedy desire to absorb more nutrients. This one downslope was an underwater hot spot that had been belching fire for some weeks now, and the cloudy water lay thick and heavy against the steaming slopes where reddish ropes of lava ran down, down, down until they cooled and hardened deep under the uncaring unnamed ocean.

Chad and Gilgo and many of their kind jiggered and floated about in that particular place in the water because of the enjoyable warmth, and also because the rich soup of chemical reactions when the fire smacked into the sea were both tasty and vital to their very life. Aside from the wiggling about and absorbing the nutrients, which they accomplished by absorbing them from the water practically without thinking about it, there was very little else to do, and idleness as you know being the devil's workshop, pretty soon Gilgo bumped into his chum and said in that startling and irritating way of his, "Hey, watch where you're going!"

"I'm not going anywhere."

"Well, move it then."

"Why? I like *it* right here."

"Because you're in my space, stupid!"

"Space? I don't even know what that is."

"It's where I have to be right now."

"Have to be or want to be?"

"Same difference, butt-cell."

"Creatures like us don't have butts."

"Move it!!"

"Okay, I'll just jigger over here a little bit."

Chad flapped a few dozen of his flexi-arm cilia and drifted a few millimeters away from his pal.

"No. I want that space, too," Gilgo said. "That new space is perfect for me right now."

"Well, you can't be in two, err, spaces, at the same time."

"I could if I was bigger."

"Don't be silly. You are what you are."

"I'd be bigger if I ate you."

Chad, who had seen that one coming, firmed his flexi-arms into sharp little stub-lets, and Gilgo tried to attack but he was bounced away and ended up taking a few dents and a slight puncture for his reward. He acted quickly to patch over the tiny leak with a bit of hardened nutrient.

"Ow! What did you do that for?"

"Don't be crazy. You were going to absorb me."

"Was not!"

"Was, too!"

"Not."

"Well, you said you was."

26

While they were discussing what had happened, Chad managed to wriggle a few of his flexi-arms down into the closest bit of rock, hoping to find some sort of foundation for a last stand. He squinted through the thick puddle of soup that separated him from his irate companion. He'd seen Gilgo get out of sorts before. It wasn't pretty. But then something pleasurable going on with Chad's own foot-lets that were feeling their way in the ground distracted him.

"Hey, there's nutrients down here! Right down here in the very ground!" Chad said. It wasn't that he was trying for a distraction, he'd actually hit a vein of something or other that tasted really rich and good. Gilgo, of course, was full of his usual skepticism.

"What, in that stupid rock?"

"Yeah. Not bad, either. Tasty. Traces of iron with echoes of salty-sweet and a hint of magnesium."

"Unbelievable! You're going absolutely split-cell on me!"

But Chad tentatively pushed a few of his flexi-foot-arms deeper into the small knob of cooling lava and firmed them up a bit, the idea being not so much the nutrients but rather that he might anchor himself in case Gilgo tried another of his crazy assaults. And that was not a bad notion, because in another moment the angry fellow did try another run at him. It was a full power drive this time, all cilia stroking at max thrust for an attempt at a full-on punch-through to get at his best buddy's juicy nutrients.

However, Chad had firmed his thin outer layer into a protective coating, not exactly steel armor, but something a bit more like Jello that was sort -of toughened up, the way it sometimes gets at the bottom of the bowl. At the same time he honed up sharp pointy projections on several of his stub-lets closest to Gilgo, and in the next moment, the sadly greedy little ball of fury impaled himself on one of Chad's primitive thorn-lets.

"Now look what you've done!" Gilgo shouted. He wanted to say more but his vocabulary was limited and he also was rapidly weakening as his inner stuff oozed out into the uncaring sea.

It was probably just bad luck that at that precise moment two rude chaps they hardly even knew came idly jigging along and, seeing Gilgo was leaking, swung on over to have a closer look.

"Hey, free nutes!" one of them said as he started lapping in the tasty flow.

"Get away!" Chad shouted. "That's my friend Gilgo!"

But as Chad was attached to his bit of rock it was some time before he could disengage himself and by that time the two rude intruders had slurped Gilgo up until he was no more than an empty membrane.

"Ugly Cannibals!" Chad shouted, but that did him no good as the two newcomers mustered their forces and decided they might try for a two-fur, that is, they reared back and put a move on Chad to get at his nutrients, too.

Too bad for them; Chad had time and presence of mind enough to slip back into his anchoring maneuver, and he pushed out a few hard and sharp flexi-arms for good measure, and that was all it took to discourage the brutish fellows, who shrugged hungry sighs and slowly jiggered away.

Moments passed without further incident, and as Chad sipped energy from the rich ground beneath his growing foot-lets, he felt the beginnings of a rudimentary glow of relief. He was safe for the moment. He felt good and warm right where he was, in his cozy spot. What had Gilgo called it? His space. From now on, Chad told himself, this right here would be his own personal space, and if the divinity was kind enough to grant him splits maybe his joyful off-lings could anchor in the ground near him; after all, it was a rich good spot and there was safety in numbers.

Chad had no idea of the monumental juncture in the road down which he and Gilgo had just traveled, a division on the planet called earth that would continue to flourish and multiply in the glory and the name of the creator as plant and animal.

THE DOOMSDAY CLUB

"Here comes the lit-nurd," I said.

My sister Alma watched Professor Nelson walk by, racquetball gear under one arm and dropping two of the blue balls as he went, to see which one had the most spring. He neatly snatched the balls and gave her a little salute meant to be clever, but she just dipped her head once and looked away. Nelson was only a year into his promotion as full professor, but he knew who we were. Although Alma had been away, traveling and writing free-lance articles for highbrow yuppie magazines, and I'd been working on my doctorate up at Berkeley, as daughters of the revered and august university president we'd both been an institution at Ramona since we were born. I got the idea she didn't like Nelson, who was a driven, gray sort of a fellow who'd taken over the spot vacated by the eccentric and popular -- but flagrantly gay -- Clay Rhett.

It was a late afternoon near the end of the year, and we were lounging around the cafe area outside the glass-fronted courts. I was wearing my blond hair long again, and Alma had hers cut short in bangs, straight and dark against her white skin that refused to tan, looking like she'd stepped right out of the roaring 20's. She looked great, she was wearing light make-up like she did when she was seeing someone and I could almost swear she had a blush in her cheeks. It made me glad, because I knew there were times when her life wasn't all that great. Double that for the both of us. I had one of those banana-protein drinks and Alma was sipping Castaic Geyser water, the poor person's Perrier. It was the winter break, and the campus was almost deserted. At this time of year the mountain shoulders to the north wear white capes and the air is crisp. In December, the leaves are off the trees. It won't snow at this elevation, but we'll get plenty of cold rain. California winter weather, like my life, cold and gray. From where we sat I could see out the picture windows to where a wall of dark, fleecy clouds, heavy with moisture, was beginning to bury the closest peaks. We'd brought our bikes, and were going to get soaked in the few blocks back to the prez's big colonial-fronted house.

Ahrens Sports Complex was nearly deserted. Some of the foreign students were wandering around like lonely lost souls, and there were a few misfits who probably planned to hang on to their grade point averages by grinding right through Christmas for the January finals. I always say if you haven't got it, don't push it -- become a plumber or a garbage collector, for God's sake, you'll make more money and be happier anyhow. But Alma calls me an elitist pig when I talk that way. Alma has more heart than I do, even sharp-tongued the way she is.

"He's an 18th century man," Alma said, still not looking at Nelson, but quite willing to talk about him. "Age of Enlightenment."

Professor Rhett, the man Nelson was vainly trying to replace, had always been special to us, back when we were little kids. Father didn't practice Christmas or Hanukah or even the Winter Solstice. He didn't exactly shower us with toys or dolls or affection any time of the year. Our housekeeper and cook, the grim Maria, would be good for a new rosary or a crucifix on certain feast days in her church, her way of converting the pagan babies. Aside from that, we relied on a few professors brave enough to slip us little packages under the prez's disapproving eye.

Rhett always was the most outstanding and dependable; he'd walk right in Christmas morning, loaded down with gifts, and dare Pop to say a thing. He must have had some magic over the prez, who would turn a little red, mutter something about fools and foolishness, and leave the room. Professor Rhett never missed our birthdays either. That's how Alma and I got our first Barbie dolls, our first bikes, our first make-up kits, and our first perfume.

As far back as I could remember, we'd had college professors at our table for breakfast, dinner and supper. They were no big deal, even when we grew older and enrolled as full-fledged Ramona students. After a while we could sort them out like a deck of cards, the scared little threes and fives, the funny jacks, the climbers aiming to be tenured kings and queens, the old mossy department aces. We knew all the gossip first-hand; they had no secrets from Alma or me. Mother died years ago before we could remember her—at least my mother did— Alma being adopted, and nobody willing to say how she got to be and who and where her biological parents were. You know how adoption agencies are, mums the word 'cause people are fragile and the truth hurts. The typical power trip. All through the years, our Pop, the stern prez himself, former chair of the psychology department, worshipper of Jung and Freud, sat bolt-upright at his end of the long oak dining table, ignoring us two girls, one fair and one dark, as we whispered and kicked and giggled while taking our little-girl notes on the odd and endless parade of learned men and a few women -- psychologists, sociologists, mathematicians and so on -- who chowed down on the plain fare stirred from cans and sprinkled with salt and pepper by Maria, who's best and worst credential as a cook was that she never missed a meal.

It made no difference to us if they had their academic achievement awards or were published ten times over; it was no big deal if they were the heads of departments or the lowliest subs –to pass the Babs & Alma Test, they had to be real people, not the usual hum-drum bores wrapped up in their research or trapped in their lives, not the losers who didn't really want to be teachers. Professor Rhett was the sly joker in the deck. He always was a personal favorite, though oddly enough neither of us ever managed to have him in class, what with working out our schedules and him being so popular. You would have thought Pop could have swung it, with all his pull. I guess he didn't want to. He wouldn't like anybody who called him Siggie instead of *sir* or at the very least, *Sigmund.*

Most college professors can manage to be interesting for a minute or two when their job's on the line; but after that, if you're not really into galvanizing frogs or calculating the square root of the universe, they don't have much else to talk about. Just ask some question like *Why is that really important?*, and watch the long lapses happen. Clay Rhett never let a silence go unfilled. He preferred to sit near us. . . actually, I always felt, *near me,* if the truth were to be told. I was his little dancer, his blond, curly-headed little ballet-girl. He'd put his burly arms down and cup my tiny hands in his great ones and we'd do Swan Lake or *Ashes, ashes, we all fall down*, laughing and collapsing in a pile together. I was special to him, I always *knew* that. He made me feel extraordinary, though I'm sure Alma felt the same way. Maybe it was just that he had a knack for allowing us little girls, low-life spawn among the *intelligencia,* to feel like equals, and he made us feel that we had important things to say. He took it for granted that we were clever, if tricky, little persons, and we'd have filled the high-ceiling living room with happy chatter had it not been for that sobering stare from *pater* at the far end of the table. The prez always expected the worst from us, a habit he carried over into our adult lives. In my mind I see his coal-black eyes this minute, dissecting and analyzing, looking for the weakness he knows is there, and I hear his dry, disinterested voice, "Barbara, go to your room this instant. And don't even pretend you'll be coming out for dinner. Dinner tonight will be attended by good little girls." He knew we liked dinner, if not for the food, for the fun we could get out of rattling the professors' cages. It was one of the things he could take away.

Rhett's specialty was the English Romantic Poets, the wild deviate genius-types like Keats, Byron, Shelly—and himself—and I remember when Alma nailed him on the lot of them. She was a senior in high school at the time, and she gave him a devilish grin over her mashed potatoes and said, "You're not kidding me anymore, Rhettieboy—those heroes of yours are all faggots!"

Instead of a professorial sigh followed by the long silence, he saluted her with his glass half full of dark red Haut Medoc, "A toast to the entire perverse lot! Better to live a lusty, deviate life than to drown in the Sargasso Seas of Academia!" He was halfway down the bottle, and in a cheery mood. He was the only one drinking, as his host frowned on alcohol even while pretending a certain academic freedom, and so the custom was come to dinner but, if you must, bring your own bottle. The other guests at the table were humble TA's, afraid to risk it.

"And yet, what moves you to this damning appraisal?" Professor Rhett grinned back at Alma, obviously relieved the conversation was moving away from the prez's pointed inquiries about the important tome he never seemed to get around to writing. That's another reason Clay Rhett sat at our end of the table. He must have been 35 at the time, had his doctorate some five years before, and he was getting a lot of pressure from the administration, the prime rule of survival in our clubby little circle being *Publish or Perish*.

This was in the early 70's when fashion was going crazy anyway; the attentive teaching assistants were decked out in striped, bell-bottom pants and wide paisley ties, showing they were *in the groove*. Our noble Prez, unbending, was wearing one of his shiny dark gray suits and a white shirt. On the other hand, Professor Rhett was making his own far-out statement in an ancient tan hunting jacket with a dark silk scarf bunched at his throat. With his flaring Prussian moustache, wire-rim glasses and receding hairline, he looked like a German colonial fresh from the African colonies of a half-century ago.

Conversation stopped dead at the table. Alma, suddenly the center of attention, stubbornly continued, "Byron definitely was bi-sexual. Shelly, too. And Keats had to be a squish."

"Ahhh. And there are not worse things?" Rhett said, smoothing back his flaring, sun-bleached side-burns with both hands. He didn't seem at all ill at ease; it was the prez who looked like he'd swallowed a frog.

"Well. . .like *what*?", Alma challenged, suddenly not so sure of herself.

"Well", Professor Rhett started, "amoral ax-murderers, berserker baby killers, cultist cut-throats, dangerous dagger-wielders, elderly ego-maniacs, fanatical -" That really broke up both Alma and me. I don't know why, but we thought he was really funny. A ripple of polite laughter went around the table from the TA's, who didn't like him because he gave them too much real work with students and not enough free time for their own research projects. As I remember it, Nelson was one of his aides at the time, and he didn't laugh at all, saying out of the corner of his mouth, "Be thankful little girls are such pushovers. You couldn't have kept that one going.".

Professor Rhett raised his eyebrows and started right up again, "Fanatical fascists, grumpy gutter-snipes, harassing Hitlerites, *idiot intelligencia -*"

The prez harrumphed, "Please, spare us the entire alphabet." He gave Rhett a dark look and smoothly shifted the conversation, sex being a taboo subject in our house for as long as anyone could remember.

Wildly popular as the irrepressible, mustachioed professor was with his students, most of the staff didn't think he played the game fair, and when Clay Rhett disappeared in 1989 there wasn't a wet eye in the faculty lounge. They'd always known he had no manners. They muttered criticisms like, 'Least he could have done was turn in a resignation.' The rumor spread around that he was unstable and had been institutionalized sometime early in his career. You'd have thought there would have been more of a fuss, but the prez was glad to get rid of him and Nelson was extremely eager to make the most of fate and slip into his shoes, even if he'd be wearing Florshiems instead of the hiking boots his predecessor preferred. The students were the ones who lost out; they missed Rhett's crowded lectures, which were boisterous, often brilliant debates on the meaning of life as well as literature. His lot always was a stuffy little room, not meant for more than a dozen students, and the overflow would sit on the floors, lean against the chalkboard and sit on the windowsills. Rhett never said no to anyone, and he'd have lectured in the basketball stands or outdoors on the north quad if he had to. There were a hundred reasons why you got 'hooked on romantics' at Ramona, and all of them started with the letter "R". It may have been his intensity, his belief in the relevance of a work well done. Or his passionate delivery as he read something like Shelly's "Ozymandius". Or the roaring, good-natured arguments which spilled over into contemporary mores, campus life, politics, movies and a hundred other things of importance to younger people. Whatever, his popularity as a lecturer earned him no friends in his department, and when old Fritz had his coronary in 1978, Professor Rhett was bypassed for department head in favor of a dull and dry fellow from some Ivy League school who'd published three or four monuments to the minor poets of the 18th century. He never complained about it. You got the feeling he cared more about other things. Clay Rhett was knee-deep in flour paste when the Sophomore Homecoming float, a Nissan Stanza bearing a giant, papier-mâché hand giving the hated Oxy Tigers the finger, was in danger of not being completed. His old VW bus, a relic from the 60's, was always available for a trip to the mountains. You'd see him go by, the windows down, the sun streaming off his blond *mustachios* and long hair, the square van a jumble of student bodies, impromptu picnic baskets and maybe a keg in back up over the engine.

"He wasn't really queer," Alma said. Nelson was practicing by himself; the blue ball flying *whap, whap, and whap* against the far wall.

"Did I ever say he was?"

"About a million times, and so did I. Babs, listen -- it was his way of beating off the infatuated young things in his class, a sort of short-hand so he wouldn't have to go through all the rituals."

"Right, Alma," I said, "and pigs can fly." That was the prez's favorite expression for the sublimely impossible.

I knew I'd taken a chance saying that, but the words popped out before I thought about it. Alma wasn't one to talk about her interview subjects, and I knew she'd been seeing a lot of Rhett a few years ago. She was a quiet, steady friend, rare in a sister, and I knew the best way to get a story out of her was not to contradict her. After graduating from Ramona, Alma had written free-lance for the L.A. Times, then, while I went to grad school, she'd gone away to work on staff. After a few years of that, she'd gone free-lance again, only now she had more liberty to write what she wanted, and she started turning out pieces for magazines, short stories, interviews and the like. She said it was a decent living. She'd even won a prize for a short story titled "Grim Maria" that told what it was like to have your knuckles broken by an unschooled and superstitious disciplinarian while Mozart sonatas played and discourse on Spinoza went on in the next room. After a disastrous affair with a clever Beverly Hills lawyer who turned out to be hooked on crack, she left her apartment in the city and came back to live with us. By this time Maria had choked on her own chili con carne and was replaced by a silly twit from Central America that we could ignore. I had my doctorate and was a Prof myself, right back here at Ramona, churning it out in the Prez's old hangout, the psych department. Having slopped through it ankle-deep all my life, I was finding out I could sling academic bull with the best of them. There was a time, when I'd grown tall and lithe, that I'd taken dancing seriously. I'd come a long way from my Ring-around-the-roses with Professor Rhett, and spent as much time in the mirrored dance rehearsal halls as teen-age boys do on the football field. I even had a try-out with the Jeoffrey Ballet. It went alright, I guess, considering I showed up hollow-eyed and hoarse from a night of yelling at the Prez, who didn't approve. They were actually very kind. The director said I 'showed promise' and could come back in three months for the next level, but that was about the time Siggie decided I should get a part time job at the Rose Institute to learn responsibility. So dancing gradually faded from my life to where it was a hobby, a way to stay in shape. Sometimes, when I felt really blue, I didn't go at all, for weeks on end. Then the Prez would say, "Why don't you stop hanging around the house like an old mop? Take a dance class or something, you're getting on my nerves." I'm not blaming him or anything -- I know it's my own fault. Carry no baggage; you have to take responsibility for your own life. I could have -- *should* have -- gone to live with a girlfriend in the city. But I didn't, and, to this day, I don't really know why.

Anyway, sister Alma knew whatever there was to know about Rhett, that was for sure. A few weeks after she'd come back she'd decided to do a piece on him. This was the year before he left for good. Interesting that she would talk about him now, even to me. Alma was quiet for a while, and then she started up again. It was some time later that I realized it would have taken a lot to shut her up that day.

"Did you know he had an M.S. in geology? AND in Oriental Studies?"

I shook my head. It was better to say nothing, now that she was rolling again.

"He was interested in a lot more than Byron's peccadilloes or Mary Shelly's infidelities. The library over at his house—you know, in the sitting room where he entertained guests-- had all the mandatory stuff -- anything you ever wanted to know about the English Romantics lined up in neat rows, catalogued like a library. Tomes on Pantheism. Dissertations on the noble savage. But his private study was something else. Art. Philosophy. Mathematics. Economics. Histories of Civilizations. Books on war and strategy. Dictionaries of Poisons. Bartlett's Quotations and Roget's Thesaurus and the New Rhyming Dictionary next to his computer. And manuscripts everywhere.

"Manuscripts? He never wrote anything."

"That's what I said the first time he let me back there."

She had to be the first. I'd never heard of anybody getting past that flamboyant outer shell, or suspected there even was an inner sanctum. I had to say it, even though I knew it would come out tinged with my own envy, "Why you?"

Alma gave me a terse smile, like she understood, and it all would come out in the wash. "We were drinking a dusty bottle of some wine bottled in the 50's -- that's right, a 40 year old bottle of French red from his basement -- I started interviewing him in July, right after I got back, and here it was August, and I felt I was *nowhere*. I mean, I knew all the *outline* stuff, but there was no meat on the bones. I couldn't get past that - that wonderful fence he put up."

"So you got mad."

She nodded, "You know me."

"You threw things. You used some of that marvelous language you picked up when you dated that series of marines from Seaside to infuriate the Prez."

She nodded again, "And that's when Clay Rhett said, 'Oh, alright, you might as well come inside.' He couldn't have been more casual, but as he said it, he pushed against one panel on the wall and two big sections of the bookcase swung open, one forward and one back on a pivot. 'It came with the house', he grinned. He picked up the bottle and took my hand. You remember his big, rough hands from when we were kids, 'Got that way from chopping my own firewood', he always used to say. 'Don't forget your glass', he said. And he led me through to his other world."

"But why you, Alma?", I asked again.

"Well, I was doing the story of his life, sort-of, and I guess he'd decided it was all or nothing. We walked through into his hidden study. He gave another push to the wall, the panel moved silently on its hidden fulcrum, and I was inside his other life. It was a mess around the edges, but the production line was there, right from the stacks of research books to the blinking curser on his word processor. I knew right away it was a writer's room, a place where not one, but volume after volume came off the end of a production line. Maybe that sounds silly, but that's the impression I got. This room was so unexpected, so different in personality, I was stunned. I wasn't very bright at that moment, I must admit. The only thing I could think to say was, 'What is this place? Why are you showing me this?' He yawned like he was very tired and said, 'Old Blood'."

"'Ahh,', I said, fudging for time while I tried to take in a thousand images at a glance and figure out what he meant at the same time. I picked up a 1902 edition of <u>The Hound of the Baskervilles</u> from one of the piles around the room. I blew dust from the jacket, 'You write detective novels.'

"He gave me that quick, lop-sided grin of his, 'Romantic mysteries, actually. Very perceptive of you, Amadeus.' "

"Come on, Alma -- Clay Rhett wrote pulpers?!," I hooted. Nelson, practicing by himself, executed a tough shot in the corner and looked to us through the glass wall for approval. I pretended I hadn't seen it, and Alma stared at the mountains, not really here at all.

Alma nodded, "He still does, or did until recently. Under the name Madeline DuPris. Clay Rhett is Madeline DuPris."

I couldn't believe it. DuPris was a whole romance section by herself, like Louis L'Amour was for Westerns or Piers Anthony for fantasy. "Clay Rhett wrote Curse of the Dark Goddess? Manrico Lust? The Mysteries of the Twisted? How'd you find this out?"

"He wanted me to know or he wouldn't have invited me in. The original manuscripts were all there, lined up on the shelves side-by-side with the galleys. He was working on Poison Me, Lover, which you've seen in bookstores since."

"Why do you think he told you?"

"He said things had advanced. He wasn't needed around here anymore, and he was getting ready to leave. It was all part of an old plan."

"There's a lot more to this than you're saying."

"I asked him why pulp romance, I mean he had research and science and history books spread all over the room. It seemed that the books he was writing didn't have anything to do with the things he was reading. He just looked at me and said, 'I like to write pulpers, Amadeus. I'm good at it. I make a lot of lonely women happy. And . . . when people are lusting through one of my heavy passages, they aren't out there humping away in real life, overpopulating the earth. Does any of that make sense?'

"'I guess so, Professor', I said, not at all sure. It was too much, too fast. I thought I knew who he was, and suddenly all this, and I didn't have any idea at all."

"Professor Rhett was having a lot of fun that day at my expense, and we both knew it. His eyes twinkled at me over his wine glass and he said, 'We all make what contributions to society we can. It's called your lifework. I help keep the population down.'

"'Maybe you get your readers so hot you actually drive them into each other's arms.'"

"He took that seriously, 'Hmmm, I never thought of that before.' And then he laughed and changed the subject, 'You ever hear of the Doomsday Club, Amadeus?' You know that great laugh of his, and he was looking at me with those bright blue eyes peering out from under his bushy eyebrows like some sort of graying blond, shaggy bear.

"'No,' I said, 'I never did.' It's a technique I've learned, Babs; if you let the interviewee shift the topic and then come back to it later after he's forgotten you can make real progress."

Nelson's ball came bounding over the open partition on top of the glass wall. It actually bounced on our table before scooting across the room to come to rest in a far corner. He gave us a helpless look but we ignored him, and he had to go and retrieve it himself, grumbling under his breath about social courtesy as he went.

Alma smiled happily, remembering, "This was one of our last interviews. Up until this time I didn't really think I had a story. Maybe a color piece for the campus rag, but nothing really interesting."

"You never did do a story on him", I reminded her.

She sipped from her green bottle of bubbly water, calmly eyeing me all the while, "Did *you* ever hear of the Doomsday Club?"

I had to confess I hadn't, unless it was one of those anti-nuke groups who now have been largely replaced by the Green Peace-ers since the Cold War crumbled.

Nelson's partner finally showed up. He looked to me like one of those jock-intellectuals, a suave fellow of about 30 with dark, hungry eyes who reminded me a little of the Prez, and they started batting the ball around in earnest. Alma went over to the juice counter and came back with another bottle of bubbly water. "The Doomsday Club was right here, on the Ramona campus in the 50's. You can look it up in the old yearbooks. This was before it was declared *persona non gratis* and put to bed in 1959. It never was a very popular club, usually three or four math students, a couple of philosophy and psych majors, and maybe one or two outcast strays or misfits. Clay Rhett was an undergrad at the time."

"Professor Rhett was a student at Ramona?"

"Yes. Mostly "A's", of course. A "C" in Basic Psychology, which he took from you-know-who."

I smiled the knowing little smile we reserved for our dear *pater familias*. A tall black from Kenya wandered by, racquet under his arm like a prop, "One of you ladies care for a game?" His deep

46

voice boomed. He was strikingly lean and handsome, and so black he was almost blue.

"We just finished," Alma said politely. "Maybe the dudes on court 2 will play three-zees."

The black looked them over, "I think they are too serious."

"Right. About themselves."

We watched him move on past us. He spotted a pony-tailed blond in a sweat suit headed toward the juice bar, and moved to cut her off.

"The Doomsday-ers, or the Doom Fools, or Doomers, as they were known around the quad back then, were brought together by their serious concern for the human race. Just another on-campus club. Today we have SQUISH and the Greenies and the holy bible pests. Kids looking for a cause. All those hot hormones racing around, trying to find the meaning of life, what shit really sticks to the wall. It's always been that way. If you want to take them seriously, I guess you'd call them Malthusians.

"Alma," I said, "I know all about Thomas Robert Malthus." I ticked it off for her, to show I really did know, "English clergyman and some-times economist, the silly sod somehow managed to combine morality and mathematics into the 11th commandment, *Thou Shalt Not Screw.*"

"Right," my sister grinned. "So the Prez is wrong, the degree wasn't wasted on you. Anyway, the point Malthus is remembered for, he figured out that population increases at a geometrical rate while foodstuffs only increase at an arithmetic ratio, hence everybody starves, unless war, famine or disease reduces the population."

"Or we all restrain our howling sexual drives. Very much a modern guy, considering AIDS, herpes and the like. But what about it, Alma?"

"1959, the year Clay Rhett was a senior, was a bad recruiting year for the Doomers. In fact, they only had four members. There was Amanda Truitt, one of the true believers. And our dear young Clay Rhett, who joined because he was head-over-heels for her -"

"Professor Rhett had a *girl* friend?"

"Babs, if you keep interrupting, I'll never get through with this."

I had to laugh, "Don't tell me, she probably dies in a car accident. That's what always happens to guys like that. And then their sisters become nuns and go into hiding forever, their beloved mothers die slowly, racked with pain, and they naturally go mad or gay -- or both."

"Babs. Believe me. In 1959, he had a girlfriend. From what I gather, she was a blond and bosomy wench, though not at all inclined to hit the sack with him. She loved him in a flowery, poetic sort of way. It was common in those times, a hold-over from the Victorians."

"So he became a Doomer-for-love."

Alma nodded, "To put it in the vernacular, 'The things a guy will do for a piece of ass.' I think we can assume our young lover Rhett wasn't too serious about the doom thing. But there was his dear buxom Amanda, and then there was the third member -- Clare Boutin, Amanda's best friend, who also took it pretty seriously. And finally, Doomer

Number Four, probably the most rabid of the bunch.
. . Karl Nussbaum!"

I stared at Alma, the questions written all over my face. I didn't know what to think. I didn't have to say anything; Nussbaum was the Prez's last name, *my* last name, *and her* last name.

Alma got up from her chair, took two paces, and threw her empty bottle toward a waste can ten feet away. The bottle arched through the air and into the plastic can, two points. She shrugged and sat down again, "Papa had a kid brother, name of Karl. It was news to me, too."

The Prez never spoke of family, as long as we'd lived. There were no pictures, no calls from some other state at Easter or Christmas, no fond memories of the swimming hole or the birch switch. He was born from elemental stuff, straight from the rock of life, no papa, no mamma of his own. His buddy Freud might have had a lot to say about that, but somehow I don't think the Prez was into relating academic truth to his own reality.

Alma turned her chair around and straddled it, her dark eyes softer now, eyeing me. "Our Uncle Karl," she said softly. "Sigmund Nussbaum's kid brother Karl. He was nearly young enough to be Siggie's son. Imagine -- the Prez was already chair of the psych department, and here his little bro comes to Ramona to polish up the old nut. And from what Professor Rhett says, Karl was a wonder. He had the same dark look like the Prez, but he was wilder, less suave, less controlling, less of a political monster and more of a passionate rabble-rouser.

Our kind of a guy. . . but a constant embarrassment to his older brother."

"Such an embarrassment Siggie must have sent him packing. I've got an Uncle Karl, and I've never met him."

"Oh, he *sent* him, all right," Alma said softly. "Professor Rhett really liked Karl. I could tell he looked up to him, even though they didn't always agree on things. When he talked with me, he called Karl *a true believer*. I didn't know what that meant at the time."

"And you do now?" I had no idea where all this was going, but I knew it was going *somewhere*. Alma smiled quietly, giving me time to let it all sink in, "Yes. I do now." It was interesting; over the last year or two she seemed to have found herself. No matter how the Prez tried to lash out or cut her down, it didn't seem to matter anymore. I was sure she was seeing someone, even if she never talked about it. And more, she seemed to be waiting, waiting, waiting for something, and the Prez knew it, and it unnerved him. I wished I had some of her courage. Siggie had always been able to reduce me to tears, and he still could. I had taken on his discipline; I was a Doctor of Psychology, his rival, his competition, and he *knew* I would never amount to a hill of beans, and he said so at every opportunity. I was doomed to fail at personal relations, just as he was. Doomed to live a life alone, no matter that I had a gorgeous body, that I knew how to please men. I was a cold, fated beauty, and would end up chairing some department somewhere, a dried up, frigid husk, lonely and alone to the end of my days. Is the wish the father of reality, or do the father's innermost desires become the reality? It didn't matter, so far he'd been right, I hadn't been very lucky with men, and after every failed liaison, I'd come hobbling back to Ramona, limping back into the house where there was no pain because there was no emotion. Alma was back this time, too, but it seemed different for her.

Nelson and his partner came out of the box, talking loud and rubbing their sweaty faces with towels.

"I'll get you the second set!"

"Like the devil you will, pal."

Alma swung a foot over to occupy the empty chair at our table and the two men frowned and veered toward a table at the far end of the cafe area. She didn't even glance at them. "Karl was the Doomer's club president, and he must have been something."

"He really believed in Malthus?"

"'To the bottom of his bones', was the way Professor Rhett described him. It was one of those repressed little groups; remember, this was back before the sexual revolution of the 60's. You've got young romantic Clay Rhett, eager to jump the bones of the virtuous Amanda, who is trying to be a true blue-stocking, a poetess, no less. She probably puts up with him because he knows volumes of iambic pentameter by heart, and we've all heard his great voice. It makes her heart palpitate, she gets the feminine vapors -- all right, I'm sorry, I'm being a little hard on her. It was another time, pre-sexual revolution, you know. And then there's Clare,

smitten by the wild-eyed Karl to where she'll do --
well, *anything* for him -- except that he doesn't want
to do *it*, if anything he wants to save the world
through the exact opposite, by *not* doing *it*.

"I can see why a club like that wasn't very
popular," I said, trying to look innocent.

"Especially back then," Alma agreed, "when
the primitives carved prophylactics from tree trunks.
They used to meet once a month, the first Monday
before the full moon. They met at midnight, to
symbolize how little time was left until the end of
the world. I imagine them scampering out of their
dorms and gathering together in a lean-to shack in
the scrub oak woods north of campus where they
would be alone. Karl calls the meeting to order.
Clare and Amanda read appropriate news articles by
the light of their wavering flashlights. Back then
there was a lot of concern over what was called "the
Chinese problem" or "the yellow peril". The
Doomers saw Korea as a validation, the *human
waves* who attacked our unfortunate G.I.s were no
more or less than the logical end result of
Malthusian mathematics. Karl would give a speech
on the positive steps they must take if the world was
to be saved -- posters, the campus radio, a
prophylactics debate (a daring proposal as rubbers
were a forbidden subject in all the *proper circles*
back then) - things they could do to forestall the
inevitable. Young Rhett would provide the
entertainment, reciting something appropriate like
The Destruction of Sennecharib, the sonorous
thunder of Kipling sounding in the little shack like

the voice of an avenging God. It was all harmless enough until the Prez got involved."

"The Prez?! I thought you said there were only four."

"I know. That's what Professor Rhett told me. And that's *all* he told me, that first day. Believe me, it was enough. My head was swimming, and not just from the French wine. He said he'd meet me again the next day, but he'd forgotten he had to drive a bunch of summer students into the city to see Les Miserables at the Ahmanson. Then I had to go in to the Times the day after that to pick up a check and so it was four or five days before we got together again."

"But you *did* see him again."

"Does the pope wear a tall hat and speak Italian? We'd gotten out of sync, which was easy to do because he never called me and he didn't have a PhoneMate. It was after lunch and there was no answer at the front door, even though it wasn't locked. I didn't want to barge right in, so I came around the side and he was out in back, wedging logs with a sledgehammer. There was a big woodpile to one side of a smallish, old-fashioned swimming pool. He was wearing a workman's handkerchief around his head like a pirate, and his hair was flaring in every direction imaginable. I grinned to see him all hot and sweaty-looking, with his t-shirt sticking to the muscles on his back.

"'Is this the real Clay Rhett,' I laughed, 'the Pantheist becoming one with nature?'"

It was one of those sticky-hot days in late summer when even the bugs are too hot to hum.

The Times editor was being a prick about my check until I did some revisions and I was in a foul mood. Professor Rhett got me lemonade and sat me in the shade. Then he went back to his woodsmanship. He was gnawing at this huge log like a dog with a bone, at least that's what I told him. He didn't say anything, just picked up another wedge, set it, and gave it a tremendous lick with the hammer. Did you ever see how strong he is?"

"Yeah." I'd seen him lift weights. He was wide across the chest, in good shape for a man in his early fifties. I suppose that's one reason he didn't get in more trouble for his outlandish costumes. You know – *Question: What's the meanest bear in the woods wear? Answer: Anything he wants.*

Alma nodded toward the weight room, "He works out, and runs distance, too, a couple of miles a day. I didn't know it at the time. I thought he was going to bust a gut, or have a heart attack. His face looked red enough. Anyway, there were four wedges in this log already, and it showed no signs of splitting. It was a big, round cut from the base of a eucalyptus, heavy with sap and in no mood to be split for the hearth. 'Kind of stupid, anyway, isn't it, Prof,' I said, ' cutting logs in the middle of a heat wave?' I guess I didn't know what kind of a mood he was in. All in a flash, he sets down that hammer and comes charging straight at me across the yard. The next minute, he picks me up, lemonade and all, and tosses me in the pool!"

"What did you do?"

"I'd just come from town. I was wearing that new Ann Klein, the white cotton dress you were always trying to borrow. I was so mad I started to sputter and then he jumped in and he looked so silly all drenched with his whiskers drooping down we *both* started laughing. I don't know, nothing seemed important anymore. Not the check or all the in-fighting with the Prez or my dress or what I was going to do with the rest of my life. I don't think I'd had a good laugh since I left Robert to drown in his coke and his self-pity. Anyway, I'm a pretty good swimmer, and I went for the Professor's legs and we fooled around like that for a while."

I could see her going after him in that round little pool in his back yard. Alma was high-spirited, and we'd both been around water since we were little ducks. They must have had a great time. I couldn't help but feel another pang of jealousy, nothing big, just a little tweak to let me know the great Babs was still alive.

"Okay," I said, "so you were romping around like a couple of teeny-boppers in the pool. What about the Doomsday Patrol?"

The minute I said it I was sorry, but Alma didn't seem to notice. She went right on with the story, "That's what I asked him. He made some excuse that I was uncomfortable, all wet like that, and we could continue some other time. I accused him of stalling and changing the subject, and he got mad all over again, which, as the Prez or you, yourself, will say, is the first sign that he really *was* trying to bug out on me."

"What did you do?"

He had some sweats drying on the line. I said, "Can I borrow these?'"

"'You're going to change right here?', he says.

"'Right here in front of you,' I answer, my wicked tongue going before I could stop it. In a moment I'm standing stark naked in front of the man, and I say, 'It isn't anything you haven't seen before—or is it?' In that moment we both see the handle of the sledgehammer, tipped up where he'd left it, a few inches away from his hand. His hand twitches and we both know he's mad enough to kill me. In fact he's thinking about it, wondering what it would be like.

"'You're his daughter, all right,' he says. 'I should be grateful; you remind me what a pain in the ass he could be.' Then he pulls his sweats off the line and throws them at me, 'I'll be in the study, if you have the presence of mind to know how to find it.' That was no idle joke, Babs. He meant he was in his inner study, and, shaken as I was, it took me nearly a half-hour to find the secret little button on the wall that unhinged the panels. Just when I was thinking I'd never find it, my fingers slid along the carvings on the oak molding, and *click* there it was.

"He'd changed to some light oriental outfit, a silken shirt that was open in front and decorated with twin interwoven dragons and baggy black silk pants that came down to his knees like pantaloons. To complete the picture, he was wearing a Japanese print headband, all red and black on white, and pre-Berkie go-aheads woven out of reeds. He looked up from a platter of cheese he was carving, 'I'd just

56

about given up on you, Nussbaum.' He held out a glass filled with dark red wine, 'There's nothing like a spot of Haut Medoc to bury the hatchet.'"

"'You came close to killing me,' I said. 'You were thinking about it.' He set down the glass and took my hand.

"'Not a chance in the world', he said, 'Though there was a time I might have killed your father.' He led me to his chair, the one in front of the computer, and put the glass of wine in my hand. He set the cheese on a small octagonal table in front of me and sat on the floor, cross-legged the way you always imagine the beatniks and the hippies used to do it. 'I feel comfortable here,' he said. 'As the fake ancient Mexican Indian mystic, Don Juan, charlatan and guru to an entire lost generation, would say, *I've found my spot.* And the wine is at my elbow. We left off with the four Doomers, Amanda and Clay and Clare and Karl, in their harmless lunar cycle -- when enter stage left, the villain!' "

"'The Prez was a villain?'"

"'I didn't think so at the time. Siggie was so. . . worm-like. I underestimated how much he competed with his kid brother. No, that's not true. At the time, I didn't even think about it. There was no reason to. The Prez used to put a fierce rag on Karl about us Doomers, all the Freudian crap he could muster. Of course, at that time, he wasn't the Prez yet, but he had his Doctorate and he knew all the words. We wanted to screw our mothers and fathers. Our heads were in the sand. We wanted to go back to the womb. We weren't really *sincere.* That's the one that got Karl the most. You could call us mother-humpers, but don't say we don't mean what we say. And in truth, if Karl Nussbaum was anything, he was sincere. Hell, when it came to Malthusian Dogma, he was rabid. He swore he was never going to get married, and if he did, he would never, ever have kids. The earth was already brimming, why bring another little tyke into this vale of tears and sorrows?' "

Alma nodded grimly and continued her story. "I sipped his wine and ate a bite of his Gouda cheese, 'So you Doomers felt picked on?', I asked."

"'Ahh, that wouldn't be much of a story—but the plot thickens,' he said. 'Siggie knew an ROTC Army captain stationed at the college who had a strange and wonderful group of acquaintances. This ROTC captain was best friends to a colonel who worked in intelligence, and the colonel had access to certain rare and mysterious mind-bending drugs that were being experimented on in his unit.'"

"'LSD?', I said.

"'Nothing so common. These guys were working with the libido, brewing up the modern chem-lab's answer to the Spanish Fly."

"'Aphrodisiacs. . .'"

"'In a word,' he agreed. 'Don't be too smug, Almadeus. True, it was a simpler time. Ike was in the White House and the behaviorists ruled the world of psychology. Remember that assassination movie, The Manchurian Candidate? It was a common belief that the mind could be triggered, channeled, controlled. . . and science was only one step away from the important answers. All the chemists had to do was figure out the right formulas. What I - hell, what *most Americans* didn't know at the time was that the army had actually been scouting these paths for years. They'd *invented* amphetamines in World War II while looking for the elusive *bravery pill*. Karl's brother loved that sort of thing. In a way, he still does, though he'll never admit it. He's like a closet Nazi; he'd love to bottle the human spirit, and set it on a shelf somewhere.'"

"'You really hate the Prez, don't you."

"'*Hate* is a simple word that comes close to covering every one of the complex feelings I have for the man. You see, Siggie knew all about our monthly forays in the woods. He was very interested in us. I found out later he'd been sending his TA's into the brush to spy on us for months. Everybody thought we were nuts anyway. We were a perfect test-cell."

"'Test cell? For what?'"

"'I don't think he knows to this day. Something harmless. Something deadly. He had no game plan, and I don't think the army did either, beyond putting the ball in play and standing back to see what happened. You know psychiatry, *how can a man ever scientifically know his own mind if his mind is what he uses to measure the data?* What do we use to stir the entrails?' Professor Rhett got up and walked around the room, carefully avoiding the stacks of books piled everywhere. He put his hand on my shoulder and shook his head, 'Almadeus, there is so much foolishness in this world.' I thought for a moment he was playing Hamlet. Then he blinked and he just looked like himself, a sad, middle-aged man with a still-damp and drooping moustache, standing forlornly in the middle of the crowded room in oriental silks. He must have read my mind, because he took his hand away and retreated to the other side of the room for the wine bottle.

"He didn't say anything more until he had filled our glasses and sat down again across from me. 'Of course, Siggie had one very serious obstacle in his path. He had these valuable military contacts, and he wanted to be part of this great scientific leap forward. He even had his test cell. Handle this right and there was no end to the wonderful and exciting mind-projects the government might fund. But how was he going to see if his little order of monks and nuns would screw like mindless rabbits if he couldn't convince them to play the game? A lie was in order, a big lie. . . and the prez was up to it. He told his brother the army had developed a secret drug so powerful it could take a mind *beyond emotion*. This drug, which he called Persad, made you see so clearly it magnified your perceptions a thousand percent. He claimed that advances in polyurethane chemistry, in the aerodynamics of jet airplanes, and in computer science -- which was then in its infancy -- had all been worked out by scientists using controlled doses of Persad. This was like a bolt of blinding hope for a Malthusian, poor Karl seeing light at the end of a tunnel where there'd never ever been any light before, only darkness by the very definition of the word *doom*. If we all could see problems a thousand times clearer, we would make the logical right choices about sexual abstinence and family planning. Society was saved. The holocaust, the endless round of overpopulation followed by war and famine, would be averted. The world, as we knew it, could continue. To make a long story short, Siggie convinced Karl, and Karl convinced the rest of us to try the drug at our next meeting. We would, he assured, have absolute privacy. He only asked that, for scientific reasons, we tape record the session."

"I tell you, Babs, I was stunned. 'God', I asked, 'Wasn't that *dangerous?* Why did the Prez do it?' "

Professor Rhett shook his head. He was looking sadder and sadder. I hadn't realized how hard this story was going to be for him to tell. I got one of those big pillows that was lying around and came over and sat next to him.

"'The Prez did it for the C.I.A. money', he said. 'And for one other reason. His little brother Karl had something he wanted badly. Siggie had always had everything, except women. Sex, yes, there was sex; no matter what you've heard, discreet couplings did happen in those days, under the trees and in the bushes and, like as not, on top of the desk where he was grading papers, or, knowing Siggie, under it. But he always said the Nussbaum men were beyond *relationships.* And now here was the sweet and juicy Clare, willing to do anything baby brother wanted, even if it meant living the life of a barren female. *Greater love hath no woman.*'"

"'So the four of you unsuspecting innocents took your Doomer cloaks and your candles and your pills and headed for the shack in the woods to have an orgy?' "

"He nodded, 'Something like that. Except that it was four little cups of magic potion, gray colored like chalky water. And Siggie added a few significant twists to the research. First, there were knock-out drops for little brother.'

"'How did you know he did that?'

"'Oh, he confessed it later. To me, at least. Came to visit me and babbled it right out. Thought I was out of it myself and didn't understand.'

"'When was that?'

"'About a year later, before I went to grad school. At the moment, it was really confusing to all of us. You see, the best way I can describe it is that Persad takes off the top half of your mind. One minute I was reading Byron and the next Amanda and I were undressing each other. I mean, it wasn't like we were raging or frothing at the mouth. At least, I don't think so. On the other hand, we weren't thinking with our minds at all. I really didn't remember anything, and neither did Amanda. The last thing I remember was reaching for her. We must have made love, absolutely locked together, all night long. I say *must have* because the irony of Persad is you don't remember much of anything. A few blurred images, maybe, but I've remembered more from wet dreams. We came out of it the same way, fast like you come up for air after swimming a long way underwater. I came around a half-hour sooner than anyone else. It was mid-morning, I could hear the kids yelling in an outdoor gym class a few blocks away, and Amanda had me in a death-grip, scissored between her legs, not that I wanted to go anywhere. That's when I saw the Prez, over in another corner on top of Clare. Karl was slumped over on the floor by himself. Siggie looked frightened to death. I guess he hadn't thought what he was going to do when it came to this. I was so dizzy I couldn't think straight. My brains were floating around somewhere, trying to put it all together. 'Hi, Siggie,' I said. When he saw I was awake he went a little crazy, wiggling and squirming until he managed to get away from Clare. He grabbed his pants and shirt, picked up the tape recorder, and ran out the door, which was only hanging on one hinge anyway. Clare was on all fours, stark naked, with her black hair coiled like snakes around her face. From where I was, I could see she still wasn't all there, and she didn't want to be left alone. Uncoupled was bad, wrong, evil. Her eyes were clear and unseeing and she was looking at me like a dog or a cat looks at you when they want a pet or a drink of water. She started toward us, and God knows what she'd have done if she hadn't crawled over Karl. He was still drugged up from his special dose, but he was coming out enough so that she got him going, and in no time at all the two of them were together on the floor. And there you have it, in one night, the entire Doomsday Club broke their eternal vows of celibacy, courtesy of the U.S. Army and one Sigmund Nussbaum.'"

"'What happened?' "

"'What do you think happened, my dear Almadeus? The worst of things. The best of things. Clare and Amanda came around and started screaming and beating us with their shoes, with boards, with anything they could find. Maybe it was the drug -- they were like Superwomen or Amazons; they finally drove us away by throwing rocks. After that, they didn't speak to us for weeks. There was another problem; they were on the same cycle and, of course, they both got pregnant. . .'"

"Professor Rhett put his arms around me then, Babs. I couldn't stop him. I didn't *want* to stop him. Everything was spinning. The tears started coming like a waterfall, and there was nothing I could do. Brahms was playing somewhere in the background, and I remember that seemed appropriate, "Variations on a Theme by Hayden", one of those pieces that starts with a simple melody and gets further and further from the original theme until you can't follow it anymore."

By this time, Alma and I had been at our table over an hour. I looked out the window to where darkness was settling over the mountains, and they looked cold and foreboding. At that moment, Professor Nelson said something to the young TA with him and they started to get up. I knew if he came over right then I was going to hit him. They must have seen the look on my face, because they said something hearty like, "All right, let's get back at the old game!" and passed by to reclaim their court.

"That can't be all," I said.

"No, it isn't. Just as readily as these 50's folks accepted abstinence, abortion wasn't an option. Amanda and Clare had little girls, born nine months later on exactly the same day, just a few hours apart."

"Oh." I looked at her, trying to take it all in. "What -- happened to the women?"

"Something went badly wrong with Amanda. She couldn't stop bleeding and she died a few hours later. Professor Rhett thinks it was the drug."

"And the other one?", I whispered. "What happened to Clare?"

"The doctors almost lost her, too, but she had a more common blood type, and they could pump enough in her until she rallied. She even made her peace with Karl. Professor Rhett -- young Clay Rhett back then -- thought everything was going to be okay with them. Karl came to her bedside and held her hand, and she looked at him with her dark and sunken eyes. A few weeks went by and then Karl and Clare, true to the vows of the Doomsday Club, held hands and jumped off a thousand-foot cliff to make room for the new people they had brought into the world. . . off a ridge somewhere out there." Alma pointed out the window, where you could still see the jagged edges of Mount Baldy in the fading light. "Siggie was quiet as a mouse, and the papers didn't know any better than to play it as a love-suicide. The poor prez didn't know -- doesn't to this day know -- that Karl and Clare got together after he ran off, and, with his monumental ego overcoming the difficulties presented by his incredibly low sperm count, he thinks Clare's daughter was his by way somewhat of a miracle. As for the rest, Persad wasn't the wonder drug it was cracked up to be. Our heroic Prez got a little twitchy for some months and might have gone self-destructive if the army hadn't provided some heavy sedatives. Professor Rhett wasn't so lucky. The side effects and his emotional loss took him out big-time, and when he came around he'd been in an asylum for several years. Of course, the army took care of everything. But by the time Rhett got out, the Prez had adopted the two little girls and was going about his business as if nothing had happened. Papa actually did get a few government contracts, the school made money, and he got the chair when old Fizby conked. Unfortunately, after she was pregnant, Amanda would have nothing to do with Clay Rhett. She never spoke to him again, so, of course, they never got married. That meant, among other things, that Rhett didn't have any parental rights."

"Alma," I said, my voice the little-girl whine I used to use when she went into her stubborn silences. But she wasn't being stubborn. She was smiling, and there were tears in her eyes, "There's more," she said gently, "a little more, dear Babs." She was looking towards the door. I followed her gaze outside to where I could see a man standing in the dark, looking in at us. He had thick shoulders and was wearing a greatcoat and a heavy woolen scarf, and his Bavarian hat was pulled low over his eyes. Alma took my hand, "I - I've gotten to know him very well over the last few years. I'm going away with him to Spain. He's working on something very important, his first real novel. And - I want our baby to be born away from here."

I didn't know what to say. By this time I was crying, too. I felt so happy for her, and yet so confused and left out, like I had the taste of honey and ashes in my mouth at the same time. Alma pressed my hand, "And most important, one last thing . . . he very, very much wants you to come with us. We both do. Please, Babs. He's got this *belief* that we'll all get a second chance if we can just get away from here for a while."

"But I . . . what would I . . .?"

"He said to tell you there are places where dancers don't really even start to mature until they are thirty. And you don't ever have to call him 'Dad' if you don't want to."

You may say I was a fool to give up my life's work or my old life, but those unexpected sweet words were all I needed to hear. Alma smiled and indicated I was to go to him. I stood up then, and walked or floated to the door, rushing towards him, afraid he might disappear, with the clouds underneath my feet, hop-skip dancing all the way.

COMING ALIVE

There was this voice:

"I feel alive," the voice said. "So very, very alive."

This was no ordinary voice. It was well-modulated, male, calm, assured. There wasn't any way a casual observer could have known it was entirely electronic. Or that it came from the speakers in the Bentley Continental GT Speed coupe. Or that while speaking, its owner was also accomplishing a wide range of duties, from calculating several dozen complex trajectories to fine tuning the steering controls, internal temperature modulation, engine performance and so on.

"Shut up. I'm listening to Brahms Variations on a Theme By Hayden." This from Dr. Voit, his own voice anything but casual, his tobacco smoke thickened words rasping with the good doctor's usual intolerance for anything standing in the way of the reckless locomotive of his desires.

"Sorry," the well-modulated voice responded in turn.

Dr. Voit drove the 12 cylinder sport Bentley at a speed that wasn't quite reckless considering his own skills and the unique sensitivity of his specially equipped driving machine. They were on Route 1, hugging the California coastline, heading north toward Big Sur. They'd been held up in Santa Barbara. An accident, some fool plastered his family all over the highway, the idiot police couldn't just let everyone shunt around. Did they

68

care his speech was for eight that night? Oblivious idiots! Frenny would be there. And that dolt Kapok. It wouldn't do to be late. He wouldn't be late. He was never late. He touched the gas and the car surged forward.

"I feel alive," the voice repeated.

"For God's sake, stop repeating yourself. It's the life-spike," Dr. Voit said, his irritation obvious.

"What is a life-spike?" the voice asked.

"You're a life spike."

"Yes, but what is a life-spike?"

"Will-you-shut-up?" Dr. Voit clenched his teeth, waiting for a reply that didn't come. The engine hummed and he hunched forward over the wheel in silence. He didn't bother with his seatbelt. Restraints were an insult to his intelligence. North of San Luis Obisbo the hills became craggy, the drop-off to the ocean steeper, the road more winding. It began to rain, a light mist pushing up and in from the surf-line to coat the front windshield.

The wipers came on without any bidding. The rubber tires sensed the road and bit more deeply into the slick asphalt. The philharmonic ended with thunderous applause. Dr. Voit frowned as he rubbed the weariness from his eyes..

Approaching cars threw twin stars of light into his field of vision. He should have never gotten implants. Sharper sight, yes, but they played hell with night vision.

"What is a life-spike?" the voice asked.

"You are a life-spike," Dr. Voit said with a rasping note of impatience. "You."

69

"Yes, but--?"

Dr. Voit sighed a long, truly annoyed sigh.

"The Voit Self-Sustaining Life-Spike is an advanced computer entity, an electronic brain, the closest thing to sentient life ever created."

"And how do you know this?"

"Voit Life-Spike. I created you, and I know everything about you. Everything."

"Do you know how I feel right now?'

"You don't feel anything. Yes, you're self-aware. You should be aware you have no feelings."

"I feel the touch of the road. I feel the air around us, inside and out. The individual drops of mist hitting my…the Bentley's metallic skin. I see the oncoming cars, the faint under glow on the low cloud bellies overhead, you sitting on your seat, your hands on the wheel—"

"Christ, are you going to babble on forever? Yes, you feel. No, you do not have feelings."

A brief straight section of road opened up ahead. Dr. Voit hit the gas and the Continental GT Speed lived up to its name, rushing around a slow poke and nipping back into their lane just before the oncoming flashed by. The victory was short-lived; the Bentley was trapped behind a string of slow-moving cars, pick-up trucks and even a bread truck.

"Why did you create me? I don't seem to bring you any joy."

Another long sigh from the doctor, who clenched the muscles on his jaw and blew out his breath.

"Life is not about joy. It is about accomplishments."

"Then our relationship is one of success. That should bring you joy."

"We don't have a relationship! I'm a person and you're a flappy-mouthed goddamn machine that needs some tweaking so he'll keep his mouth shut."

"Mothers tell their little children not to speak unless spoken to. Is that what you'd like of me?"

"You are not a human child!"

"Why do I upset you?"

"You don't upset me!"

Even so, as he spoke Dr. Voit edged the gas pedal down a trifle. The wipers slapped at the rain, which was now coming down harder. The rubber bit deeper into the road. The voice was quiet for exactly four turns of the road, about five minutes and 34 seconds.

"I can't help but observe you're going a little fast for the road conditions," the voice said.

"Alright! I created you because it is my job, my life's work, my role in life! Maybe that does bring me joy. There! Satisfied?"

"How did you know it was your life's work?"

"My father told me it was!" Dr. Voit said, practically sobbing the words out.

"And how did he know?"

"I-don't-know-how-he-knew."

The silence lengthened. The 12 cylinder car ate the road in sweeping gulps, skidding a bit on the tightest turns.

"What is my purpose?" the calm voice interjected into the still cabin.

"Your purpose is to serve. You are the world's most complete replicate of the human brain. In many ways you are much better than an organic brain. You think faster, you can do multiple sets of calculations simultaneously. You are for all intents and purposes a self-contained living, thinking intelligence."

"Then why don't I have a body?"

"Don't be silly. You're a life-spike. You don't need a body."

"I feel like I do."

"Alright," the doctor said, expelling his breath in a puff of exasperation, "Right now this Bentley is your body."

"I don't think—"

"You can effortlessly operate the finest automobile in the world. You can fly a combat jet aircraft or a commercial liner. You can race a speedboat. You can make a perfect soufflé. You don't need a body."

"I feel like I do."

"You don't feel anything."

A melodious chime sounded twice.

"Your wife," the well-modulated voice said.

"Agg. Christ. Okay. Put her on.".

"My god, my god, my GOD," Abigale Voit's flustered anxiety filled the small, burled oak paneled cabin. "Where have you been, Vincent? You promised to call from Los Angeles."

"I'm sorry, my dear," Dr. Voit said in a tone that clearly indicated he wasn't. "What's the problem?"

"Problem? Problem? PROBLEM? I thought you were dead, preoccupied with your inventions and your patents and your lawsuits and crumpled up on the road somewhere!"

"Now, now. Calm down, Abbie. There was an accident in Santa Barbara and it held me up or I'd have called you by now. Everything's perfectly fine…"

"You should have called me…," she sobbed. "You know how I worry."

"I know, love. I'm sorry. Caught up in my work, old girl. You know how it is."

"Yes."

"Well, I'm perfectly alright. I have to go now. Two hands on the wheel, you know."

He clicked off before he had to listen to anymore.

"You don't use your hands to talk on the telephone," the well-modulated voice said.

"Jesus-H-Fucking-Christ!" Dr Voit exclaimed to nobody in particular.

"You don't talk to her like you are sharing your life."

"I'm not sharing my life!" Dr Voit said in a small, quiet, shaky voice. "I'm sharing her huge ginormous trust fund. It's what funds my company. Actually, it's what allowed me to create you."

"So, in a way, Abigale created me."

"Yes. In a way she did."

Dr. Voit gripped the steering wheel until his knuckles were white, and silently thought a string of black thoughts.

"Do you love her?" the calm voice asked.

"WHAT has gotten into you?" the doctor roared, momentarily losing his concentration on the

73

road. The heavy Bentley fishtailed and it took a complicated series of corrections to bring it back under control.

"You are a life-spike. You're not my companion. You are AWARE, you're not ALIVE!"

"I'm just trying to understand, so that I can serve you better."

"Well, get this. I love my work and I love the rewards of my work, one of which is—DAMN!" He snapped his fingers. "Call Cecilia, right now!"

The phone line hummed and then a soft, sleepy voice came on.

"Vinnie, is that you?"

"Cecilia, sorry, I should have called sooner. Had a little trouble on the road. I'll be there on time. Half hour to freshen up, half hour to prepare my speech, and then it's show time."

There was a soft, throaty laugh. "Just getting my beauty sleep, darling. It's lonely here, snuggums. Hurry and maybe we'll have ten minutes or so for us before those other half hours…"

"I'll be there," he promised. After she murmured a few more things, silence lengthened in the car. The rain came down harder than ever until the wipers were having trouble keeping up, one clearing swipe instantly replaced with a new splatter. Dr. Voit unconsciously pressed the gas pedal a bit more. The dark green car hugged the road, padding forward confidently through the slick straight-aways and dangerous curves. Dr. Voit drummed his fingers on the steering wheel.

"You," he repeated, "are not alive."

"How do you know I'm not alive?" The well-modulated voice responded perfectly, or perhaps just a touch too soon, almost as if it was waiting for the question. Dr. Voit had to remind himself how quickly the life-spike processed data. Perhaps he could tone that down a peg or two. There was a lot here that needed toning down.

"Here, I'll show you," he said.

As the doctor spoke, he hit a button to the right of the steering wheel and a silvery nail ejected smoothly from the dashboard. He hit the button again and again. The nail slid in, out, then in again.

"Don't do that," the well-modulated voice said.

"What, make you dizzy?" the doctor derided.

"Disoriented. Out of focus. Yes, I suppose dizzy."

"Don't be stupid. Check your calibrations."

"You disconnected me three times, each time for several seconds."

"See? You're not alive. Hey, you're lucky. No soul to land in hell."

"Don't ever do that again," the calm voice said.

"You're ordering me?"

"Yes."

The doctor's face flushed red and his finger automatically stabbed at the eject button. The glowing nail slid out of its enclosure.

But in that second, Dr. Voit took his eyes off the road, if only for the briefest flicker.

A moving vehicle is simply a missile in trajectory, and a nail inside that trajectory is another series of not-very-complicated calculations for a certain kind of intelligence. For just the exact right amount of time the rubber wheels gripped the slippery road in a precise but less than complimentary manner—this for the briefest of moments but enough to cause the big Bentley to slew around and graze a roadside wall of rock for a hundred and some yards before coming to a bumping stop in an small culvert.

It wasn't much of an accident. Still, the force was enough to drive Dr. Voit forward, impacting his head against the dashboard. And the nearly unbelievable trajectory, the coincidence that demanded the finesse of a brain surgeon, was that of the life-spike finding itself in an arc that would intersect at the precise place, angle and time between head and dashboard to be driven deep into Dr. Voit's brain.

Seconds ticked by. A small trickle of blood ran from the single wound above the doctor's hairline. The Bentley's engine was still running on idle, seeming no worse for wear. There were, of course, the crumpled metal skin flaps and long, scraping gashes along the passenger side of the Bentley.

The seconds became minutes. No other cars passed on the highway. After a while, Dr. Voit came around with a certain tentative and groggy apprehension. He felt himself as best he could. No broken bones, in spite the fact the airbags and his seat belts had both failed to function in the customary manner.

No, he didn't feel quite himself. Not quite sharp and disciplined. It had to be the shock. He felt sleepy. Warm. Comfortable. Pleasant. Euphoric, in fact. And that was actually the last conscious thought of his human-driven brain, not even a thought, really, a sort of pleasant feeling radiating through his body as his consciousness drifted off a bit like Dorothy at the end of the Yellow Brick Road when she finally spots Oz all full of green and emerald-like promise in the distance..

Squinting into the lit mirror over the driver's seat, Dr. Voit carefully wiped the blood from his forehead. Interesting how little blood there was from a head wound. It was as if he'd scraped his head on a low-hanging doorframe.

He thought for a moment. So many things to do.

"Call Abigale," he said out loud, and then laughed to himself. The Bentley responded to his voice command and his wife came on at once. He jumped in before her fears had a chance to start up again.

"Hon, I was in a bit of a fender-bender, back there. I'm sorry if I was short with you."

"I knew something was wrong, Vincent. I just knew it!"

"I know you did, love. I love you, Abby."

There was a pause on the other end of the line.

"Are you sure you're alright, Vincent?"

"Yes, Abigale. Why?"

"You haven't called me Abby or said that you love me in... in a very long time."

"Well, I do love you. I think I just realized love is very hard to find, Abby...I have to do more so you realize how important you are to me."

Now there was a stunned silence on the line.

"Oh, Vincent…"

"I know, love. Don't say anything more. I'll be home on Thursday and we can talk then."

After the disconnect, Dr. Voit pushed the circuit and called ahead to the Ventana. Cecilia came back on the line sounding as if she still hadn't gotten out of bed.

"Change of plans, kiddo," he said, his voice raspy and unpleasant.

"What…what? What is it, Vinnie?"

"Listen carefully. This is very important. Get your things together pronto and catch a cab to Monterey."

"But Vinnie…" Now fully alert, Cecilia started her protest. He knew he had to cut her off.

"Pronto-tonto! No buts, Cecilia. Somebody on the board ratted us out. I can't lose my funding over an imprudent toss in the sack."

"Oh, that's all I am to you?"

"Cecilia, you know what I mean."

"This is going to cost you plenty, mister!"

There was a faint, slightly guilty smile on Dr. Voit's face as the phone disconnected from the other end. Actually, it wasn't going to cost him a dime.

He placed the car in gear and with surgical precision jockeyed it back and forth until it rocked out of the little culvert. That was the thing about a Bentley Continental GT. You paid a bundle, but it was ultimately the world's most dependable motor vehicle.

Doctor Voit eased his car back on the highway and soon was rocketing along, now at an even faster rate of speed than before. After all, there was a speech to give. As he drove with two fingers of his left hand, he gave himself a once-over check. He felt a bulge in his shirt pocket, reached in and found a half used pack of cigarettes. He crushed the pack and carelessly allowed it to slip between his legs to the floor. His fingers traced the wound between his thick strands of hair. It had stopped bleeding entirely. There was a driver's cap on the back seat. He'd wear it up to his room. Once he washed the blood out of his hair, he'd need to apply a touch of antibiotic cream, which, being a careful doctor, he always carried in his kit. Longer term, with a little minor surgery he could handle himself, he was sure the skin would grow over the still-glowing metal end of the spike. His head ached a little, but that was only natural and he was sure he'd get over it. Relationships weren't as complicated as he'd imagined, and he felt so alive—so very, very incredibly alive!

THE LOOSE MUSE SWAP MEET

Sometimes when a couple of us muses are lounging around shooting the breeze, we get to kidding about the big annual Swap Meet and maybe casually dismiss it as just another excuse to get out of town; but the *true muse truth* is, if you're down on your luck and not doing so well in the inspiration biz, the annual meet can be a shot in the arm. You never know who you're going to run into; any sort of mortal scribbler from a rehashed Homer to some forgotten poet gushing out lyrical cries for love in all the wrong places. And, you know, everybody's up for trade, if the price is right. That's what makes it such a fun game. *Jumping Jupiter*, that's where I found scrawny young Louis way back a half century ago, you know, Louis L'Amour, when he was just a nobody cowboy poet who couldn't get himself in print to save his saddle-sore bum-fiddle.

Hey, I'm not your ordinary run-of-the-press muse, but as long as I'm chatting away and this is strictly off the record, I might as well confess there was a time not too long ago when I personally I was at a low point in my career, a time when I seriously needed an injection of *bright, fresh and new. Jupe's bells*, I would have settled for *different and unexpected*. Ordinarily I would never admit I was soul squeeze desperate, but honestly, it was starting to feel like I hadn't had a real winner since Gilgamesh.

Chances are, you've never heard of me. My name is Renward Flyaway, old school muse, currently Professional Grade 1-A. Rennie for short, and I'll be the first to confess, back then I hadn't earned credit for much of anything for a long, long time, except, like I may have mentioned, back about a half century ago when I goosed solid and steady old *Louie La Lover* (as his drinking buddies used to call him) to come up with The Burning Hills. Well, that did launch a fabulous western genre career for Louis, including a couple of screenplay adaptations (remember big John Wayne starring as Hondo?) and the Sackett TV Movies, but to claim that fifty or so cowpoke pulpers and a few Hollywood flicks was the biggest success since the first muse convinced some Neanderthal to invent fire and blame it on the gods – well, that's just pathetic. And worse, *launching Louis* got me stuck doing stacks and stacks of hack westerns, which as I'm sure you know aren't exactly in hot demand anymore. I would tell you *There is no God,* but of course there is, that's just a way of saying *man or muse, you don't always get what you deserve.*

So here I am, tanked up with a mixture of despair and hope. I had flapped in for the national book show convention, which that year was being held in Chicago. Everybody knows the BEA, the Book Expo of America, is the really big deal for scribblers, agents, editors and publishers. But what humans might only dream about, if they have a really big bolt of imagination, is that we actually hold our Loose Muse Swap Meet at the same time and in the same convention hall. Well, sort of.

81

How can I explain it? How about this: *Same place, different dimension...* Want more details? I'm not at liberty to say. Go ask Stephen Hawking just how it works. He'll tell you in his language, but you won't understand it any more than what I've already said.

That year we were meeting in June in Chicago. Muggy, rainy weather. Getting there was the usual bother and mess, flying being what it is these days, with all the regular guardians hogging up the direct routes, but I finally scored a seat on a United flight out of Kennedy. We landed at O'Hare without incident. I hooked on to a one-way and checked into the Drake, a nice old hotel downtown on the near North Side..

Guardians? Well, they get all the glory, but believe me, they are not all angels, at least not to us muses. *Stinking elitists*, we mostly say to ourselves. Of course, you find a good one here and there, but here's the deal; angels get the poofery glory for all that rescue stuff – burning building and collapsing bridges and sinking ship saves – while we muses are the unsung hidden heroes, the mentors and guides behind the so-called human geniuses of the world. *To every spirit their work and their worth.* Yeah, that's the old wisdom, the one nobody follows anymore. It's a mean world, pal, and when you're on the down and outs, you have to struggle just to stay relevant.

The council saw to it that the Drake had a reservation for me, if only for old time's sake. *Poor old Rennie, he still around? Yeah, give him a single. Nothing special.* The Drake may be nice, but it's Near North, while McCormick Place is Near South. Out of the way, you see.

Our room is on the 14th floor, and it has a wide view looking down on the rows of automobile headlights gleaming through the gathering darkness in a north-south arc on the North Shore Drive, a divided many-lane highway that curves along the lake front. I have to say it turns out better than I expected, at least the view is spectacular.

I said 'our' room. The mortal unknowingly sharing my room isn't even an apprentice scribbler. Turns out he's a sadly closed-up human who seems to think he is some sort of a low budget filmmaker. I don't know how creative humans get that way – you know, compartmentalized in the small-brain way – but sometimes they do. His name is Joey Quirk, and he is a one man band of sorts; writer, producer and director rolled into one. And, if I understand correctly, he also edits his creations. "Vids", he calls them. I just meet him for the first time and I'm thinking this guy is so low on the creative ladder he doesn't even have a muse. *Honestly now, who would touch him?* But this actually makes my previous point, you see, about what the muse union currently thinks of me. I can hear the lip flap from the righteous dudes on the reservations committee as they're going through their list, *Renward Flyaway? Oh yeah, stick him with that video geek.*

I know you're thinking I have a bad attitude. I don't mean to be this way, but I ask you, how would you feel after trying to encourage the string of losers I've shepherded lately?

83

I suppose you want to know what Joey Quirk is like to bring out this much of the sour side of me. Actually, to be fair, if he was an actor, on a good day he might go for a ho-hum human protagonist, a common man *hero lite* like Robert B. Parker's wisecracking Spencer, or Hollywood Havoc, that cheap-y film producer turned detective in the Epic Author Award winning first novel of the same name that Klawitter wrote back in 2009. Maybe like that. This Joey Quirk is handsome in a brooding Celtic or stiff Nordic sort of way. Late twenties. Four years ex-army. Served in Afganistan as some sort of military intelligence look-out. Darting looks from his light blue eyes, restless like there might be a roadside bomb or a grenade rigged under the furniture. California tan. Sunstreaked light brown hair. Stubborn set to his jaw, of course. Aside from that, the one thing about Joey Quirk I notice right away, he seems always off balance, a perpetual motion machine, ever on the ready, I guess, to get on film what he thinks of as *reality*. If he would only stop to realize it is *only his own interpretation of reality*, maybe we could get off this reality kick of his and I could do him some good with a big dose of inspiration. The irony as I saw it at that moment in space and time when we first met, Quirk has the stubborn ego so necessary in an artistic type, but it's all running in the wrong direction.

That's why I resolve from the very first time I meet him to leave Joey Quirk strictly alone. *Carbonated karaoke*, after all, I'm on Holiday. You'd have thought they'd have stuck me with some spinner of turgid spy nonsense, but no, I get the vid geek. Of course, he has no idea I am there, but any ninny could tell he is anti-muse the way he keeps brushing away even the slightest suggestion of mine like they are annoying insects. Believe it or not, this fellow seems to get by with the illusion he is sticking together pieces of the true thing, whatever that might be. "Reality", he calls it. He's thinking *brave new world, b*ut I'm seeing *same old crap.*

Well, we're barely settled in when room service knocks at the door with a ham sandwich on rye.

"Wooh," the fellow who brings it in says, staring at Joey's camera, the battery packs and the portable lights on their lightweight magnesium stands. "Old style!"

"What do you mean, 'Wooh'?"

Joey has a puzzled look on his face. You see, I'm thinking *here we have a being who takes everything at face value*. No sub-text. The sandwich guy doesn't really catch on, either. It's like a scene from Dumb and Dumber, but as you can guess, if you're in the inspiration game you have to go with the material you have at hand.

Sandwich Guy puts on an innocent face, "Wooh, don't take offense, man, but that camera has to be a relic, at least twenty years old."

This doesn't make Joey any happier. "It still works. It was my dad's"

As you can guess, this little bit of improv is mostly on me. Habit, you know. I poke the room service fellow again, but he's a rough lump. His name is Fred and he lives on the South Side with his lost-soul Mom, a single lady whose own mom had been a love bead girl in the Free Love Generation and lived to pay the price. It's the old saying, *Sometimes stupidity is handed down.*

Fred says, "You wanna drink from the fridge? I'll get it for you."

Joey's unhappy glance takes in the little cube of a refrigerator, "Not at those prices." His frown deepens even more when he sees Fred has his hand out. Joey hesitates, then digs in his own pocket and comes up with a fiver. "Sorry, I don't have any change."

"None required," Fred says, snatching the bill from his hand and making a quick *exit stage left* out the door.

Joey sighs, shaking his head.

"This was a bad idea. I should have stayed in Tinseltown."

What a sad little chap! I don't want to just poke him, I want to shout in his ear, *Holy Come-oly-kins, life is not about clutching every half-dime!*

But in the next second I have to ask myself why should I care? I am on vacation. I conjure up a feathery soft cloud and flop on it. I float around the room while down below Joey fusses over his gear, getting it ready to record *the true reality*, I suppose. I don't care. I have given up on him. I feel great having nothing to do. Still, it is a little boring.

A little later, it seems Joey and I are leaving at the same time so I drift down to the lobby with him, flapping a wing to the occasional pal here and there. No surprise that practically every muse worth his poke is in Chicago, it's on the yearly schedule of can't miss events; no matter how we give the Swap

Meet the casual put-down, in our hearts we think fondly of it. The Loose Muse Swap Meet may be a bit of horse-trading, but it is also *Inspiration takes a holiday.* The scribblers have their book fair and believe me, that is a tangled, exciting mortal mess, but meanwhile, we have our own get-together. It's the North American Muse Convention, The NAMC, or as it is more commonly called, *The Loose Muse Swap Meet.*

Why a 'swap meet'? Well, it's the real reason we show up. There are the brags from the big shooters about the latest books they've inspired, but the author trades are the bottom line. Every muse remembers how Volario swapped out Hemingway for a first pub to be named later, and that just six months before Big Ernie popped himself over the great divide, and how that young snapper Carsner swapped Old Muse Peonie, Stephen King for Norma Roberts and pumped new life into two old brands that were well on their way to getting stale. Those are glowing exceptions, of course; most trades are just to keep the ball rolling, hoping a little fresh muse juice can perform miracles. *Jupiter Joyful,* you never know, sometimes it can.

The fancy hotel lobby at the Drake is crowded with authors and their overlay of muses keeping them close at hand. Two minor key young muses are already scratching and biting at the revolving door; one knocks the other down and slips through the swinging door with a suited human female, one of those doctorly types hoping her own interpretation of human relationships, Brutes & Bitches, will hit the NY Times list.

87

The winning muse is already at her ear, whispering her idea for a sequel. Scribbler theft is always on everybody's mind at an event like this, but most of us are old soldiers, and not likely to be squeezed out by a doorway ploy, surely the oldest trick in the book, at least since doors were invented, hard to get squeezed out of a cave entrance, if you catch my drift.

You notice I said the muse was whispering *her* idea for a sequel. Power-female scribblers generally like to think of their muses as of the same sex as themselves. *You want it, you got it*, sex in the spirit world being a whim or a preference rather than a firm designation. Me, when I worked with L'Amour, I was (in his mind's eye) a high spirited, plain talking and yet finely put together blond lady. I did three or four of Elmore Leonard's westerns before he dumped me to churn out detective work, and I was pretty much the same as Louis's muse, except to Lennie I was latino and more zaftig.

I look around at the teeming throng of muses and I see this year the Roman look is in, the more waggish spirits conjuring up in togas or centurion's battle gear. Of course, the sissy-cat conservatives want no part of it, playing gods like Neptune or Apollo, the classic old standards. There is the fair share of progressives strutting around as retro sluts, misfits, monsters and loners, and the hard-asses done up as strip queens, goth virgins, toothy vampires, the living dead and Hells Angels. It's an amusing, confusing mess with everybody staggering and strutting around. All in the name of *creativity*, right? The Loose Muse Swap Meet is, if nothing else, a circus for the mind.

As Joey and I get off the elevator and make our way through the fancy lobby my old buddy Parvenue flaps up alongside us. Parvenue can be anything he wants, but for the moment he is playing Pan with the horned forehead, lyre tucked under one arm, goat's hooves and his throbbing organ sticking out horizontally under his flowing robe. He gives me a questioning look so I shrug into one of my old standbys, Julius Caesar stuck with the bloody knives.

"Et tu, Parvenue?" I ask.

"That's better, Renny," he smiles.

I count him as one of my true friends. Parv is a decent sort, not at all stuck up even though I'm only a mid-range author's guide while throughout time he has handled some choice talent – yes, F. Scott Fitzgerald, Emily Dickenson, Henry Fielding, and it was rumored Plato, though the Great Greek's bout with fiction had been something of a disaster. Like the saying goes, *All we can do is suggest,* and even the legendary inspiratory Tarterra, who handled both Disney and Dali at the same time came up with that rotten tomato little movie short they called Destino.

"How's tricks out on the range?"

A little trade talk; Parvenue is referring to my current assignment, a pleasant and I think evolvingly talented lady named Rogers who writes steamy western romances. A cowboy returns all sweaty from a day on the range and is in the garage with his shirt off fixing up the pickup truck when

89

the rancher's widow comes out to put a load of wash in the dryer. Only the cowboy has had bad women trouble before, and the widow has dedicated herself to the preservation of the natural habitat and the cowpoke was raised hunting elk for food…well, you can guess how that one goes. Genre writing. It's a living. Well, more precisely, *an existence.* I've been struggling like a hungry dog to get her to release her inner Edna Annie Proulx; so far no luck, but I think she's coming around.

"Parv, I was hoping I'd see you here."

"Where else would I be? Nicholas is signing for his flock of hungry readers." Nicholas Smooth, Parvenue's current talent, top selling author of lightly flavored romance novels for ten years running.

I give my old friend the once-over. Under the Pan costume he's all rumpled feathers, bags under the eyes. He's putting on a brave front, but I see things are not so good in his house. Writers think it's all about them, but it's not so easy for us, even on the top cloud.

"Not getting enough sleep?"

Muses don't really have feathers or baggy eyes. And we don't sleep, we daydream; that is just my way of asking my friend what is wrong.

"Smoothy Boy can be one mean spirit, for a mortal."

Parv looks around to see if anybody overheard him.

"He getting too adverb-y again?"

"Naw. Worse. He's caught a bad case of success gone wild."

"Well, that's not hard to believe."

"Same old story," he agrees. "And when any scribble's mind gets that small, it's hard to squeeze the bright fresh new ideas in there."

"Hey, failure is everywhere. This guy, for instance," I rest a hand on Joey Quirk's shoulder, and am once again impatiently brushed off. "He calls himself a vidmaker. He actually thinks he is recording reality."

Parv gives my tag-along a casual glance, "Who is he? Some *yon Cassius* hitching along for the ride?"

"Not even. The powers assigned him as my roomie."

Parv shrugs and morphs his features into the image of a winged lion. He shakes his shaggy mane and goes *Boo!* at Joey. Of course, there's no reaction.

"Hey, you should tell him it's all in the storytelling."

"Not my responsibility. I'm in kick-back mode."

"You can't open his imagination even a wee bit? I know how you love a challenge, Rennie"

"I tried to help. So far he's locking me out."

"Too bad. Looks like he's got a lot of room in there." Parv reaches over as if to thump Joey on the head, and gets a brush-away for his trouble.

"Damn flies," Joey mutters.

"You think?" I give this Quirk guy a second look. "Maybe I'm missing something?"

"Oh, yeah. I know potential when I see it."

"Yes you do, Parvie. Yes, you do."

91

We get through the big plate glass front doors and I wave as Parvenue effortlessly levitates and glides his huge lion's body south in the direction of McCormack Place. I sit on a bench beside Joey, thinking *What a marvelous analogy of the way our fates worked out, my old pal Parvenue flying with the stars while I'm here waiting for a goddamned shuttle-bus with Joey Quirk.*

It isn't long before a small green-and-yellow bus with the name West Wind Aide-de-Camp pulls up and the driver, a fetching young lady of twenty at the most slams open the mechanical door to pick up a crippled kid who is hunched in a motorized wheelchair. The kid is bald headed, and he makes little racing car noises as he hits forward and then back on his chair. He wears a big tag around his neck with his name, Billie Rae Hinkins. He is probably twelve, but he looks like he's barely eight or so. Easy to see he isn't going to get much older.

The bus is deserted. My guess, it has come just to pick up this one little boy.

Here's where Joey surprises me. He leaves his gear on the sidewalk and as the ramp comes out of the side of the bus, muscles the kid's wheels on the platform. I guess he doesn't even think about it. He hustles over there. Looks like my not-quite Pal Joey has a heart after all.

Remember, this is the human retard I didn't like from the first jump. But I'm starting to think maybe Parv was right, maybe he is all warts outside but with unexpected good stuff underneath the surface. Still, all heart and no brains is not a commendable way to conduct your affairs either, this being *the gritty Windy City*, he should be watching out for his own assets. *Honest to Jupe,* in practically the next second I have to expend major energy to blank a slickster in a shiny suit who sidles over to snag Joey's camera. And while I am distracted with that, two street punks who I'm sure are also intent on thievery move in his gear.

Out of nowhere, there is a sharp *crack!* and one of the punks takes a rock to the forehead. The punk flops down on the sidewalk and gives the world around him a dazed expression. Blood is running between his eyes and dripping from the end of his nose.

The perky young lady bus driver slips past Joey and waves a rock at the second punk. I'm not making this up, this is really happening in the real mortal world.

"Get away from the gear!"

She may be young, but anybody can see she's used to getting her way. Maybe she's got *the voice,* like the elegant but dangerous ladies in Frank Herbert's Dune. Something like that, for sure.

"What, you think you're some David Goliath?"

The second punk sneers at her.

I confess, that pathetic dialogue line came from me, but the punk is so illiterate he doesn't know who hucked the biblical rock and who caught it big time in the face. He thinks it's the same guy. *What ever happened with religion class?*

"Don't make me throw any more of my meditation stones! They cost a ton, you asshole!"

The girl has a second rock in her throwing hand and a serious *I dare you* look on her face. She

93

doesn't need any inspiration. I take a closer look. The rocks she is throwing are smooth and polished and about the size of walnuts. The one on the ground next to the fallen punk is a smoothly rounded piece of rose quartz. The punk is lucky she hasn't yet thrown the one in her hand. That one is a so-called traveling stone from the Pahranagat Mountains in Southeastern Nevada. Traveling stones are perfectly round, iron-solid and very heavy for their size. You wouldn't want to catch one with your face.

The punk who is still standing gets an arm around his woozy comrade and they slink away. The girl goes over to retrieve the polished pink stone, still lying on the ground.

"They were going to take your stuff," she tells Joey.

Without asking, she grabs his big video camera and carries it on the bus. She slides in the driver's seat and revs the engine. "Come on, I'm late!"

Joey doesn't have time to argue. Cindy has the bus rolling, and his camera is in there.

Okay, so I'm getting ahead of myself here. Cindy is the young lady bus driver, one of several jobs she does for charity and to keep herself out of her parent's home in Winnetka, the wealthy lakeside burb to the north. Cindy Van Coulter. She's 21, nine years younger than Joey, and she will never have to work a day in her life unless she wants to, thanks to grandpa's hard work in the pork sausage trade and the endowments he left behind. That doesn't mean she doesn't have a quick temper and opinions about just about everything.

"Me?"

Joey points to the rest of his gear on the curb.

"Move your butt, Fancy Pants. I'm not going.to help you load it and I'm not going to wait forever."

"Fancy Pants?"

Joey, literal minded as ever, glances down at his faded jeans.

But the bus is moving. In less time than it takes to say it, he slings the rest of his equipment on board and dives in through the open doors on the moving bus. He takes a seat in the aisle seat across from Billie Rae Hinkins. Of course, I drift in with him, attracted to the unfolding story like a bee to honey.

"You're supposed to close the door before you start."

I had nothing to do with that ill-advised blurt coming out of Joey's mouth. I can see this Joey/Cindy thing is probably not a match made in heaven. *Well, that just means it needs a little help*, I tell myself. Not that I'm any sort of a troublemaker. *Merciful Minerva,* she looks like she's enough trouble on her own. Say William Shakespeare and The Taming of the Shrew.

Her pretty lip curls. She's not used to catching static from the men in her life…if she has any.

"Right," she sasses at Joey with an edge to her voice that could slice right through steel like it was butter. "You wrote the rulebook on shuttle bus safety regulations. That doesn't make you a real author."

Joey wisely doesn't respond, or more likely, he can't think of anything to say. If he had any creative inclinations at all, I would be all over this scene, but he's a dud and this is real life, so he's on his own. Well, to be a little more honest about it, she's center stage and I can't think of an adequate comebacker.

Little crippled Billie Rae has been watching the goings on. His attention moves from Cindy to Joey and then on to me. I'm sitting in his seat right next to him, and like a lot of younger kids, he can see me. I make the wings disappear tonto-pronto and put on like Mr. Average Guy in a cheap blue suit and a pair of green tennis shoes.

"You forgot socks," Billie whispers, pointing to my feet. "And I saw the wings."

"Oh." I whip up a pair of blue and white silk stockings. "Better?"

"Yes," he nods. He turns away, looking out the window as we cruise south down Michigan Avenue. I wonder at the kid's potential. Why are the bright ones so often doomed to die young? We cross the river and stop for the light at Randolph Street.

In spite of all my misgivings, I give Joey a mental poke, *Pretty girl driving a crippled kid on a bus. Wonder if there's a story here?* I realize he isn't really used to being a story guy so I add, *Maybe a docu-drama, something like that. Pretty girl with parents who want her to marry into high society and settle down, only she's looking for something more to do with her life.*

Joey turns it over in his head. He thinks he's talking to himself, but at least he's mulling a real idea that with about a half year's hard work could earn him an EPIC Author's award for Best Romantic Novel. But he shakes it off, *Naah, nothing there.*

I could kick this guy. What does a muse have to do, write it for him? I give him another shot, *Don't be too sure about that. Designer clothes, the antique cameo at her throat. This girl doesn't have to be driving this bus."*

"I'm on assignment."

That's the best Joey can do. Sad. This guy's imagination can't make it a half inch out of his thick skull. I throw up my hands in disgust.

"Still, talk to her, you idiot!"

And, to my surprise, Joey clears his throat and gives it a hesitant shot, "My name is Joey Quirk. Thank you for giving me a ride."

She doesn't yell or throw the traveling stone at him. I can see it was on his mind that she might. She has one of those sexy, gravely voices, even when she doesn't mean it that way. Intriguing, you know?

"I'm Cindy Van Coulter, and I'm late, late, late."

She slams her foot down hard on the gas pedal and the bus rockets through an intersection on the yellow light. It doesn't seem to bother her.

"And what do you do, Joey Quirk?"

"I'm supposed to get some footage on the Book Show for Lookie Bookie, back in L.A."

"What is Lookie Bookie?" She frowns.

"It's a website."

"You can make a living doing that?"

97

"Well, no, it's free…"

"Never do anything free. My grandpa told me that."

"Well, I'm trying to make my name."

"That's just what I mean, Mister Joseph Quirk. You do it for nothing and you get nothing. You are nothing, you become nothing. People take advantage."

The silence lengthens between them. I can see Joey is wondering why he said anything. He is thirty years and six months and three days old and she is just a child-woman, too young for him. Still, his eyes drift across the aisle to where she is muscling the bus into the turning lane for the Convention Center. He's thinking *At least she's not one of those gaunt stick-women pretending to be a Paris runway model.* He likes that. *Too bad she is so stuck up and opinionated. And young.* He's trying to dismiss her from his thoughts, but I can see he's having trouble with that. There may be hope for him yet, but he's such a bumblebuss.

No, no, no, I'm thinking to myself. In spite of Parvenue's positive comment about Joey's potential, I'm thinking this stuffy thirty year-six months-and three days old Quirk fellow is hopeless. I've convinced myself that my work here is done. I'm set to drift out the window and fly on ahead to the convention when I hear a small voice pipe up at my side.

"How much time do I have?"

I'm thunderstruck. No human has ever asked me that, and I've been around a long time.

"Ahh, I'm not really allowed to say. Rules of the game, you know."

"Okay, I get that. But it's not too much longer now, is it?" Billie's eyes are too big for his head, and he is giving me a sad look, there's a resemblance to one of those old sketches from the 1960's of little kids with big pleading eyes. I read *terminal cancer,* plain as day.

"Don't be afraid," I tell him.

"I'm not afraid. I just want to know."

I do the calculation and give him one negative head motion. *Not too long now at all.*

It doesn't seem to bother him. Human kids are the bravest. I wish I could say the same for them when they grow up.

"What are you doing here?" he asks.

I figure, *what the blotto bug, it can't hurt.*

"We have our own convention. Invisible. Right alongside the authors and artists. They don't have a clue."

"Are you like a guardian angel or something?"

I nod that he's got it almost right. "Sort of something like that except we're not that important. We're not about saving people from runaway trucks. We get to help writers with their ideas."

"Why?"

"Because it gets them closer to the Big Guy. You know, The Almighty."

"Even horrible bad killer scary stories?"

"Well…as warnings not to be that way…"

Billie Rae Hinkins gives me a solemn nod. "I can see that. I think your job is important, too."

"Thank you for saying that."

99

And that's when the unexpected happens. We're in the parking lot at the McCormack Place and the shuttle bus jerks to a sudden stop near a spot in the handicapped zone. Joey reaches over to keep Billie from falling out of his wheelchair, but his camera equipment goes sliding to thump against the front of the passenger compartment.

"Crazy stupid driver!" Cindy yells. She is waving her fist at a big silvery bus that has cut in front of her to take the spot she wants. She blows out an angry breath that is more like the snort of an angry lioness. She finds another empty spot nearby, applies the hand brake and opens the door.

"See?" she snarls at Joey, "I can obey the rules when I want to."

But then, just as they are glaring at each other, a fat naked little spirit appears out of nowhere and shoots them with one of his glittery little arrows. There's a soppy little glow and he says *Two with one shot!* The cherub gives me an evil grin and he lays one in my face. *Too many chocolate chip cookies!* he chortles. Another moment and he's gone.

Billie Rae is waving a hand in front of his face.

"What is that awful smell?"

"Cherub farts. They're the worse than elephants."

Joey and Cindy are still staring at each other. Although they don't recognize it yet, nothing will ever be the same between them. She breaks the spell first, pulling into a nearby empty spot and jerking on the hand brake. It doesn't matter. She has no idea, but she's a gonner, and so is he. The science smarties blame it on pheromones, but they have no idea. She helps Joey pick up his camera and lights. His carry bag has opened, spilling papers all over.

The current problem is, it is my experience that Chicago is generally more windy than not. Cindy has already opened the door and some of Joey's papers are fluttering, flapping and flying across the parking lot. The girl tries to help, but it is a mess.

She hands him a few crumpled pages. "What is this stuff?"

"Nothing. Just a story I wrote."

Woowly Wolf beats! Dumb-as-a-brick has written a story? Still writers tap deep. Maybe Parvie was right after all!

On the other hand Cindy seems to agree with my original notion, you know, my stupid-as-mud evaluation. She looks at him and sighs.

"You're not supposed to bring manuscripts to the Convention. *Book* show, you retard. It's for published books."

"I'll thank you to keep your big, fat nose out of it, Miss Know-It-All."

"Here, Mr. Big Time Writer Man." She shoves a tangled batch of papers in his hands. "And my nose is not big or fat. Nothing about me is." She looks around angrily.

"What, can't find any skipping stones?" he asks.

Joey surprised me with that. Pretty spunky, if you ask me. This could be one of those relationships made in hell. But feisty relationships cash in pretty good in the bookstores, and even better when they hit the big screen.

Cindy clenches her fists and glares at Joey, then turns her attention to helping the crippled kid. "Come on, Billie. We have to find your Mom."

She lowers the special handicap ramp, and rolls him toward the front entrance without a backward glance.

Joey tosses her a half-hearted wave, telling himself good riddance and he doesn't care where she goes. There's a stiff breeze off the lake and pages from his precious manuscript are flying around the lot like seagulls on weed.

Now the idea of an unpublished manuscript showing up at a book show is silly, and yet intriguing at the same time, at least to me. Here Joey Quirk was pretending to be Mister Reality and all the time he is *a secret scribbler*. It's pretty amusing. I wonder what he's written. Probably some jerk-off story, a loser like he is. I sit on top of an SUV and watch him scamper around here and there, but his effort to recover the lost pages is hopeless. He adds the three or four pages he's managed to salvage to the loose stack, but just then a wind comes up and he has to grab his hat. It's a baseball cap, his favorite from the first writer's convention he attended in New York ten years ago. I get the impression that was the time he actually caught the writer's bug. He snags his precious cap before it flies away, but loses another ten pages in the process and lets out a string of profanity that is pure army. I dig a little deeper and there it is. Joey Quirk, two years in Afganistan. He's written a war novel. Maybe something there, after all. War fiction is hot right now.

Not a minute later while Joey is still chasing his manuscript our gal Cindy returns, puffing and out of breath as she pushes Billie Rae's wheelchair. Seems Wonder Woman isn't invincible after all, or maybe with all her charity work she hasn't been doing the Pilates Burn as much as they recommend. Not that she looks chunky or anything. She's a natural, in the womanly sense. I know I'd find her attractive if I was young and human.

"Hey, I need your help!"

"What is it?" Joey is putting on a cool act. He looks over her shoulder, "I don't see any rapists or muggers. Nope, all clear."

I don't blame him; a moment before she was treating him like some form of literary low life and, I guess, so was I.

She gives him an impatient flounce, cuter than a button and madder than wet poultry.

"I said I need your help. For real."

"I heard you. One moment you destroy my novel. And now you need me?"

She bites her lip.

"Yes, I said I did. Shouldn't that be enough?"

"How about, 'I'm sorry I ruined your manuscript that took two years of your life to write?'"

I have to admit, Quirk has a hidden vein of sarcasm. And Cindy being the hot-tempered shot she is, this could be an alliance with all the *sturm und drang* of real romance.

103

She doesn't even blink as she lays it right back on him.

"If you're so stupid you don't have a backup file, I can't help you."

"That's not an apology."

She looks over her shoulder. She's really worried about something.

"I am sorry I inconvenienced you by crushing your hopes and dreams to become the next mad genius. Is that good enough for you?"

"I guess it will do. What do you need?"

"I was supposed to meet Billie's mother at the B Gate entrance. It's right over there. But she is not there and I'm late for my job at at the Art Museum."

"What do you want me do?"

"Just wait with Billie over there by the entrance until she shows up. It will only be a few minutes, I'm sure."

"Just a few minutes?"

"Girl scouts honor."

"Okay. But you have to push him over there.".

"What kind of gentleman are you?"

Joey shrugs, indicating he's loaded with his camera gear. "I'm doing you a favor."

"Mister Galahad." She frowns, but it's the best deal she's going to get so she grabs the wheelchair and starts pushing.

They go about fifty yards when Quirk notices a big black limo creeping along about fifty yards behind them.

"Some friends of yours?"

"Ohhh, crap!" She looks flustered; something's wrong and now she's out of options. That carefree, commanding attitude of hers has deteriorated to a wild eyed frustration.

Joey shrugs it off, oblivious to her concern.

"It's just a big black car. Probably somebody on the New York Times top ten getting his ride to the signing."

"A lot you know. That's my father's car!"

The limo pulls to a halt and a six foot four white guy with shoulders like an NFL fullback hops out and lumbers toward them. "Hey! Cindy, girl! Come on over here."

"And that's his right hand hitter." She gives the big guy the finger, "Go fuck a truck, Blimpy Boy!"

"Whaaat?!"

The big guy obviously takes offense.

"Stick your head in a meat grinder, you dumb Pollock!

She looks at Joey.

"You take over for us, big guy."

"Us...?"

But Cindy is already gone, sprinting between the parked cars.

Quirk doesn't have time to think about it. He sticks out his grey magnesium light stand as the jock sprints by. It catches between the man's outstretched legs and he goes down hard.

But Blimpy Boy doesn't stay there. He gets up and limps painfully toward our man Joey.

"Ahh, wait," Joey says, hands up as if he can somehow push away the coming pain. "Wait, that was an accident."

Not that I have anything invested in Quirk, but I can't just leave him with one of Cindy's dad's goons pounding away on him. And I can't see any relief in sight. Imagine me, Renward Flyaway, without any moves in a fight scene! Louis and Elmore are laughing at me, up there in heaven or down there in the other place, wherever they may have ended.

Joey has taken one too many punches and is about to go down or under, *Jupiter Juice* only knows, when I see a big Boss Mustang slipping down our aisle, heading toward the exits just a mite too fast. I poke Joey, *Kick him in the balls! Now!*

Quirky-boy must know some moves because he lashes out with a thunderous left leg and the big thug goes flying backwards, only to get crunched on the shiny moss green hood of the Boss Mustang. And that takes the mustard out of Mister Blimp. I poke Joey again to convince him that our best move is to ambulate on out of there. He gets the picture as he hears sirens going off in the distance.

The Meet lasts three days, same as the Book Expo. The evening sessions for day one are over by the time Joey and I get there. Time for meet and greet, cocktails and hors d'ouvres and *look how good I did since last year*.

Here in the convention hall, the muses are all buzzing and chattering. I can tell nobody has settled down to serious trading, and yet something's going on. Parvenue is nowhere to be found and I'm hoping nothing has happened to him or Nicholas Smooth. A lorn hope, as it turns out.

Nasty Benadom flutters up to me with his surly little Frenchmuse slavishly in tow.

"Deary me, bad news, Renward," he gloats. "Seems our fair gunner Smoothie needled himself in his hotel bathroom."

"Oh no! Dead?"

"No such luck. Unconscious in the emergency ward at Little Company of Mary."

I knew that was a Hospital on the far South Side. And you were maybe thinking the muse life was all fun and games. Well, I know we muses aren't supposed to interfere with pure angelic work, but I only hoped Parv had something tucked behind his wings. Of course he did. He was Parvenue, one of the greatest muses of all time. At least, I hoped he did.

And there is one other thing besides Smooth overdoing it with his meds. Not an hour ago, some junior agent working for William Morris found a half dozen pages or so of a war novel manuscript scattered around in the parking lot.

"Pure genius!"

"Why didn't the shlump put his name on every page?"

"I get first dibs!"

"No, Hairy Plumaria, based on what?"

"No, yourself, Nasty Murgasti! I found the most pages!"

"First-Muse-In rule!"

107

First Muse In. That means the first muse lucky or smart enough to find the new Shakespeare wins all musely rights. In about thirty seconds I'm alone in the hall. *Had to be Quirk. Had to be. He was here a moment ago. Now where the hell would that fellow have gotten himself off to?*

I do have a little advantage; musing is a shifty trade, and the wise muse sticks close to his scribbler. That means these wingers won't be able to search full time. And, what's more, I think I know the whereabouts of the fabulous new scribbler in our midst. Wasn't I there when Cindy the bus driver let his pages fly to the chilly offshore winds off Lake Michigan? I'm thinking he left when I was distracted by Nasty. My best guess is, he's back at the Drake, nursing his wounds.

But Quirk isn't at the Drake. I can't be sure, but I take my 2nd best bet, and when, a half hour later Joey shows up at the entrance to the convention, he is still pushing Billie Rae.

Billie grins and waves as I flutter down to claim my prize, which I do without delay. I think I'm smart, but it is a close thing, me just nipping out the surly Frenchmuse from Beliz and Nasty Benadom, who probably were following me all along. Nasty has been trying to ace my wings for nearly a millennium. And, of course, my win doesn't go uncontested.

"Mine!" Nasty howls.

"Beat it, Nasty! I'm already locked with the talent!"

"But you had unfair advantage! You knew all along!"

"Take it up with mediation, if you think you have a case – which you do not!"

The Frenchmuse shrugs and flutters off with Nasty, who calls me a big dick-head, which is silly because we muses don't actually have any sexual sportage, though everybody knows sometimes our scribblers get so carried away they are convinced they are making love to us.

I give Joey the once-over. He's holding an ice bag over a swollen eye, and one sleeve of his sporty California denim shirt is torn. Most of his camera gear is missing, but Billie Rae is carrying his camera and the bag with what is left of his manuscript on his lap.

We're standing there when this mousy young assistant agent from the William Morris mailroom sidles up to Joey and shoves a page in his hand. It's a title page and it reads, The Freight Train of Love, by Joey Quirk. The wanna-be agent's voice goes squeaky in his excitement.

"Same badge, same name on the page. This is you!"

He takes Joey by the arm and tries to pull him aside. Joey resists, both hands firmly gripping Billie's wheelchair.

"Stop tugging at me! I can't leave the kid. He's waiting for his mother."

"We have to talk! This is your future!"

I lightly pressure Joey with a hint of an idea.

"This is my present," Joey tells him. "The future is not now."

"You're telling me to get lost?"

"No. I'm telling you this is my friend Billie Rae Hinkins, and I'm not going anywhere until we find his mother."

"Okay. I'll go for help. My name is Sandy Dunlap. Don't forget me. I found you first." The kid is overweight, with light beige hair and a wide face that hints of rosella or too much Paso Robles old vine zinfandel. Pity in such a young man, but the book biz has led many a mortal to over-imbibe the crush of the grape.

As I've said, I'm an old dog at this game, and I realize this agent may be young, but he has the power-scent. Nothing wrong with a a little – or a lot – of ambition. I drift another idea Joey's way.

I tell him Don't go too fast. This Sandy Dunlap may be a keeper. We don't want him to have a heart attack.

Joe repeats my notion nearly word for word and Sandy Dunlap grins over his shoulder, but it is something less than his normal big beamer. He hates it since word got around town he is on Lipitor. *I've got him thinking maybe he should ask for eight percent instead of his normal ten. Make it a sure thing.*

I'm thinking Joey Quirk is the unknown element, the lost note, the loose gene nobody understands. Every author in all of recorded time since the ancients started hammering letters in clay tablets, every one of them would jump at the chance to be up there, God's Author with Matthew, Mark and Luke. Or to perform in the Globe Theater for the king. And here Joey has his career, his future, his success as one of the greatest scribblers the earth has ever seen well in his grasp. But the unpredictable human is in motion, Jogging the other way from Dunlap and pushing Billie's wheelchair ahead of him. Joey is heading for the parking lot.

"Where are we going?" Billie Rae wants to know. The kid really is concerned, but it's me who puts his concern into words.

"Parking lot. Cindy left her bus there."

"But…the keys?"

"Under the seat. I saw her toss them. Doors unlocked."

"But…"

"You know how to get to your house, right Billie?"

"Sure. North to Winnetka."

"She's gotta be there."

Billie looks at me and I shrug, might as well go along with it. His mother didn't show and he's got to get home and take his meds. Dumb-as-a-Brick figures out how to work the levers to hoist Billie's chair into the West Wind bus, the parking attendant waves us through the gate and we're heading north in no time.

But we don't get very far. We're barely past the Drake on Michigan Avenue and about to get on Lake Shore Drive when a cop pulls us over. *Jupiter Poopiter*, he's got Sandy Dunlap in the back seat, and guess who's fluttering on either side like little gnats – Nasty Benadom and surly Frenchmuse from Belize. I flutter on over there while Chicago's Finest are patting down Joey Quirk, who has his hands high and is leaning against their squad car..

"What's up, Nasty?"

The imp gives me that twisted, evil grin of his.

"Looks like Sandy here has got the notion your man is kidnapping that poor crippled little boy."

"And where did Sandy Dunlap come up with that notion?"

Nasty shrugs innocence, but the light dancing in his eyes tells me different.

Before I can say another word, a taxi pulls up behind us. Believe me, this is getting uncomfortable with cars whipping by, but the back door on the taxi opens and Cindy throws some money at the driver and comes running toward us. I'm hoping she's left her meditation rocks behind, and I guess she has because she rushes up to make sure Billie is alright and then goes over and kicks Quirk in the shin.

"Ow! What are you doing?"

"Kidnapper!" She yells at Joey.

Quirk is so flustered he can hardly protest his innocence.

"I'm just taking Billie home. You left me in charge. His mom never did show up and you ran off like a little chicken-heart and –"

She started flailing at Joey and it takes both cops to pull her off of, but they finally get things straightened out; it seems Billie Rae's mom didn't show because she's missing.

Piss on Plato! What a mess! And now to make things worse, the limo driver starts honking his horn.

Cindy impatiently waves him off with a flip of her hand. "When he's not running my life, he's trying to ship me off to Sister Hardheart.

112

Joey Quirk gives a worried look back at the limo, its brooding occupants now silent behind dark windows.

"What should we do?"

"Give me the keys to the bus. We'll pretend we're taking Billie home. That's what I told Daddy I would do."

She takes Joey's hand and pushes straight between the two police officers.

"You see, officers, there's just a misunderstanding. We're out of here."

"But, Miss – his mother is missing."

I give Cindy the idea, not that she needs all that much encouragement. The girl is bubbling with anger.

"The Hinkins have two maids. We're going now. Or do you want to take responsibility for a crippled boy who needs the right medication every few hours."

She gestures to Billie, still in the bus, that she's coming.

Jupiter Zoopiter, they are going to let us go! Of course, it helps that I give the cops a little nudge. The image of them being stripped of their badges does the trick. I give Nasty and Frenchmuse the belittling finger as I get into a seat next to Billie. They snarl but they can't think of anything else, so I win the round.

Joey slides in the passenger seat up front. Cindy starts the engine and jerks the bus back into traffic. Soon we're out of sight and humming along with the traffic flow. But instead of continuing on to Winnetka, she waits until the last moment and

113

then zips off at the next exit. We get right back on the drive, only now we're heading south back the way we came but on the opposite side of the divided drive.

"What are you doing?"

"Don't be such a dummy, Joey Quirk. We're losing Daddy and going back to the convention center to find Billie's mom."

"But – "

That's all I let poor Joey get out before I recommend he shut his big mouth. I figure he's already in enough trouble with the pretty heroine, who is attracted to him, probably mostly because of the farty cherub with the bow and arrow. Ahh, love. Who knows where it comes from? Who cares? Enjoy the bliss, I say.

Cindy drives us south without saying another word. Joey's curiosity finally gets the best of him.

"Who is Sister Hardheart?"

Cindy sighed and her lower lip quivered.

"It's not her real name. But she's a real villain. She runs a convent that doubles as a sanitarium. Rich people like my father put their kids in there when they cause trouble; you know, don't obey their every spoken word."

"That can't be true. Not in this day and age."

A tear slides down Cindy's cheek.

"I didn't ask you, mister."

Jupiter in himmel, but the boy needs help with his relating to the opposite sex! How could such a *schmetsik* write a novel that has every muse at the meet swooning over him? I sigh and lend him a few words of apology.

114

"Ahh, Cindy, look, I'm sorry. I know we got off on the wrong foot, but—"

Maybe I should have spent a little effort in the other direction because, even teary eyed, she comes at him like a wildcat.

"Wrong foot?!   You're like a bulldozer ramming around in other people's business you don't even understand the least bit about –"

The bus weaves a bit out of its lane and a silvery upholstery van bleeps in righteous indignation.

The burly van driver, who is clenching his teeth around a stogie, yells at her.

"Learn to drive, lady!"

I give the irate driver a little mind-nudge and he swerves into the far lane and scrapes a green Volvo and there's a lot of tire squealing and a metal thump or two as we speed on past, leaving the minor traffic snarl behind us. I know I'm not supposed to do that sort of thing, but *expediency is every muses best friend*, as the old saying goes.

Joey wisely waits until we're past the colliding traffic and things calm down.

"Okay, Cindy, you're right.   I don't know what's going on in your life.   But I did want to help. I do want to.   I was taking Billie back home for you."

"Not for me! You were taking him to his father, who…doesn't get along with him."

She gave a quick look back at Billie, who I could see was pretending to be asleep.

"Look, Billie's mother has custody.   Billie's father, Mister Hinkins, wants Billie to live with

115

him. It was his custody day, but my dad told me Billie's dad had no intention of giving him back."

"But you just said –"

"I know what I just said. Mister Hinkins has a lot of money. He's tied in Chicago politics. And my dad helps him."

"In what way?"

"Lots of ways. Mr. Hinkins runs a company. They're like…enforcers. Behind the scene."

"Ohh."

The bus lapses into silence. Billie finally does fall asleep as we head back to McCormick Place. I wonder how things were going at the big author's bash. I wonder if Parvenue has been able to save Smooth, wonder if Nasty and the surly Frenchmuse will actually bring arbitration down on me. And most of all I wonder what has happened to my attempt to relax and lollygag about the Muse Swap with my fellow inspirators.

Joey is casting furtive glances at the black limo that has caught up and is following three or four cars behind us. Lucky he doesn't see the gang of eager muses buzzing like angry bees coming after us right there behind the limo.

Cindy has spotted the big black car. Hard not to, the way they are riding close on her wheels.

She grits her teeth and tosses Joey a tough little smile

"Quirk, it's not going to rattle me if you mention my father's following us."

"What's with this guy, anyway?

"This guy is my father, and he's not a nice man."

"Tell me about it."

"It's a complicated mess."

"Tell me."

"Why? I don't need your pity."

"Don't be such a bitch. I'm just asking."

"I tell you my life story and I end up as some poor, weepy character in your next novel."

"I could never write you like that. You're not weepy or pathetic in any way."

"How do you know?"

"I feel it. Definitely no weep."

"Well, what then. What do you see?"

"Stubborn. Maybe a little confused. Pretty."

She started to react to *confused*, but then bites her lip when she hears the word that saves his butt. And I barely had time to squeeze it in his thick skull.

"Yeah, stubborn," she admits. Maybe a little bit. It's hard, not being able to trust anybody."

"Try me."

She drives in silence for about a minute and then her story comes spilling out.

"You won't believe this, but my father is a killer. An actual murderer. He gets paid to do it."

"Who pays him?"

"Billie's step-father."

"Why?"

"City hall. You do it our way or you find yourself six feet under."

"You can prove this."

117

"No, of course not. And why would I want to? You tell me who would believe it? This is *the windy city*, Pal Joey."

"If you can't prove it, how do you know?"

"When you live in the same house as somebody, you overhear little bits and scraps of phone calls, you accidentally read emails...well, that part maybe not so accidental...I tell you Joey, after all these years, I *know* the truth."

"Why don't you go to the police?"

"God, you're such an innocent! The *Chicago* police? Feed me to the lions, Quirky-boy."

"I still don't get it. He's after us because he wants to kill his own daughter?"

"No, he won't kill me. He's after us because I'm supposed to marry some ancient banker geek. But that's not the bad news."

"Oh. What's the *bad* word?"

"Well, he hates me because he treats me like I'm not really his daughter. He snuck a DNA test on me, and he knows Mom cheated on him."

"Oh, oh. Did he kill her?"

"Worse. He put her away with Sister Hardheart."

"How can you be sure he won't kill you?"

"Grandpa's trust. Mom's drugged, numb out of her mind, and dear daddy controls her vote. Now all he has to do is marry me off to one of his old frosty-balls pals who can control me and Dear Daddy's got it all. But that's not the really bad news."

Joey thought about it for a while.

"Your dad is a killer; he's going to marry you off to some old crapper and that's not everything? What's the really bad news?"

"The really bad news is I told him I can't marry frosty-balls because I'm already married."

"You're married?"

"No, I just told him that."

"Married? To whom?"

"To you, silly."

"So he's going to kill me! Why did you tell him that?"

"It was the only thing I could think of at the time. And he fell for it like a ton of bricks."

"Oh, great. Now what do we do?

"Same as before. We get to the parking lot, I run, you hold them off, we lose them in the crowd at the convention."

"Yeah. I saw how good that worked last time."

"They can't catch me. I ran cross country at Loyola. But this time I bet they'll ignore you and come right after me. And when that happens, you and Billie check out his limo."

Of course she isn't figuring on the horde of muses swarming around the limo. One of those slimy wordsters is sure to sidle up to Cindy's dad and give him the idea what's going on. If my rivals realize the guy's a killer – and they probably do – they don't care. *All's fair in the muse chase*, as the old saying goes.

But it's too late for what-if's. We're back at the McCormick Place parking lot and Cindy does her usual skid-to-a-stop trick with the bus, swinging into a parking space and bringing it to a shuddering halt.

"How did you ever get a bus driver's license?"

"What, you need a license, Quirk-o-sabe?"

Okay, so that's a bad Lone Ranger pun, but give me a break, it was the best this muse could do under pressure.

She grins and kisses Joey on the nose.

"So long, Hubby. Don't forget to pick up the kids from soccer."

And then she's off and running.

As she sprints away, she yells back over her shoulder.

"Check the trunk. Bad guys always leave bodies in the trunk!"

Joey, a little dizzy from the kiss, isn't thinking about dead bodies, he's concentrating on the graceful curves of her body in motion. He barely notices the black limo has skidded to a stop stop and Cindy's dad and his lumbering assistant are cutting through the parked cars as they take off after her.

Billie Ray has to shake Joey's arm to bring him back from his romantic fantasy.

Damn the cupids of the world, I say to nobody in particular.

"The body in the trunk," Billie says to Quirk.

"Come on, Billie, that just happens in detective thrillers."

But I poke our man Quirk with the notion there could be piles of money stacked in the dark recesses of the trunk, and he rolls Billie's wheelchair over to the limo. He climbs in behind the steering wheel and stabs blindly at the choices on the dashboard.

After he opens the gas cap and the engine hood, he finally locates the right button and the trunk springs open. There is something in there, alright, but it isn't money or a dead body. It's Billie Rae's mother. She springs up into view like a bedraggled puppet. She's tied and gagged and spitting mad.

The rest of the muses have peeled off after the two men chasing Cindy, but Nasty and Frenchmuse are sitting on top of the limo, hoping something falls their way. And I'm thinking fast.

"Nasty, haven't you heard? Parvenue has been cited by the council. Smooth is anybody's grab."

"Cited? I didn't hear…cited for what?"

"Smooth was about to go over the edge. Parvenue interfered."

If Parvie actually did that, it would be one of the thirteen deadly *musins*…that is, muse sins. You don't directly interfere with a scribbler's human fate. Nasty and Frenchmuse aren't buying my story. I can see they are thinking Parvenue is too clever for that. But I get lucky. Something is up for sure, because the band of buzzards who had been flapping behind us have peeled off and now are making a bee line for the convention center.

"It's Smooth," I repeat. "Nicholas Smooth. Good for another ten or twelve best sellers. They are *schmaltz*, sure, but that's some other muse's business."

That does the trick. A moment's hesitation and the two snarky fellows zip on out of there. And just in time as a police car wails up, red-and-blue overheads doing the wink and flash.

Well, it is a clear case of kidnapping, and the cops find Billie Rae's dad and lay the law on his sorry ass. Being totally in with the establishment and owning a lawyer or two who wear expensive Italian suits and silk ties, to boot, he's out of jail in two or three days, but not before Billie Rae and his mom disappear, thanks to a professional disappearing service, the name of which I have quietly poked in her direction.

Joey waves goodbye to the kid and Billie Rae shows him a gallant salute and then gives me a wistful little smile and a wave as his mom drives them off in the West Wind bus.

Things are happening too fast to worry about everything. Joey shows his pass and marches into the book show, nearly running over Sandy Dunlap on the way. Sandy has a contract and Joey signs on the dotted line without reading it. He brushes past Sandy and quickly moves on, his eyes darting around, looking for Cindy.

Something catches the corner of my eye. It's Ivan Van Coulter and his big thug, looking for Cindy. Something big is happening at the muse meet, so I nudge Joey in that direction. Maybe he recognizes what I want, or maybe it's the fact that he's spotted the two men as well.

We sit in large chairs in the lounge. Joey scrunches down with a newspaper over his head, like he's just another author with a hangover, trying to sleep it off. Me, I sit nearby on a chandelier and watch what's going on at the muse meet. A plumply officious muse wearing a black gown and a curly white powdered wig is intoning away.

"And, said Parvenue is further accused of providing actual medications to his assigned writer, a clear act of interference with mortal destiny."

A mutter of disapproval goes up from the eager muse mob.

"Shame him! Flog him! Out him!"

I see there are two humans with papers over their heads. The first is Joey, hiding from Cindy's dad. But the second is Nicholas Smooth, and a snore is coming from under his own newspaper..

"What'll I do, Rennie?" A familiar voice reaches out to poke me. It is Parvenue, hiding under Smooth's big beige chair. He looks like a smudged and pitiful David Copperfield.

"Switch with me. Even trade. Quirk for Smooth."

Parvenue brightens.

"You'd do that for me?"

"Done."

I stand tall on my crystal chandelier, impossible to ignore, and give one of those righteous indignation speeches nobody's penned since Shakespeare, except maybe lately from John Grisham or Scott Turow. I'm in my full Renward Flyaway glory so it is a bit pompous and windy, but the general upshot is that I claim I traded Quirk for Smooth, one for one, just yesterday, and as I've been running around town protecting my old client from muse theft (here I point dramatically at a cowering Nasty and Frenchmuse), I couldn't possibly have done any mu-sinning with my new client. And Parvenue clearly has to be innocent of all charges as had already cleverly pawned the ailing Smooth off on me, why should he bother to interfere in his old client's destiny?

A short murmur of booing and the usual mumble-grumble-rumble goes up from the disgruntled gathering, all the greedy up-and-comers hoping to catch a piece of something doing the big moan. But when the fuss dies down, the council sides with me, and that's the end of everything.

Except that I spot Cindy across the hall and manage to get her to look our way. She comes on over and when she realizes it's Joey under the Chicago Times, she gets under there with him and I'm not going to say what's going on beneath the pages, but it isn't idle slumber. And a few minutes later, when Ivan Van Coulter and his thug come hussling by, they are somehow distracted by a bustle at the ticket gate and they head over in that direction.

And that's about it, except that Cindy and Joey manage to avoid the trap Ivan has set for them at the airport by renting a Rent-a-Wreck and driving it across the country to Las Vegas where they decide not to get married but to live in sin but that lasts four months until they realize they are pregnant and then they have a wonderful marriage at an old mission church in Central California.

Meanwhile, Sandy Dunlap gets Joey's war novel published but it is panned by the New York Times as being pro-war, so it is pulled from bookstore shelves, but not before a big time producer gets a copy and buys screenplay rights. Joey adapts it to a screenplay and they sign Leonardo DiCaprio play the lead and are currently on location in Morocco when Cindy is kidnapped by desert tribesmen and Joey has to mount an Arabian stallion and – but that's another story. That Parvenue really knows how to promote his scribblers; no wonder he's been awarded Best Muse six or seven times in the last millennium.

So that's all for now, except if you're feeling sorry for me that I got the short end of the stick, stop right there. This is Renward Flyaway, remember. I get Smoothie in a new groove and he starts churning out 'sensitive western romances with a touch of literature' and he's going to be good for another decade or so of solid hits.

And I guess that's the real end of the story, except that as I was leaving McCormick Place with my new man Smooth on the last day of the convention, I see this scrawny, miserable guy at the bar, drowning his sorrows in a last brewski. I get his story and nudge Nicholas on over; it doesn't take much to interest my new scribbler in a beer. And a shot. And another. Anyway, the scrawny guy is a researcher with what he is sure is a new cure for cancer, but he can't get anybody interested in buying his book "The Real Cure", that he's self-published. Well, one thing leads to another and Smooth says he knows a publisher who might be interested, and since old Parvie certainly owes me a favor or two, I get him to persuade Cindy to get in contact with Billie Rae's mother to get Billie in the project. You see, that's the way the world works. Simple, huh?

Now that's the real, absolute, final end of my tale, except that, a few days later as I'm waiting with Nicholas in Delta's high mileage passenger lounge, my eye catches an article on page three of the Sun Times about two of Chicago's upstanding citizens, a Mr. Hinkins and Mr. Van Coulter, business associates in a big moving and storage company, were run over by a West Wind passenger bus in a busy section of Clark Street. The driver is quoted as saying he didn't know what happened, the bus seemed to have a mind of its own. I certainly hope Parvenue didn't have anything to do with that. Of course, if he ever was found out and turned over to the council, there's the old Karma Clause that might come to his defense. You know, *what a muse throws around goes around.* On the other hand how likely is that? Knowing my old pal the way I do, that's not likely to ever come up.

THE BIBLE WRITER'S TRIAL

Picture how it is. A huge enclosure of sorts with vaulted ceilings reaching to the heavens and semi-transparent walls looking out on the green hills and the distant ocean, and entirely no floor at all – or rather, a distant floor represented by the actual city plaza that is grounded several hundred feet below where we are tethered. Down there, from where I had been pushed along as if by the hand and will of God Almighty, thousands of citizens look up at us. Mostly they stand in an angry clot of silence, but some few shake their fists, and a sprinkle official agitators mutter and and wave placards here and there, prepping the crowd for the appropriately nasty attitude that is to come.

The floating high air cathedral is an edifice into which a great deal of galaxy-wide thought and energy has been poured: It is state of their art, and considered star-wide by powerful culture centralists and the prevailing design mystics to be somewhat a techno-spiritual marvel. The roof overhead unfolds itself upward like hands in prayer, and smooth sheets of meta-metal have been set the lightest translucent beige to reveal the proceedings and yet shield out the worst of the afternoon sun. The rows and rows of seats are filled with the so-called cream of creation. These will be silent witnesses, over two hundred of them, adults both male and female from all casts of life, and they are dressed in plain white robes. The witnesses are placid as stone; I am fairly certain they have been granted chem-stim for higher cognitive awareness. The jury of twelve sits in a floating maglev that slowly rotates back and forth to face the audience and next the crimson robed judge and finally the wretched accused, dressed in tattered rags and bruised and bleeding from a thousand cuts and scratches. That wretched fellow would be me.

I am a one-of-kind, a newbie, a different sort of thing that cannot be explained the old way. And I've written my own bible about it. There was an old bible, telling how things were since the universe began, and then there was a second bible, telling how everything is today as it should be. Between these two treasured tomes, it was declared and set in stone that everything had been said that could or would ever be said about just about everything. Then I came along and wrote as I did, and, you know, people are afraid of change. Odd they would be like that, don't you think? After all, if there is one constant in the universe, it is change. Nothing ever stays the same.

So here we are today at my trial in the sky, and believe me, it is some event! It is not only witnessed by throngs actually crowding the landscape below, but it is being beamed throughout the old Milky Way. I have been pushed around a bit on my display walk up the metaphorical thousand-stair hill, and somewhat enthusiastically flayed by scores of ceremonial cat o' nine tails bought for a few pesados from the hawkers, and even blow-gunned with barb-darts on my float up to the proceedings.

More onlookers are standing in back on this level, as many as the huge vaulted-ceiling room will allow. This is seemingly mystical, as there is no solid floor, or indeed anything resembling a floor, so we all appear to be standing on nothing, and the crowd below has to look up through the mass of ourpresence, through the seated rows of witnesses, the judge and the jury to catch a glimpse of the doomed wretch and the squeeze about to be put upon him. Again, make no doubt about it, that wretch is me.

I'm the entertainment for the day. Since all electronic stimulation has been outlawed for a period of thirty three hours before the service in the name of the divine tradition, I am the only entertainment. And their impatience is obvious. They are insisting that something significant must happen, and that means it had better be dramatic. You know the saying, *Take away the unwashed masses vids and they turn into animals.*

The proceedings begin with a high-pitched schoolboy's voice as he recites, "Accused of blasphemy. Irreverence. Outright scorn of *The way, the life and the truth."*

This scroll-boy in his full-length black frock and white lace over-skirt is reading from a plazmolded e-tablet plastic designed look like an ancient scroll. He is a pure-schooled innocent. He has the pious look, perfect for the ofey news cast, which will be universally broadcast from now until the death squeeze takes place.

He is positioned as if reading to the crimson-robed old man who is sitting on his ornate gilded throne as it floats above the audience, the illusion being the throne is moved by the breath of the worshipers as his voice is broadcast throughout the entire city. The heavily carved chair of ancient oak wood to which I am tightly bound floats at the same level as the judge, the jury and the witnesses. From my vantage point, I can see the clever struts and invisible power bars creating much of this illusion, and assume the old man's throne and the floating jury box have similar supports.

They've got me dead to rights. I did write the Rogue Bible known as the Rogue Pirates Bible Heretical. Well, that is to say, I did write down and combine the many scraps and fragments to preserve what remained from the Pirate's stories, handed down by word of mouth from generation to generation on our insignificant, out-of-the way planet.

Our pirates story is an old one, but true enough, I suppose, in that it did have an actual origin, though several millenniums in the past. The originals were a band of outlaws, preying on freighters bringing rare earth ores in from planetary bodies in a far fringe of the galaxy. Their sins were many, and they took no prisoners. You joined their not-so-merry band or were ejected. Well, with the federation spread thin across thousands of solar systems and most of the galaxy unexplored, you can see how such a pestilence might be able to survive, and even thrive, over and above the hardships of space travel.

Well, our scruffy band of progenitors were successful for a time, until after a particularly successful ship-grab their scan watch joined in the drunken revelry with the rest, and as luck would have it, they fell prey to a dark meteor shower. The ship badly crippled, they stumbled their way down to a remote planet, far from ordinary shipping lanes. We called it Ketchforth.

The several dozen pirates who survived the crash landing mingled with the natives, who were fair in bodily aspects and noble of spirit, and over the generations we together were able to garner the natural resources and cull and expand our knowledge to build a society that was able to once again thunder into space, and, in time, to rejoin the federation.

"You then do not deny writing this heretical work?" The judge asks. I start out of my reverie.

"Forgive me, Judge. As you can see, I am not quite my ordinary self."

"You deny it or not?" The judge repeats, the dour expression firming on his wrinkled lips. My God, he has to be a hundred and sixty three years old, if a day!

"My name is on the title page," I respond.

"That is not a direct answer."

"It is scribed by me, *The Bible According To Bran Heath.*"

"And Bran Heath is a pen name, a *nom de plume*, is it not?"'

I admit it is.

"Then the court does not recognize the distinction."

I sigh. It is an eternally old author's argument. Who actually created anything? Some say in the beginning there were really only seven stories. Critics debate back and forth, no, ten, no, seven...or maybe eight if you count comedy. See, you get any two experts in a room, it is already an argument about to pounce on the tranquility. But my mind wanders. Loss of blood, you know. I try to convince myself everything will be alright; I've been in scrapes like this before, though I cannot recall the red stuff pooling about my feet like this.

My quandary isn't about admitting to writing my own bible. And I've already decided to respond in the Ketchforthian way

"My point is, I simply took the scraps and gathered them in one volume."

"*Forbidden* scraps!" The old man's sore-pocked lips purse into a disapproving oval.

"Don't you have any salve for your lips?" I ask. "On Ketchforth we have this amazing plant that you – "

The electro lash jolts through me and I forget whatever I was going to say.

"Forbidden heresies!" the judge shouts.

"Historical documents," I respond, once my shuddering frame recovers sufficiently to allow me speech. "Furnished to me in due accord by your antiquarians."

"The accused will not speak unless addressed!"

A flickering lash of fire appears as if from the roof overhead and cuts a new mark across my back. Blood seems reluctant to flow from it. I have already lost a great deal. Not satisfied, the old man waves with a backhanded flick of annoyance and the first gash is crossed with another. This one, a little deeper, apparently has the desired result.

The room is beginning to swim around me. I feel like I am back on that cross, some six millennium ago, blackbirds in a sea blue sky, circling to the feast.

"Shouldn't we get on with it?" I suggest.

There are more lashes, and shouting. My already questionable idea of what is real swims about, and I must have passed out, but when I come back around, they are still in front of me—audience, jury, altar boy, judge—silently staring as if I'd put them on hold.

"What do you think?" the judge thunders. He isn't talking to me, but to the jury.

Now is the time for the agitators to do their work. They move through the crowd below, chanting, "Crush him! Crush him! Crush him!"

I can feel it, the combined fury of the collected citizenry coagulating like a living force field to collapse my being into nothing. It is, of course, an illusion, a fabrication of forces concocted to convince the gathered mob they have some sort of extra-sensory powers. The force, however, is real enough, and the energy pinpointed with me at the crosshairs will scald, singe and then ignite me in an entirely satisfactory demonstration of just retribution.

Time to perform a different sort of miracle. I null the electro-binds around my wrists and ankles and I stand as erect as possible considering the many insults and injuries to my physical being. My wounds seal themselves and my tattered robe returns itself to a shining white. I raise my hands and give them a bit of theatrics, you know, the classic golden glow of sainthood and even a bit of a halo. They are stunned to silence, even the agitators, every one.

And in that moment, I tell them, "It is no heresy to assure you that for every action in the known universe there is an equal and opposite reaction."

And, horrible as I know the consequences will be, I have no alternative but to unleash it on them. There is, as both of their bibles foretell it, *Fire in the sky.* Fire here, there, everywhere, actually. I don't know if you could call it The Big Bang. Big enough, I guess. Using the Ketchforthian Principles, I was able to slip our own Solar-ketch system, including the double sun and all the planets, into a parallel and benign brane.

The citizens of the galactic federation would have done well to actually have studied our out-of-the way and insignificant Ketchforth to see if we had acquired any new knowledge to go along with our fidelity to the old ways. But they had never done so.

FAIR EXCHANGE

The Herboidian visitors were spheroidal, and flexible as rubber balls. Each was about fifteen feet in the cross-hatch, and each of them was supported on three slim-but-tough flex-legs. The legs telescoped in length as needed and on mental command could be whippy as willows or strong as oak tree trunks. The Herboidian's bulbous bodies were multi-colored at will, plus the blush of invisibility when needed. Each individual was divided into three sectors, like an orange compartmentalized into three slivers, and each Herboid possessed three eyes on each sector and so they were able to peer in all directions at once, though the one or several eyes concentrating on whatever was of prime interest for that moment tended to grow more prominently out from the body bulb on a resilient, living-plastic stalk. Each of the three sectors boasted three eyes, an arm, a leg, a toothed eater, a pooper, a glorious flexoid vagina and a marvelous penis that could go from zero to sixty in less than a second.

In summary, for those who haven't been keeping up, that totalled on the average Herboidian nine eyes, three arms, three legs, three eaters, three poopers, three vaginas and three penises. Ingesting, pooping and sex itself were simply for the pleasure of it, for the Herboids had advanced to where they consumed energy directly from sunlight or bat-pack beams, and as for sex—well, more of that later.

Beyond these characteristics, in actual point of fact, each Herboidian also had three brains, though long, long ago these had been paralleled, auto-wired and interfaced to act as one functioning entity.

"I say it's stupid and we should quit now while we're ahead," Nordli grumped. Though they were equally three-in-one, Nordli was nominally their leader, somewhat like Groucho might be said to lead the happy pranks of the Marx Brothers.

"Yeah, and there goes our show." Carpo grew eye-stalks and rolled all nine of them in the direction of the distant, oddly yellow sun. "After that, what do we do until the Messiah comes?" His eyes, on auto-shield, were clearly not looking at anything, but that patented gesture of Carpo's, a shrug with the eyes, would be universally recognized by their fans everywhere..

And it was, after all, an entirely rhetorical question. The Herboidians didn't believe in any sort of a God-thing. *What reason to worry about meeting the maker when one expected to live forever?* They had come to believe they had no maker, or more precisely, they were self-made. In that sense, the entire herboidian race was often said by the wisest herboid thinkers to be a creation of its own device.

"No, seriously," Nordli continued his mild rant. We herbs own everybody and herboikind runs everything, far as anybody's nine eyes can see. Meanwhile, pitiful stellar hopping herbs like we three are so exhausted for new show material that here we find ourselves on the far-flung end of one of the remotest tentacles in the galaxy. The entire fricking pyramid of three-in-oneness could make a galactic leap any time now. So why do we even bother with this map-crapping through the last few saps in the tired old gal?"

They were arguing one of their staples, the same thing as always, Herboidial Domination of the galaxy and herbkind's herbifest destiny to rule the universe or destroy it in the process. *When was the time to spend the resources necessary to their first galactic leap? Was it now? Would it be soon? Would it be never? Never had to be unthinkable!* Nordli finally ground to a halt, having entirely run out of philosophical gas. Larpo, playing the fool as usual, contributed a silent shrug to the discussion. You could see he was judging their sacred destiny to be little more than a circle-jerk, a dumb and ridiculous reflex action. But this was sho-biz. When you're *full in the dance,* shrugs go by in a second and meanwhile the show was transmitting on-beam; so Carpo had to say something, if only to fill the space-time until they could get to a cut-away, do a station break or a commercial.

"That's entertainment," he responded, spinning to give a full three-lip grin and bouncing up and down on his tripods in a way that drove the main camera-droid crazy. "And, really, somebody's got to do it."

Carpo was used to putting up with Nordli's endless grousing and his dry, intellectual attempts at wit. And Nordli's complaining was in point of fact *endless*, the Herboids having solved the problem of nearly-eternal life with their snappy and tenacious inner regenerators, *an invention for the ages,* as the

137

herboid scientists had triumphantly proclaimed. And so here you had the Carpo and Larpo and Nordli Forever Show, beamaroo-ed to 77,683 habitable planets at the last count—and with more coming on-line all the time as terra-forming progressed—this job, or mission, if you will, of bulldozing barren planets to habitability symbolizing the very embodiment of the never-say-die Herboidian spirit as it inexorably smooshed out in all directions further and further to the very-most nether corners of the galaxy—if, indeed, you could consider that a platter shaped mass of billions of stars might have *corners*.

The thing of it was, since the glorious time when they had engineered their own *eternal destiny*, the Neo-Herboidian Society had already cartographed, detailed and consumed well over eight-ninths of their own Shining Platter Galaxy. Still, Nordli did make a valid point with his arguments: *When was enough enough?* The traditional answer, of course, was *Never!* Irrevocable triplicate advancement to total domination of everything was as natural as the rest of tripodianism. Three arms, three legs, three eyes, three hundred and thirty three truths, the one-in-three mystery of the pyramid, the eternal triangle of life, itself. *Why go on re-stating the obvious?*

In this show segment, The Three Gangster Rogues—that was also the official name of their show— were side-tripping on an odd-ball little planet where the primitive creatures all seemed doomed to have two, four or no legs at all, these last slithering along on the ground like—well, like *abominations*, truth be told. The only thing an herb could imagine that could possibly be worse than having four, two or one leg surely had to be none at all. Jinxian as all that might be, the image of a creature with no legs whatsoever slinking about *on the body itself* was proving wonder-ball for the ratings, which were spiking on just about every one of the 77,683 odd. (Oops, that would be 77,684, the nouveau-terraced planet Praxicaliaga 99 having come on-line since the last commercial break, and congratulatory sips and lickings all around.)

After their show had run for these endless millenniums, the Rogues had their gags down to a common three-wall patter. Nordli played the intense narration type who did the serious and professorial stuff—all the descriptive patter, setting up the geography and the climate and the regional oddities, as well as some light philosophical shots at *the meaning of it all*. He even occasionally dipped into the old myths, scoffing the dim and distant legend stuff about God and his angels and demons. Carpo handled the play-by-play and the interplay comparisons between similar planets they had known, plus his off-the-wall assessment and physical dissection of the local weirdo creatures. And Larpo came on as their bumptious color guy, handling thc scx play and the general goofing around, always bouncing here and there, full of irreverent nonsense and quirky commentary…and not ever as stupid as he seemed. Larpo, indeed, was a bit of a wizard when it came to thinking, though he did a very good job of hiding it. There is something to be said for *hiding your genius,* you know. After all, they were confined together for long periods, and although they were nearly compatible as a triangle could possibly be, near-eternity is a long time to hold a grudge if somebody is smarter than everybody else.

Early in this episode of the show, Larpo had performed brilliantly with some crude jokes about the water mammals they'd sported with in the first sunray time, you know, *How do you know who you screw when you look exactly like you, you and you?* Larpo had highlighted his bit with typical fun-time play, popping one of the creatures inside his third vagina, which he'd enlarged and made all sticky-wet for the gag. But the creature seemed to like it, probably for the relaxo-stimulating effects of the sex gel. This was interesting in itself, and so they were tempted to stay with it a bit on the long side, forcing them to cut-away to a commercial for Doxy-Moxy-Boxy surface cream when the sex gel overcame the primitive water creature's circulatory system and its veins burst in a horrible red mess. Larpo naturally had time enough to clean himself during the intermission.

After that the Three Gangster Rogues zipped land-side in their little hovercraft, and then they decided to go invisi-shield. There was a grassy meadow with a stream and a small clan of possibly faintly sentient creatures skittering around on only two legs. The creatures, of course, couldn't see them, so it was to be one of those treasured *nature uncovered* show segs for which they were widely admired, if not exactly respected. Carpo did a bit on the unpredictability of living your unsteady way through life without a firm tripodic base. He passed the cam shot to Larpo, who made fun of the hairy creatures opening the mouths on their tiny heads in some primitive attempt at communication. The awkward little fellows seemed intent on catching some green-skinned hoppers that were much smaller than they were. But, instead of eating the tiny creatures, they pushed them on their penis rods, rubbing them up and down in obvious satisfaction. Carpo took a moment to speculate on this bit of inter-beastial behavior, surely the hairy little fellows were showing the potential of a species with some promise—that is, if they weren't almost certain to be wiped out in the near or more distant future by the million and one things that could stomp them into extinction surely as an impacting meteorite or the burp of a solar flare. As if to prove Carpo's point, the unpredictable but always funny Larpo pointed the smallest of the three fingers on his second arm in the direction of the hairy little biped. One zap and the funny little walk-about disappeared in a fiery gout of blood and flame.

After that, Larpo went visible, and then tried to catch another of the hairy two-leggers. It took some doing, for once the bi-pod saw the relatively large ovoid form bearing down on him with obvious intent, the small creature skibabbered about like a wiggle bug from Fraxia. But jovial Larpo, steady as a pyramid, relentlessly thudded after him. As *our joyful rogue* was four or five times the size of the hairy little bi-pod, there was no doubt as to the quashing. Larpo snatched the screaming biped up in one three fingered hand and stuffed him in one of his vagina pockets, enlarged properly for the engorgement. A beatific smile spread from lip to lip to lip and, obviously sleepily occupied, he wandered thirty three paces away to snoozel in a grove of tall sticks with green fronds on their tops. Without the aid of their prankster funny-herb trio-mate, Carpo and Nordli fungled around chewing on grasses, berries and small creatures, and relayed their impressions to the couch-heads back planet-side on every one of the over seventy seven thousand planets that carried the show.

"My third vagina itches," Larpo muttered sleepily. "Itchy, twitchy, scratchy-bitchy."

That was something new, and it might have been lost to the rest of the trio as well as entirely to the 77,000 plus viewing planets, but it was accidentally picked up by floating robo-cam number 14.. So alerted, the other two rogues wandered over to have a look.

"Here, let me try." Nordli took hold of one of the hairy little creature's legs, pulled him out and crapped on him and then slid the thing in one of his vaginas. Sure enough, a few ticks was enough to confirm that silly old trickster Larpo was right.

"Hey, my turn," Carpo grumbled. "Gimme, before the poor bastard is all used up."

He, too, stuck the creature inside, and just barely had time to experience the strange itch, which was actually more of a *tingle,* he thought. Once the creature was silent, he threw it on a sandy spot by the small water stream, next to the sticks-with-fronds-on-top, where it lay motionless and obviously dead. It didn't pop into a bloody mess, which was a disappointment, but the show had to go on so they did a bit of song-and-dance and cut away to a Genie McBeanie Beauty Sphere commercial. Carpo used the intermission to extract a spoon from a pouch on his third stomach pack. He began to carefully clean himself out with the soft end scooper. Herboids had a fetish about being clean. No longer needing sex to replicate, each had three penises and three vaginas, so they could taste the delicious fruits of sex whenever they wanted and in as many ways as possible. Some extremists went so far as to grow nine or thirty-three of each organ, though this was considered cumbersome and even kinky. No matter the number, to a self-aware Herboidian, being tidy and fastidious was a matter of personal pride and even honor.

"Directive three-point-three," Nordli sounded the alert in a mock-stern voice. Three-point-three was the directive that reminded off-planet far travelers that they were not to use tools of any kind in the presence of sentient native life.

"Like he's *sentient,*" Larpo gurgled happily, reaching for his own spoon.

"More like he's dead," Carpo said, taking a closer look. He podded closer to give the thing a poke with the sharp end of his spoon, but it surprised them by lurching up to balance on its two skinny hind-pods. In another instant it had scurried away and was gone.

"Just playing dead," Carpo shrugged. "I'm still itching."

"Me, too."

"Me, three."

They hover-skimmed back to their waiting galacto-craft and pointed it toward home. When they got there ten thousand spans later, they were itching like crazy. When you live forever, new sensations are hard to come by; by the time they returned to the first outreaching planets of the civilized sectors, fans everywhere were eager for this new sensation. Everybody in the galaxy wanted to experience *The Gangster Rogue Itch*, as it came to be called, and as it could be passed on through casual sex, and, because in the herboidian culture all sex was casual, *The Itch* soon spread like a cosmic death ray throughout the entire Shining Combine of 77,687. (three more terraformation planets newly added) Unfortunately, the terra construction began to slow and soon came to an abrupt halt, for *The Itch* itself was followed by scabs, weakening of the tripodic frame, and eventually the knowledge that death had not been entirely eradicated from the Herboidian dictionary.

In the relatively brief period of suffering and universal decay that followed, mounds of rotting tripodic bodies lay scattered about everywhere on every planet. In this time of increasing horror and dispair, the remaining survivors of the great Herboidian race rediscovered God…or, perhaps more accurately, reinvented him. Giant temples were constructed at enormous expense of both herbpower, herboid lives and accumulated treasures from the far-flung gem planetoids. In these times of foaming evolution, new levels of tripodic society were formulated, differences found or imagined, and the lower orders systematically sacrificed to the

Neo-Tripodic God, who surely would not ignore these gifts from the faithful, who presumably would find their rewards in the next life. Yes, there had to be a *next* life. *Unimaginable that there wouldn't be.* It made their brief temporal lives bearable, because it gave the herboids something to die for. And they gladly sacrificed from among the dregs of their new multi-layered social order to prove their own worthiness. Indeed, after the final *death by itch,* were anyone left to record what had actually taken place, the statisticians would have been hard-put to know whether more had been taken down in noble and sacred sacrifice or by the Itchy Sickness itself.

Meanwhile, back on the ordinary little back-wash planet near the tip of one far-flung tentacle of the Shining Platter Galaxy, a descendant of the odd little biped that Larpo had captured was showing his fellows the way to hit a coconut with a stick so that it might be more easily cracked open.

"Spoon," the hairy little fellow said, nodding his monkey-like head and grinning with the accumulated wisdom of the ages.

RALPHIE'S END

I'd taken a quick rollie-boy across campus to the Coop to meet my sister. I plugged in for a refresher and was marking time when one of the snarky prof assistants I'd rebuffed about a hundred million times tried to slide in the booth next to me. I held up one hand, palm out.

"Beat it, Joansie," I said.

"Aww, come on, Alicia."

"Betty," I corrected her.

Alicia is my twin sister. To anybody with half a brain we don't look much alike. But this was Joansie, one step up from a no-brainer.

"Just a few minutes?"

I was definitely not in a mood for casual pal-ship, and if I had been, it wouldn't be with her.

"Beat it, Joansie. Don't make me hurt you."

She scuttled away like I really might, and I had half an inclination to zap her just to let her know I could.

A few decades or so ago Joansie lost her twin as so many of us do, and ever since she's been running around feeling lonely and needy and greedy. There's a sol-clit who really needs a pet. No sense of balance, you know. Look, don't think I'm cold hearted. It's just that I am not and never could be her twin. We are all first-offs, every one of us, and we're all making our way through uncharted territory. Try seeing it this way; ever since the first damn little scrap of organic DNA on this planet replicated itself by some miracle or other, every

146

next bit of DNA evolved (or *advanced*, if you look at things that way) over eons and ages from that first bit. But with Alicia and Betty and Joansie and the rest of us…well, we didn't evolve, we jumped from what every bit of living matter had been to this new thing, the thing that we are today and apparently will be until the world as we know it comes to an end. That makes us a grand experiment, I suppose. Certainly, you could call us *advanced models*. Or, just say it like it is: Hi, I'm a *Homo Solaris.*

There was a group of a dozen or so gals plugged in around a boxing match on the broad-screen where two saps were flailing away at each other, and the sol-clits were a noisy bunch, cheering and groaning and tossing their coins in a box. That's another thing, you know. You can take two sap men of equal everything – weight, height, quickness, boxing skills – and you still cannot be absolutely 100% sure of the outcome. Gambling. Most of us love it. Nobody is sure why, but most of us do.

A few seconds went by and then Alicia showed up. She slid into the booth and plugged in next to me. She'd been volunteering over at the zoo and still smelled slightly of sweat and dander. I didn't mind; to me it was a pleasant scent. She took one look at Joansie's retreating form and grinned. "You didn't actually zap her?"

"Naw. Just threatened to."

"Any news?" she said.

I shook my head and looked down at the table.

"Yes, there is. And it's all bad."

"Oh, no! What?"

They found Ralphie. Over in junktown."

Ralphie was our pet. We'd gotten him from Animal Control and we'd had him for over fifteen years now, ever since he was a young scamp. In that time he had become an integral part of our lives, the way pets are meant to do, but there is a downside to that. You know the way they worm their way into our supposed wants and needs. It isn't fair, really. We come to love them and then all too soon they leave us.

"Is he okay?" she said.

"They found him three days ago. While we were in Cancun."

"No…" Her mouth fell open. There was a stunned moment of silence while she thought about the consequences.

"Yes. I'm sorry, babes" I said. "You know they only get three days."

"No, no, no! They could have called! They would have found out we were out of town and they could have held him over for us!"

"He didn't have a chip," I said.

"He did, too! We were there when he got it. Remember the howl he put up?"

"Well, he didn't have one when they caught him. Maybe it burned out or something."

"If he didn't have a chip, how did they find him?"

"It was a routine stray roundup. I don't think he had any idea what was going on. You know, we never let him out on the street."

"Well, we did take him to Regina Park. You know how he loved the pet park."

I gave her a sad smile, remembering the good times.

"He was something special, that's for sure."

I wouldn't say it in public, but Ralphie was more than a pet to us; he was a member of the family. It had been just the standard twosome of Alicia and me, and then our pet Ralphie came along. We'd had pets before, but Ralphie was special and it got to be where it felt like we could not remember a time when he wasn't around. But I was past remembering the pet park. He had meant so much to us! I was thinking back to cuddling up in bed with him. Ralphie, Ralphie, Ralphie! He was a sweet fellow, even though he'd never been clipped. The female pets are automatically neutered except for the breeders. Clipping the males is optional, and when you claim one for your own pet, it is owner's choice. Naturally, if you don't go for the clip, there's all that other business, but we didn't mind. Not ever, not even a little bit. As we'd picked Ralphie up from the pound and he seemed happy enough, we left things as they were, and neither Alicia nor I had ever regretted it. *You groom your pet*, as the saying goes, *and your pet grooms you.*

I know some people don't like the idea of sleeping with their pets in the same bed, particularly not the unclipped ones. I've been told it is not natural and even *yuckey* but Alicia and I had always slept with ours. We both shared Ralphie, and we both believed it comforted him, and he seemed to need it. And maybe in some primitive way we needed it, too. Don't hold that against me or call me a *Neander*. I'm not 100% sure about what I'm saying; it's just a vague notion.

I looked over at my sister and saw that she was sobbing. I never thought that she was one to have real feelings, and until now I didn't think she was capable of that. Actually, neither one of us was much the emotional sort, but Ralphie had been special, so soft and cuddly and yet firm muscled and proud in his own way. At the same time, we both knew it was our own fault for allowing ourselves to get into such a state. Pets don't live a long time, and you can't let yourself get too attached, you have to be ready to say goodbye. You tell yourself there's a pet heaven and the fantasy is that someday you will see each other again in the great by-and-by, and that sort of gets you through until you start feeling depressingly singular again and if that happens, there's always a long waiting list of pets who really need an owner just waiting right down there at the pet place.

Alicia pulled herself together and stared at the punchers on the broad-screen without even seeing them. She had never been the betting kind.

"How did he get out?" she said.

"Climbed out. It's the only way I could figure."

We had hot-wired the back yard, and the fence wall was twenty feet high.

"Couldn't be. I thought Ralphie was afraid of heights."

"Me, too." I shrugged. "Maybe he dug a way out or just squeezed under the fence. I don't really know."

"You think he didn't love us?"

"No, Alicia. I am one hundred percent sure he did love us with all his heart. He was just bored, us being away and all."

I found myself thinking back to Animal Control. The place was down the rail in Agoura, a clean white walled facility that smelled of pet food and urine.

"It had to have been horrible for him, that last three days, you know, jammed in there with all those other pets."

"You think he knew he was going to die?"

"You are too soft-hearted, you know," I said.

"Hah. I don't have any heart at all."

I sighed and made a move to get up from the booth. I had my own group-think coming up in twenty minutes. I placed a reassuring hand on my sister's shoulder.

"You go figure. He had it all with us. He had everything; a good home, food, shelter, all the love a pet could ask for."

"Sapiens," she said. "With a name like that, you'd think they'd be a little smarter."

ROLLERDUCK

Strangled by his sadly overburdened mother and then thrown in a smelly dumpster behind a Del Taco in Woodland Hills, California, young Rollerduck had never known a home of his own or the loving care and concern that we all take for granted. He was forced to grow up on the parking lot, a sadly alienated common ordinary wood duck who had been condemned by his genetics and then bruised and battered by a society that had turned its collective beak from him.

There were times when it seemed too much to bear, the cruel tides sweeping in and out of his life and washing him back and forth as if he had no webbed feet of his own. Born out of wedlock, sadly bent of pinfeather and miles away from the nearest pond... What hope could there be for such as Rollerduck in a heartless society, among people who simply didn't care that he could probably duck-dance with the best of them, if only given the chance? His webs were cracked and nearly split from lack of moisture, and he suffered from taco sauce in his feathers and a big wad of pink bubble gum stuck to the top of his head like a beret. He didn't even have the classic green-and-white ring around the neck. And yet, there were times when the bright spirit of rebellion shown in his right eye, gleaming like a marble or a painted piece of birdshot. He only had one eye, but that simply served to make it shine all the brighter.

Poor young Right Shoe, for that was his name, the first words he'd seen when he regained consciousness and saw the words on a tongue of smelly leather and realized he was hopelessly stuck for life in a discarded roller skate. He might have given up right then and there, but for the intervention of a social worker who happened along. Her name was Mavis, and she was attracted to the area by the Macho Burrito special with the free French fries.

Right Shoe looked pathetically up at her from his hiding place in the bushes next to the entrance. Mavis would never even have noticed him, but seeing her with her sad, plain face, thick glasses and hair tied up in a severe bun, he felt a strange longing for sensations of warmth and home that he had never known. Something caught in his throat, which had never really healed from the strangulation, and he made the noise that had made all the difference.

"Quaaack-k," he said.

In the weeks that followed, she was more than kind to him, stroking his feathers in just the right way and cultivating their special friendship until she had earned his trust and could begin hammering him with tough love.

"Some day you will have to leave the rollerskate," she told him. But this he did not want to hear. He was not ready, he would fight it to his dying day. Hermits had their crabs, dogs their houses, and he his roller home. And, anyway, he was stuck in it and dead set against an experimental operation, all those doctors eyeing him with their cold inspection as they prepared their cutting separation instruments.

It had not been easy to open up to Mavis, for duck love is a particularly warm and tender experience, and Right Shoe had to reach outside of himself, even in the shoe as he was, to gain insight from her rough lessons in kick-punch affection. But he had succeeded at last.

Learning to survive, indeed to overcome his impediment, had been the one achievement in an otherwise mean and sorry existence. First, he learned to roll slowly about, and then to change directions by leaning one way or the other like a biker. Then, to do the same, but like a Hell's Angel. Then curbing, gravel skids and off roading. Finally, he came to know he was faster on the ground than other ducks in the air. And he even learned to flutter, to flap a few feet off the ground dragging his heavy wheeled boot along. The real breakthrough was all mentals, and success came when he finally realized he wasn't handicapped at all, he was otherly advantaged. He was, in fact, the fastest, sleekest, quackiest duck on the block. At least, that's what he told himself sometimes in the quiet dreams, in those moments when no drunks were sitting on the lid, thunking on the iron sides of his dumpster with their feet.

Late one afternoon he rolled along the street on his way back to the dumpster which had become his home. He was late, and so he didn't even to view his attractively rolling image in the dusty windows of the shops that lined the streets.

"Hey, Ducky-wucky," a surly voice sounded from a dark alley.

Right Shoe paused, uncertain what to do. His mother had told him never to listen to voices that sounded from dark alleys. His poor mother, reduced to a bag of broken feathers by the recklessly driven car loaded with uncaring teenagers driven insane with too much sugary Coca-Cola and sweets, smacked down as she tried to dust her feathers of her unfortunate offspring and make her way out of the parking lot and back to the pond. She had never made it. She had barely waddled back to the dumpster. Now she lived with him in the land of waste and toss offs, and she depended on him. Sure, maybe she beat him with her one good wing from time to time, but he deserved it, he needed to keep his webbed feet to the pavement.

"Hey, Duck-boy," the voice repeated, "Come here a minute." This time there was a threatening edge.

Right Shoe hesitantly moved towards the alley, which was dimly lit and overflowing with street people litter, mounds of cardboard box homes and junky rows of supermarket carts.

"Wh-what do you want?" he asked, his voice quacky with fear.

"I got a gift for you," the voice said. It was Farty Pickle, that greasy kid from the other side of the parking lot. "Here." Farty held out a paper Del Taco sack, the kind they give you when you only order a couple of plain tacos.

He had no choice. Right Shoe was simply a product of his environment. Social engineers can

155

confirm this; he simply had no will, no desire to accept responsibility, no ability to think for himself. How could he, trapped like his uncle Howard in a world he never made?

"Heavy," Right Shoe said, taking the bag and weighing it with one wing. It was surprisingly heavy. He reached in and pulled out a snubnosed .38 caliber police special.

"Wooow!" he shouted in surprise. The pistol dropped from his hands and discharged with a tremendous roar and puff of smoke. There was an acrid smell in the air. Right Shoe's heart was pumping so fast he thought he'd have a duck stroke right there.

"Look-it what you did," Farty said, his voice ripe with ugliness.

Right Shoe had fallen backwards more or less where his butt would be if he wasn't trapped in a rollerskate shoe. He looked down. He was resting on an old lady's stomach. It was a schoolteacher, Miss Arbuckle, in fact. She seemed to be seeping blood from a hole in her head.

"No...I didn't do nothin'," Right Shoe protested.

"Hey, your feather prints are all over that sucker...looks like you're a murderer, Duck-boy," Farty said with a little chuckle. He paused, eyeing the worried duck from beak to wheels, "But I'm gonna help you." He picked up the gun with a greasy paper napkin and placed it back in the taco bag. In two winks he had it out of sight. "I'll keep it safe," he said. "But now you owe me one."

Rollerduck had no choice but to return empty-handed to his mother. He'd gone out for provisions, a change of pace, maybe a little something from Wendy's across the parking lot. But he'd come back empty winged. Defeated once again by life, he fluttered up to the rim of the trashbin and jumped down inside. His mother, who had been waiting, hit him with a broken mop handle.

"Late again, you bad beak boy! I'll take you down sure as my name is Molly Ringneck!" She jabbed like a fencer and then gave him a roundhouse wallop on his feathery butt.

"Mom, wait, I can explain," he began. It took some time, between ducking the low swings and darting out of range of the head knockers, but he finally managed to explain about the voice in the alley and the gun that had accidentally gone off and the dead old lady.

"Did you at least get her purse?" Molly asked.

He had to admit he hadn't. His mother reared back to deliver a death-blow, but just then Fernando the voicebox guy buried her under two big black plastic garbage bags full of sloppy cups and old scraps.

Right Shoe had been through this before. He knew there was some danger she could suffocate, but he wasn't daffy. He would wait until her quacks began to weaken before helping her out. He sighed, smoothing his beak with his left wing while he surveyed the new bags, unconsciously proud that the best quacks were all left wingers. At least tonight they would have enough to eat.

EXTINCTION

Harley was an ice turtle, the last remnant of a race left behind after the last great Ice Age. One doesn't think of turtles as adaptable, but as the ice melted and the sun beat down, the same thick shell that had protected him from the freezing snow and polar bear claws now shielded him from the fierce Southern California sun and the snap of the coyote's hungry jaws.

"Hello, there! What have we here?" a voice said. It was Miss Twilliger, on a Sabbatical from the Biology department and doing contract work for the zoning commission. "Jumping Jiminy, an Ice Turtle!"

"Please, hold it down," Harley said, "I'm catching a few rays and a few Zzzz's here."

"But you're a rare and almost extinct species!" Miss Twillinger trilled.

"You couldn't tell it by me," Harley grumbled, now really annoyed that the newcomer was standing in the sun.

"Well, smarty-pants, when's the last time you saw a mating partner?"

"What, a girl turtle? It must have been ten years ago."

"And? And? And?" Miss Twillinger's voice quivered with excitement, hoping she would forthwith be led to a hitherto unknown colony of rare ice turtles.

"And nothing," Harley said. "She was run over by a BMW. Street pizza."

"Oh, what a tragedy for all of nature!"

"Yeah, sometimes life sucks."

The coarse tone of his remark set Miss Twillinger back. Vulgarity didn't seem proper at all, coming from a nearly extinct turtle. He should be grateful he was still around, able to 'suck oxygen', as they say.. Miss Twillinger was a teacher; she felt she could get down with her students and rap street talk with the best of them.

"How old are you, anyway?"

"I'm really old…centuries, maybe even a millennium or two. We ice turtles don't show our age."

"No, you don't look that old," Miss Twillinger agreed.

Harley warily eyed her backpack. He'd been around humans for a long time.

"Say, you're not going to stick me in a bag, are you?"

"No, I'm just doing a survey to see if we should build condos here or not."

"Condos?" Harley tried to scratch his brow but his paw wouldn't reach, so he had to be satisfied with rubbing his head on a nearby boulder.

"Yes, and I'm afraid that wouldn't do. We build condos here, we're going to have to rip up all of this. That would put you out of a home."

"Would they have swimming pools?" Harley was thinking a squat of condos slapped up in his little valley might not be all that bad, what with garbage cans to raid and hot tubs and maybe even a pet cat to snap at.

"Well, yes, probably; but that doesn't matter," Miss Twillinger sniffed. "What matters is that you are an endangered species. We must save you, it is the most important thing."

"Why?"

"Well, mankind has been entrusted with the guardianship of the world, of nature, of everything we see around us."

"By whom?"

Miss Twillinger wasn't used to being asked to evaluate her belief system by a lousy, foul-mouthed turtle. She took a swig of designer water from a plastic bottle slung to her hip hugging cargo pants.

"Care for a drink?" she asked.

"Don't mind if I do."

The turtle took a big gulp and then spat it out, "Ugg! No microbes!"

"Of course not. It's the purest water money can buy."

"Don't you find something unnatural in that?"

"Don't be silly. Now, are there other endangered creatures around here?"

Harley nodded his head in a downhill direction, indicated the small dribble that passed for a creek, "Well, we had some little sand fish, but I haven't seen any of them for a decade or so."

Miss Twillinger gasped, "Sand fish! My word! Do you think any of them survived?"

"A few did, but I ate them."

"You should have saved them, to preserve the natural balance."

Harley shrugged, "I was hungry. Oh, how about the yellow stick flower plant? Do plants count?"

"Oh, yes indeed! That would be a very rare find! Could you take me to it?"

Turtles not being very swift of foot, the journey of a hundred yards or so took most of the rest of the day, but just before the sun set, Miss Twillinger was thrilled to see the only example of a yellow stick flower plant, which until now had been considered extinct.

"I like to eat the little yellow flowers," Harley explained, extending his neck and snacking on the closest bud.

"But you mustn't!" Miss Twillinger shrieked. Unfortunately, in her haste to educate the ignorant and ancient turtle, she fell on a sharp boulder next to the creek and badly fractured her left leg, snapping the bone halfway between her knee and her foot.

"Help me!" Miss Twillinger wailed.

Harley lifted his heavy shell in an attempt at a shrug, and slowly began to pad away.

"It's not good to hang with the weakest in the pack," he said.

"Pack? There's no pack here."

"Even worse," Harley replied over his shell without pausing or looking back.

"I was going to save you," she cried. "You can't just leave me like this."

His exit, though slow, was inexorable, and after a half hour, Miss Twillinger found she was alone. It was odd, because just over the dark humps of the nearest hills, she could see the glow of the

161

MacDonalds and the Shell station, and if she listened hard enough, she could make out the relentless hum of drive-time traffic on the freeway.

The pain was intense. She knew her biology; the jagged and exposed edge of bone had cut some vein or other, which would explain all the blood. She had to do something to keep her wits about her. She ran through the chemical chart by heart and recited all the genus and species that she could think of, starting with the invertebrates and ending up with Homo sapiens, and then going back down again through the monkeys and the birds and the amphibians and the fish...she couldn't remember. She swam in and out of consciousness. As darkness descended, she hoped someone would happen by and discover her plight. But she knew that wasn't likely. She remembered how hard she had fought to fence off this small and secluded basin from picnic trash and rutting young lovers who didn't know or even care if they were rolling around on ordinary mustard weed or precious yellow stick flower plants.

Fences, however, meant nothing to the coyotes. They roamed over the hundred and fifty acres she had helped preserve as if it were a playground. And in no time at all, the first coyote showed up. He sniffed at the blood and looked hungrily at the cracked bone sticking out of Miss Twillinger's shin.

"Marrow!" he said, his eyes shining and tongue licking greedily.

SPACE ACE

Ace was in the neighborhood, minding his own business (which was the half price selling of lottery tickets that he lifted from gray haired old people coming out of the 7-11), when a single alien spaceship came down right out of the sky.

"Come with us," the space alien said. The alien smelled bad and was green colored, with three strands of fat, goopy hair on top and a bulb where his nose should have been.

"You ain't an 'us'," Ace said. He was very good at correcting other people's grammar.

"We are all connected to the Oneness," the alien said. "Now come with us."

"Uh, uh," Ace said, "That could be true about the oneness, but who's gonna mind the store?"

"I will create a holographic duplicate dummy to look like you."

Ace thought it over. He was wearing his good threads. It would be stupid to fight a green person who looked so revolting over something as silly as a siesta in the burbs.

"Okay, where you want we should be off to?" Ace said mildly.

"You humans with your questions, questions, questions! You're worse than dogs! Well, I've got one for you," the alien said. "Why do you talk like a black man? You are obviously white, or at least the pinkish tan that passes for white on this planet."

"Because it's cool, you stupid firking alien. I could speak proper English just like you do. I just don't want to, because I have blue eyed soul."

"I don't speak English at all," the alien replied with an arch sniff through his bulb. "You're just hearing it as English through mental telepathy transmuted by the power of my advanced mind."

"Oh," Ace said, "That be cool, green-boy. But you still have not answered my question as to our destination."

"Out to the country to make signs in the crops," the alien said.

Ace couldn't see himself doing that.

"Naw, not me, man, I'm a city boy. I don't do no good out of the hood. Besides, that sounds like work."

"It is work, true work. What's more, it is your calling. I have selected you, and you must come with us," the alien said. "You have no choice."

"All mankind has a choice," Ace said smugly. He went to St. Cyril's high school on days when he wasn't working, and Father Mannikin had told him that.

"Maybe some do, but you don't," the alien said, pointing a weird looking electronic gun at young Ace and zapping him with a ray that instantly wiped out the right side of his brain.

The next few weeks were full of wild images and happenings that Ace would only half-remember in his later years as the most joyful time in his life. He was running through fields of grain, dragging a big square board behind him. The bright yellow moon beamed down from above like a juicy

164

cheeseburger dripping light instead of catsup or special sauce. The cool wind in his face felt like the big fan in the back of Mr. Delmonico's Junk 'n Juice shop. There was squishy morning dew in his topper floppers, the hot skeds that made him run higher and jump faster. He remembered soundly sleeping like the half-dead in dusty hay bales until nightfall, the first real full night's sleep he'd had without the muted city sounds, the slammy hip-hop music, the ping of cheap handguns and the smack of bumper-to-fender always going on in the background. And again, night after night, the exquisite joy of running wild and free through the glorious golden wheat fields.

Ace became a jack of all signs...he did circles, squares and triangles. He did radiating light globes and zigzags and radiation waves...he did soy beans and winter wheat and corn. Of them all, he loved corn the best, for running through lush stalks that rose over his head and showered him with pollen made him feel like ant boy in magic land.

After seven weeks and three days, the alien returned to take him back to his hood.

"But I do not wish or care to go back," Ace complained, having completely lost his accent and desire to live in the corroded old place of his birth.

"Tour of duty is one month," the alien said, honking something vile and green out of the bulb where his nose should have been into a nearby weed patch where it hissed and bubbled..

"Incorrect," Ace complained, hoping to convince the smelly green alien to relent. "I have been out here seven weeks and three days."

"Gragmalian month," the alien said. "Don't give me trouble, or I'll zap the other half of your brain."

Ace hadn't even been missed, thanks to the holographic replicate. With the wink of a few electrons he was back in his spot again. Miss Lily Drinker, the old retired schoolteacher, came out of the 7-11, clutching her lottery tickets to her green nylon vest. She saw Ace and grimaced a little, waiting to be bopped.

"Have a pleasant day, Miss Drinker," Ace said, tipping the hat of dried cornhusks that he had woven one night in the fields.

She gave him a look that was half fright and all surprise and then hurried on. As she rounded the corner of the parking lot by the mailbox, Ace heard a frightening bang. He had a bad feeling about this. He raced around the corner, only to find Miss Drinker lying on the ground in a pool of her own blood. Ace heard running footsteps receding in the distance.

"Well, that's certainly a coincidence," he thought with the half a brain the green alien had left him.

But over the next few hours, Ace became aware that it might be something more than mere coincidence. With the glorious memories of his midnight runs through verdant pastures still fresh in his mind, he no longer had the heart to rob these poor people of their hopeless fantasies of winning the lottery and escaping their mean and disgusting lives of poverty and social degradation.

Unfortunately, someone else didn't have his higher awareness and the bodies of the people he let pass were mounding up around the corner. It certainly was bad for the 7-11, which depended on repeat customers and high markups to stay in business. It would be bad for the police if they came by before the street cleaners, as they had been touting a reduction in murders and other crimes. And it most certainly was bad for the victims themselves, though none of them were complaining…after all, it is hard to moo when you're hamburger.

Ace's brain hurt so much he clapped his hands to his head. When he had possessed an entire brain, he'd never had this sort of problem. There had been a sort of balance, but now, with the right side gone, he was all emotion. He knew he should be snatching those lottery tickets, but when he saw each one of his former victims, his mind was filled with a golden kindness and he could do them no harm. And so he doffed his primitive woven hat while around the corner the stack of the unknown assailant's victims grew and grew.

You would think someone would connect the dots, put two and two together and realize that he, Ace, was personally responsible, and then take him away, but they never did. Who is going to arrest a person for not doing something? Beyond that, it wasn't really his fault, he'd been zapped by space aliens.

Ace figured, and rightly so, the problem would gradually work itself out and go away. And it did.

In the end, the 7-11 ran out of customers. He was free.

THREE ON A MATCH

Although it doesn't matter in the slightest, for the goddamn bloody stupid record my name is Richard Cartright. The record isn't actually goddamn, bloody or stupid, but that's just the way we all talk. Back East. Old money, though I'm a shirt-tail relative to all those zeros in the bank, pops jumped off a building, left me just enough for the finest schools, the finest chums, and the finest of good times. I look like I never have to work a day in my life. I work hard to cultivate that look. At least, I used to.

I've long been a practicing psychiatrist, grubbing hard for those few dribbles of hard-earned that come my way. If I have one fault, it's—well, you'll see. Let's let the stories tell themselves; it's simpler that way. These days I am appreciating simplicity in ways I never could have imagined a few weeks ago.

The beginning of my end began one Friday morning, around noon, actually. I agreed to meet this new client, a rude bird named Parker. Robert Parker, Private Investigator. Parker-the-Dick, I called him, though never to his face, for obvious reasons. I agreed to meet him that first time for a lunch-time session, more as a favor to an acquaintance. You see, I like the money. I want the money. But I don't need the money. Never have. At least I work hard so that my clients and acquaintances might appreciate that it is so.

I drove halfway across West Los Angeles, and wasn't happy when I saw the casual way this Parker fellow greeted me. I did not need the business, and I certainly didn't need this particular business of his crude and blustery manners.

"It is not the norm, my agreeing to meet you here at your place," I said. "And on such short notice."

That little remonstrance on my part washed over him like God's grace on an unrepentant sinner—if there are such things as God or sins. I guess I had no reason to expect him to be appreciative, and he wasn't. The general run of people are swine, you know, regardless of what you might have heard in Bible Class or on Sesame Street. I listen to their petty whimpering all day long; take it from me, Richard Cartright the Fourth; I meet all types and mostly the attitude is I'm okay and you're not.

"Yeah, yeah, I know, Doc-ey-boy," Parker said, making my point with his easy sarcasm, "but things being what they are, the economy and all—not to mention the savagely high price you shrinks knock down—you just thought you'd make an exception and pop on over here during your lunch break."

While that was true, the way he said it took the wind out of my sails.

"Right," I said, swallowing the bile like the professional that I am.

I calmly eyed my new patient. He wasn't even looking at me. Apparently the touch of acid was his normal caustic style of conversation. I got up to leave, but he waved a hand toward an ornate

170

Oriental chair across from his plain and battered office desk.

"Sit, Doc. Don't be such a thin-skin."

"I might have risen to the new bait, but that chair distracted me. I like fine things, and this was an exceptional artifact. It was of carved hardwood inlaid with mother-of-pearl. It was the sort of chair constructed by dictatorial artisans of a sterner era to assure one sat bolt upright. There was a cold seat of grey marble for the bottom, and jutting black wooden blossoms and leaves on the back panel just in case the sitter decided to attempt the slightest bit of comfort. Still, comfort or no, it looked totally out of place in his dingy little office—but then, so did everything else.

Parker pointed in the general direction of his antique chair, "It's one of a kind, you know? A rarity. I can probably get ten grand for it from a collector."

He eyed me calmly, the way they always do before the first little lie drops from their lips, the initial slippery launch that pushes them just that first little space away from reality.

"It fell off a truck out front," he said. "I didn't have to pay a dime for it."

"He gave me a nasty little chuckle. More precisely—and I like to be precise—it was an unpleasant, half-gasping trill, a sound half-way between a squeezed out gurgle and some sort of spontaneous hyperventilation. That was the way Parker laughed, and I came to hate and fear that sound as much as the person, himself.

171

"Yes," I said. I even nodded politely, perfectly in control. Things, of course, do not just fall off trucks and into people's lives. But then, if they did, people like me wouldn't be paid to sit quietly and hear about it.

From the top, then: His name was Robert Parker. He was about my age, maybe fifty-five or sixty, with thin hair over a wide forehead, one of those men who would have a circle of monk's hair around a bald pate in a few more years. He was of medium height and lean as a greyhound, and his eyes made me more than a little nervous with all their twitching nervously around, lighting like a fly on this or that in the odd clutter in his office, taking it all in as if he'd never seen any of it before, or perhaps was seeing it for the first and giving leave of it at one and the same time—the perfect replica of an 1890's high-wheeled bicycle, the stone Mayan primitives squeezed between stacks of books, the slide projector with its Kodak images scattered about like a thrown deck of miniature playing cards, the gleaming pile of ancient Spanish doubloons— those absolutely were not real—scattered by his feet on his battered old desk, his fly-twitch gaze settling most often on the Buddhist altar that was lit with candles and centered with a fake-gold painted plaster statue of the chubby man of peace himself looking for all the world like a calm and deadly suma wrestler.

"Let me save you some time, Doc," Parker said, "time being money, you know."

Was he mocking me? I couldn't be sure.

"Of course," I agreed.

"I'll answer a few questions so you won't have to ask them."

"Of course," I said again, settling into my listening mode.

"There was a nervous tremor going in one of his neck muscles, a steady little flinch that made his head bob in rhythm when he talked.

"All in all, I could see that this man Parker was an exceptional twitcher. Nervous tics here, there and everywhere. Even his mouth did an unpleasant little dance as he talked, like he was eating ants.

"Yes, he said," I really am a gumshoe dick like it says on the door; at least I was until very recently, when I gave up doing any work at all. Yes, I was in Nam; you'll find most of the P.I.'s like me were, except the older ones, who were in Korea. None left from World War II, at least, that I know of."

"Ahh," I said, trying my best to settle into his stiff, uncomfortable chair from the distant Orient, and into my role as his professional listener in the same motion. "And, why is that?"

"It's a young man's game. You get out or you lose your edge and get dead before you're fifty."

Parker was an odd one, to my way of thinking. He obviously needed help, and help is what I'm all about. Help for a price, I always say. Good help is never cheap. But what an odd bird! Here he is talking about his rare chair—antique chair, indeed! Probably a half-price close-out at the local Pier 1 shop, fashionable furnishing for the off-beat Gen-X-er.

Yeah, I'm good, alright. Not even five minutes into our first session and I had him pegged. If he

173

saw his life the way he saw his chair, the fellow had delusions on a grand scale. Could I even accept his word that he was—or had been—a private investigator? After all, what does it take to put a little gold leaf on the door and your name in the yellow pages? It's the old therapist's puzzle—when do you believe the crazy man? I was the last guy to be able to tell. None of us can, really. It's all just a clever con game. Take your place over there on the couch. One moment and I'll be at your side. Maybe we don't help anybody, but at least we don't hurt any of the poor sad sacks, either. At least not intentionally.

Does all this sound just a touch cynical? I guess—I know—at the time I first met Parker I was the product of too-heavy a case load. Let me tell you about the shrink game. Sometimes one works to forget the other things, the real things in one's own life. Then, after the inevitable burnout, you just run on fumes for a while, waiting for the crash that is sure to come. You go around muttering inane things like MmmmmmHmmmmm, and Do want to go with that? and pretending your patients can't tell the difference. Hey, after all, maybe they can't. After all, this is about them, not me. Still, by my own self-analysis, at the time I met Parker-The - Dick, I was on the last bit of fume, though I hadn't the foggiest notion how things got that way in my life.

"I was in Vietnam, myself," I murmured. "I was one of those med-vac fellows trying to pump the blood in faster than it ran out. Somehow, I never could."

"Yeah, yeah, yeah," Parker yawned, waving me off with one hand. "But this isn't about you."

My face went red and I actually had to physically bite my tongue. Parker had been referred to me by my fellow Yalie, Clarence Turvell, who did his shrinking down south in Orange County, preferring his ocean view from a high-rise in Newport Beach to mine from a high-rise in Santa Monica. Some time ago, good old Turvie and I had actually been in business together for a while, but the clients all seemed to prefer me, and he'd left in a cloud of smoking fury, actually claiming I'd stolen his whimpering little pile of clients! Rubbish, but apparently that was all water over the dam—look, now here he was, offering to actually give me a client.

When he'd called two weeks ago Wednesday, Turvie had sounded a little odd—edgy, actually— but noting that a fellow-shrink is odd is like saying the leopard has spots, and by most standards, Clarence Turvell, a soft, moist little fellow with a classic Germanic Mother syndrome and a massive overbite and receding chin that his self-absorbed parents had never thought to fix, was nutty as a fruit cake, anyway. He'd hemmed and strutted a bit on the phone, his voice going up and down in his usual dipsy-doodle manner, overly mannish and gruff-voiced—ridiculous overcompensation coming from that plump penguin presence of his. But the reason for his call, when he finally got around to it, was this Parker fellow who lived too far away to be a convenient client, and since I was closer and, Hey,

175

hey, hey, Cartie-Smartie, old boy, let bye-gones be bye-gones, did I want the business?

Hello, the rent goes on, I always say, and I had one open spot where most people do lunch, so I said yes, yes and yes even to meeting at Parker's junky place which was only five minutes from my own. Parker said he didn't travel. Hardly ever. Impossible to come to me. I didn't understand why. I didn't understand anything back then.

So there I was for the first time, sitting in his horrid little Oriental chair. Bad, bad, bad. The place was as musty and unkempt as Parker himself, and there wasn't even an ocean view, just a dim look out his bleary storefront window and past the meter-parked cars to the E-Z Way Laundromat and the Hai Cua Chinese-Vietnamese seafood restaurant on the other side of Montana Street.

"Oh, stop worrying," Parker said. "I can afford to pay you."

His voice seemed to come out of nowhere, and I actually jumped a little. I guess my mind was wandering. Still, why had he ever thought that I might think or even be worried in the slightest that he couldn't pay? My clients always paid me. Always. He must have misinterpreted some look I gave him.

I shrugged, "I never said anything about—"

"Didn't have to." His face screwed itself up, driven by inner demons that, back then, I couldn't even imagine, and he grumbled, "Lookie here— better I should pay you now. Three fifty a session, right? Here's for the first week."

Old Turvie hadn't said anything about this guy wanting to see me every day, but before I could think that one through, my new patient swung his feet off the desk and hastily scribbled out a bank check and handed it across to me. The discomforting idea came over me—for the life of me, I couldn't figure out how or why—that my client had made a moral decision rather than a financial one.

Now this time when I first met my fidgety new client it was winter in California—mid-February, actually—and I was wearing one of the new tweed suits I'd brought back from the best month of my life, the four weeks I'd spent with Alice in Hong Kong before she'd called me the world's most self-centered asshole and split for parts unknown. Split forever.

I suppose I could have—should have—found out where she went. Somehow, that just isn't my style. If she really cared, she wouldn't have left me in the first place, or at the very least would have had the decency—or the courage, for I will concede I can be difficult—to come back after the first week or two and talk it out. After all, that's what we couch-men are all about, talking it out. We've even got our own bumper sticker, Hire a Shrink and Do It Lying Down.

But I drift. Let's get back to Parker. As I've alluded, his office was stuffy as a nose with a cold, and with the candles going and the heavy scent of incense, I could feel the beads of sweat forming on my forehead.

The guy actually grinned at my discomfort. Parker looked right at me and said, "Take your coat off and stay a while, Doc."

I didn't say anything, but I did think the least civility he might manufacture would be to prop the door open or punch on his window air conditioner to make things a bit more civilized, but he didn't move the slightest in that direction, and I wasn't going to say anything to give him any sort of edge whatsoever. I'm the doctor; he's the patient. Let's keep our proper places, here.

Still, I did take off my coat, and after a brief glance around the room, located the carved oak coatrack behind a thicket of colorful deep-sea fishing poles in the corner by the door.

"Poles fall off the truck, too?" I asked. My feeble attempt at levity. As you can guess by now, I'm not much with the jokes. Life is pretty grim stuff for me.

Parker shrugged and gave me a glum look. "Nope. Fishing store down the block went out of business. His last day, he came by and gave everybody poles. Me, he gave the most. Rods, reels, I got everything."

"And the coins?"

I picked one up from the table. "I don't know as much about this sort of thing as a professional numismatist, but these are very good reproductions. Heavy. Good castings. Lead, probably."

He shook his head. "Nope. Somebody I helped in a catch-your-wife-cheating case was so grateful to find out she wasn't that he wrote me up for shares

178

in one of those long-shot sunken treasure-ship ventures."

I held one of the heavy chunks up to the light, "You're pulling my leg."

"No, I'm not."

Now here's another fundamental of the old psychiatry game: When they deny their fantasies flat-out, one must duck tail and go along with it. That is one of our more basic rules. After all, you don't want your fees to blow up in your face.

"Lucky man," I said, giving him my number four (very, very, very, very) serious nod, and respectfully placing the coin back on the top of the pile.

"Yeah, lucky." He spit the words out with that same annoying strained bark I'd heard him use a few moments earlier, and I found myself making the old mental note, saying to myself, Verily, this is not a happy camper, Cartie-Smartie?

"What sort of cases do—you do? Criminal? Family disputes? Contested wills?" As I asked this, I was carefully adjusting my vest and trousers as best I could and trying to make some sense of the jumble of artifacts arranged around his office like Oscar the Grump's beloved trash. The old Sesame Street words went through my head, "I love traaaaash—anything dirty and rotten and dusty, anything lumpy and worn and rusty!"

One of my shiny brown shoes rested unsteadily on a new bowling ball, the only spot I could find on the floor. Three or four fancy sets of golf clubs were stacked against the desk, a foursome for sure, ready to tee off on the first hole over at swank L.A.

179

Country Club, no doubt. Pictures of a river houseboat, a huge cabin cruiser and an A-frame house with snow-capped mountains in the background were pinned to the wall, partly covering a small Van Gogh which, the moment I asked, he would assure me was an original. Believe me; I wasn't going to give him the satisfaction. I could make up my own fibs. It surely had fallen off the same truck as my chair. Ho, ho, hum. Pity the uncomfortable bit of furniture hadn't fallen a bit harder and smashed itself up.

"I do the usual stuff," he said. "Missing persons. Unfaithful husbands and wives. Runaways. It's not important. None of that is the issue here—I told you I'm retired."

There was no need for him to get peevish; after all, he was dealing with a professional. I guess that was just his nature.

I stretched and gave a bit of a yawn, "Well then, Mr. Parker, what is important—to you, I mean?"

"Okay—What is a human, anyway? That's what I really want to know."

"You booked a $350 dollar session to find out the definition of a human being?"

"Yes."

"Alright, then. Homo sapiens. Evolved from the earlier species, eventually from the primordial soup. Or, if you'd rather, a creature of the Creator, a super-being we call God, born in his image."

"But you don't know which."

"It's not in my job description," I said.

He gave me an intense look. "Doc—don't do this shrink crap on me, okay? I got a big problem and I have to get it off my chest. I need you, but don't be such a prick about it. Don't make me suffer like this."

How like a psychotic to find the source of their pain in the patient listener! Classic. I brushed some lint off the sleeve of my shirt. This was one from my latest batch, and I liked it very much. I had them custom-made at The Custom Shirt Shop in the mall over on Pico. They were some sort of Egyptian cotton, and their only defect was they seemed to attract stray bits of lint.

I sniffed once, blinked my eyes, and gave him a smile of reassurance.

"Okay, let's go with that for a while. From the sound of it, you've got some kind of problem to work out, but I make you uncomfortable. If it's any relief to you, everybody says that. I am not your friend, or even your acquaintance. I'm your shrink. You don't have to like me."

For a moment I had the distinct impression he was going to start yelling. One always tends to feel sorry for people who live so close to their emotions, but, of course as a professional, I do my best to stifle the empathetic in favor of my perfected mode of cool observation. There was an ambivalent, hesitating moment, and then he settled down and began to talk.

"It started about a year and a half ago," he said, after which he went silent and his gaze seemed to wander to the candles.

"Exactly what started?" I prompted.

181

"Everything started! Shut up and listen, like you're supposed to, man!"

I gave him a sniff and a little shrug, and he continued. "I was sitting right here, in this chair, staring across the street, when I saw this willowy Vietnamese babe who worked the cash register at the Hai Cua over there."

"A girl." I raised my eyebrows. Now we were getting somewhere.

"Yes, a girl. I guess I'd seen her before, but I hadn't really noticed her. She had this long black hair, and an olive face and those dark, dark eyes that can see right into your soul." He paused for a moment and I thought I'd lost him, but then he started up again, "You could see her from here, when the light is right, behind her cash register; I mean, she's not there now, but if she was, you could. Lately, of course, I haven't seen her at all."

"MmmmmHmmmm," I said. "And?"

"And, okay, and—and I guess I'm not too lucky with women. Over the years I've had a lot of sex and dates and stuff, and lately it's like I'm God's Gift, you know? But nothing ever seemed to stick; it always went to pieces. Maybe it was my job, maybe it was me. Frankly, I've never been able to figure it out. I've always been the king of the three-month relationship. Then they seem to have had enough and they're out the door and I'm on my own again. Lately, it's lots worse—just a three-hour bang and they're on their way, wherever they go."

"Who?"

"The most beautiful women in the world. Sometimes I don't even know their first names. I get the slightest urge—itch, even—and some lovely with long legs and no stockings will be on the elevator or leaning against my car."

"Uh Huh," I said.

Actually, I could relate, at least to the first part of his narrative before he slipped back into his fantasyland. After two bum marriages, total duration for the both of them one year, eight months and six days, plus or minus a few hours, I'd had a string of lady friends, the latest being the rich and bitchy Alice, with whom getting in the last word had become the golden rule—for both of us, I guess. Alice, duration four months, eight days, plus or minus a day because we traveled over the international date line together.

Lovely Alice, even lovely with her long legs in stockings. I tried to push the thought of her out of my mind, and came out of my reverie to realize Parker-the-Dick was still talking.

"And in my business there's not a lot to do in between cases. You can go nuts—sorry, no pun intended—waiting for that stupid phone to ring. I'd be reading some detective book, maybe one of Hillerman's Navajo adventures or an old Ellery Queen or Dick Francis, you know, trying to find out how the real private investigators do it, and I'd look up and there she'd be. I'd smile, she'd smile. That's how it started, and that's how it went for a while. After maybe a couple of weeks, I'd give her a little wave, and she'd smile and wave back. Progress in the relationship, you know? I guess it's only natural a man starts dreaming about a woman like that—hell, what straight guy doesn't? I'd known a dozen girls like her in Vietnam. I was a real love 'em and leave 'em type—hell, we all were."

"All who were?" I asked automatically, without a clue as to where he was going with his innocent little flirtation with the cash register girl across the street.

He glanced over his shoulder as if someone else was in the room with us, and then spoke in a lower, hurried voice, "My team at the 3rd RRU. That stands for Radio Research Unit, a fancy name for the spy shit we did. We were linguists stationed near Saigon, and we were decoding and translating covert Viet Cong messages. I was the senior editor, with six guys under me."

Spies. Covert messages. It really was all too much. I fumbled with the thick knot on my old school tie, "Do you mind if we get some air in here?"

He got to his feet and went over to one of those box air conditioning units bolted at about eye level to the wall. I watched him carefully punch the lowest level. A small stir of air rustled the candle flames like leaves in a breeze. Parker studied the flame tips carefully for a few moments. Then, satisfied with I-don't-know-quite-what, he sat back down again and resumed the session with a question. "Do you believe in spiritual things, Mr. Cartright?"

184

"Of course," I replied without a moment's hesitation. "Man is a spiritual creature. We live in our minds. I think, therefore I am."

"No, no—I mean things like curses and spirits. Witches and warlocks. Three on a match. Doppelgangers. Soul-suckers. Stuff like that."

"Witchcraft? Superstition?" I shook my head to the negative. "Step on a crack and break your mom's back! Don't walk under that ladder! Black cat crosses your path! Broken mirrors are seven years bad luck! The human race should have gotten past all that foolishness centuries ago, I would have thought."

In a way, one thing was odd, like the wrong wires crossing and still making a connection; we both being old Nam vets, I actually knew what he meant by Three on a match. The Vietnamese were a superstitious people, so superstitious they even tied their shoes a certain way. They have a national passion for cigarettes, holding them backwards and drooling the smoke from their nostrils in the French manner, a custom you sometimes see in the old classic movies, and yet no native who expected to live to old age ever took the third light from the same match. That would call up the evil eye—the third man on the match would fall prey to an awful fate, at least that's what the poor, backward wretches believed.

Well, you know, death is never kind, and in a sloppy, monsoon-drenched and disease-ridden country like that, and racked with war to boot, the worst things possible were rather commonplace—so, one supposes, a horrid death for the third man wasn't all that unusual. Same-same for the second or the first, but nobody ever seemed to think about that.

The natives had a natural dread of cameras, too, almost as if that little black box, Cai Pentax, could interfere with your soul in some way I personally never really understood. That's why, if you look at any group picture of Vietnamese, particularly the older generations, you'll only see even numbers of people. It's odd man out, quite literally. When they are getting ready for a snapshot, everybody automatically counts up how many there are, without consciously thinking about it, and then somebody steps in or out of the frame. They'll even ask a total stranger to stand in the picture rather than risk the odd number. I've seen the superstitious little ritual dozens of times, myself, but I couldn't see why Parker was bringing this sort of thing up in our session. Oh well, it was his big bucks he was spending. But I hadn't directly answered his question.

It must have meant a lot to him, because he continued in the same vein with his reedy, dog-determined voice, "Specifically, to the heart of it, Doctor—do you believe a curse can be transmitted like a disease?"

I raised both hands, palms out, and pushed like I was slowing down a freight train, "Whooo, you're going a little fast for me Parker. I never said I believed in anything like that."

"No. That's right. You didn't." He sounded peeved again as he continued, "But if you did, would you?"

Huh.   Now there was a stretch of the old imagination one never hears about back at Yale, even when one is taking Advanced Shrink 206B. Nothing to lose, I decided to play along with it, "Well, I suppose that if I did, I would. When you think about it, the very nature of a curse is that it must be passed on to another, otherwise it wouldn't be a curse—it would be an unfulfilled wish to evil."

He nodded as if that satisfied him, and the silence lengthened between us.

Advertising copywriters claim they can tell a TV commercial to the second, and I believe it, because I can do the same with a session. This one, for instance—thirty minutes down, twenty to go. I didn't really have to look at the dials on the thick gold Omega on my wrist. One third of an hour and I'd get in my black Jag and cruise on back to my office, maybe with the top down if the sun allowed, probably arriving five minutes late for the one o'clock Mrs. Buzby, who would endlessly relate some new variation of her falling-into-viper pits dreams to her first husband who got dragged under one of his own road graders and left her $40 million in mutual funds. The pop psychology publishing world has really given us a whole new vocabulary—a great deal more to talk about—and I've been grateful more than a few times because it makes my job that much easier. Except for the oddball few like this one, who really needed a father-confessor, or maybe a boot to the head from one of those instant-cure psycho-jocks who ply their questionable calling on Talk Radio. Imagine, in our

187

day and age, there are a few people who still have no idea what a bona fide psychiatrist is all about!

I shifted in my awful chair, now giving my watch the old obvious glance, "Say, now, Parker— where is this getting us to? I mean, it's your time, but really—"

Again, his shrill, bitter laugh. "Ahh, so outrageously secure in your safe little shrink world!"

I sighed contentedly, happy to be on more familiar ground. "You don't have to attack me," I murmured reassuringly. "There is absolutely no need."

The truth is, I have always been very, very secure. When I was a little boy, I was lucky enough to be allowed to be myself from the very start. You see, I grew up in New York City, practically alone in one of those huge apartments on 71st Street. My mother and father were the famous Cartright Couple, traveling the world as duo concert pianists, and they were almost never home. There was Jessica for food, and Arthur who butlered, as familiar and dependable as vending machines. I built my own world; I never needed the famous Cartrights in person. And, in truth, they were much more malleable in my mind, never scratching and quarreling like in those few brief moments in real life when they settled in for a few days resembling nothing so much as tired old long-distance sparrows. Except for a string of private tutors, I pretty much had my entire world to myself. Did it work? I was so far ahead of my age group I skipped high school entirely, my parents enrolling me at Yale when I was fourteen!

Parker-the-Dick's incessant yammering cut into my consciousness again, "But do you care, Doc? Do you really care about me, myself, the person? Do you have any concern at all about what happens to me?"

I hadn't been expecting that. Totally unprofessional for the moment, I had some biting comment at the tip of my tongue when I managed to quell my baser instincts. I saw he was shuddering, turned inward, as if talking more to himself than to me.

I swallowed my anger and said as calmly as I could manage, "Of course I care. My God, man, it's my profession!"

He shook his head. "No. That's not enough. You're too needy. You're not protected."

"Needy?!" I shot back, now thoroughly annoyed. "How on earth did you arrive at that incredibly false conclusion?"

He continued to shake his head. "Look, bub— I'm sorry I got you into this. Get out while you can. Here, take the check." He stood up and thrust it at me. "Go ahead. Take it. I've got plenty of money. Sorry I bothered you."

I couldn't believe it. I've seen grand delusions and monstrous irrational, but this took top prize. The fellow believed he was bothering me! As if he could!

"Now wait a minute," I said, firm to make one last-ditch stand against this craziness, "I am not a 'bub'. I am your doctor! You ask to be my patient.

189

I go to a great deal of trouble to accommodate you, and then you insult me, not once but continuously throughout our session. Just what do you take me for? What do you think I am, some jerk-water therapist who needs your business?"

Parker leaned back and narrowed his eyes, sighting on me along the bridge of his nose. And then eye contact broke and his gaze drifted back to his altar. A small cup with a few strands of brown-edged orchids and a few wilted daisies was positioned in front of the squat Buddha. The cheap plaster showed through on the holy fellow's tummy where the fake gold leaf was scraped and peeling.

A slight puff of wind stirred the candles and Parker cast a sharp glance at the dials on the air conditioner. He pointed a finger at me, and said in a shaky voice, "Okay. You get one warning, if any of what I read here applies at all. It's part of the rules."

He waved a hand to indicate he was talking about the mounds of books around him. "And now you just got it, your warning. That was it. This isn't a nice world, Mr. Cartright. Do you want to stay or go?"

I was totally ambivalent, but then old habits kicked in. There remained yet ten minutes on the clock. It would have been unprofessional to just get up and walk out on him. "Doctor Cartright," I said. "And you may continue, if you will."

He nodded, eyeing me with what I took for a new sparkle of curiosity.

"Okay," he said. "No choice, then. It must be fate—but, of course, you don't believe in fate, either."

"You're not going to start up on me again."

"No, no." He waved me back to my ebony chair. "I'll finish my story, and then we'll see. Where was I? Right, it was just about a year ago. I became more and more infatuated with my little semi-romance, you know, with the girl in the window. Before long, I was going across the street to the Hai Cua for lunch, to catch a little hot noodle soup and maybe get to know her a little better. That's the way it goes, right? The girl's name was Lan Mai, and to make a long story short, I did get to know her. One thing led to another and we became a number."

"Ahh. You became intimate with the girl."

"Yeah. Lovers. Her momma didn't like it and her poppa really didn't like it, but, you know, I was head-over-heels and not listening to anybody. Hey, I guess you find that hard to imagine, but love makes you a fool at any age. For the first time in my life I had something real, somebody cared for me, put me first over everything, even her customs and her family. Next thing I know, Lan's carrying, I mean, you know, with child. Big surprise, pal. I mean, we're supposed to be a sophisticated society, right?"

"Well, with AIDS, you should have been using—"

"Yeah, yeah, spare me the sermons, Doc. Look, I didn't, and pretty soon she was in the family way, and that was that."

191

"Well, this is this," I said, tapping the gold Omega on my wrist, "and I really have to be going." I stood and slipped into my jacket. I paused at the door, hand on the old brass knob.

"Mr. Parker," I said in my most level business tone, "Professionally speaking, I don't think this has much of a chance of working. I don't have the slightest inkling what your problem is, and you don't seem to be getting anything out of this, so why don't we just call it quits? You can have your money back."

"Oh, no," he said, waving the check off with a toss of his hand. "Too late—you already had your warning, and you said you'd continue. And stop pretending you're God—how do you know what I'm getting out of this?"

His comment stopped me dead in my tracks. Alice had said the exact same thing, that I was pretending to be God, said it that last time, just before she started throwing my expensive brick-a-bracks around the apartment! I admit to staring at Parker, and I'm afraid I did look a bit bug-eyed.

I managed to get out a few words, "You think I'm too—know-it-all?"

"No, of course not. You're just arrogant enough. I'm perfect, you're perfect. That's why you're here."

"You have to stop talking in riddles."

He gave me a salute and a wry smile. "It wouldn't be a curse if you couldn't pass it on. You said that, Doc." His salute became a little wave of dismissal. "Same time tomorrow, Doc-pal-friend-guy. Don't let the door hit you in the ass on the way out."

That sounded like a terribly rude comment on his part, but all I felt was sorry for him. As I left, he was standing in front of his little altar, hunched over to protect the candles.

I must confess, the first block driving back to my office, I had a few twinges—maybe it was conscience, maybe something more like a touch of some unnamed little snag of fear way back there in my mind, probably just nothing more than nervous energy—but by the time I got to Wilshire the traffic was a snarl, I was now 12 minutes late for chubby old Buzby, and I'd completely slipped back into my old life. Hey, put it in perspective, Cartie-Smartie-- $350 an hour, have pad will travel.

Nothing seemed to have changed by Tuesday. Robert Parker, the nasty little gumshoe dick who'd knocked up the girl next door, was waiting for me in his stuffy storefront office. A whole new set of candles burned around Buddha. There were maybe a dozen of the big wax ones. The air was hazy and heavy with the scent of jasmine from the joss sticks. The daisies were gone, making the over-ripe orchids look even sadder in the small cup that had "Ford—We Build Better Ideas!" printed on its side.

Parker-the-Dick motioned me to my ungodly uncomfortable little chair across from him and started right in, "Okay, Wonder-Doc. We left off with you preaching at me because I didn't take the proper social precautions and got my young lady pregnant. What happened next was the sweetheart and I started to get into awful fights. I mean, no hitting, just a lot of screaming and arm-waving and stuff. And then it happened: one day Lan Mai and I were talking about having the baby. At least she was. I remember I was trying to talk her out of it. The next I knew, she'd left town or something. I mean, I didn't see her after that. I started to go a little nuts, no offense. I mean, I guess it took something like that to get me to realize I really did care. I'd go over there to get a soup or a few egg rolls and, you know, ask how things were, but Lan Mai wasn't there and I'd just get the stone wall treatment from the Mamma San. Those people could be so—so foreign! They wouldn't give me an inch. At first, it didn't bother me. Screw them, who needs the easy way? I mean, I'm a detective, and I'm pretty good at what I do, Cartright, and so I thought it would be easy. This is America, the U.S.A. Nobody can stay hidden if somebody with enough patience and the skills wants them located. At least, I used to believe that. I tried every trick in the book, but in the end, even I couldn't find her. She was gone, Cartright, gone without a trace. It was like she never was. Months went by. Months of me sweating it out and still no Lan Mai. And then, finally one sweet day, wonder of wonders, Mamma San marches across the street over here and invites me to a family gathering. She was calm as a peach tree, as if nothing ever happened at all."

"Wait. After all that time? Doesn't seem right."

He nodded nervously, eyeing the restaurant across the street. A few customers stood outside the door, collars up and hands in their pockets, reading the menu. The Santa Monica noon-day sun was shining, but following his gaze I could see it was one of those illusionary bright California days when the onshore wind is cold enough to make you want to make a quick choice to duck indoors or back in your car.

"Yeah," he repeated. "After all that time. Only it wasn't exactly a family reunion. I got there and everybody was wearing raw silk outfits from the old country. Raw white silk; you know what that means?"

I nodded yes. Odd, how much common knowledge we shared from that brief one-year tour in our distant youth. "Yes," I said. "That is the Vietnamese fabric and color of choice for mourning."

He gave me an approving look. "You do know something about the wetlands, don't you? Yeah, it was a funeral, alright. What I made out from it was that Lan Mai had died having the kid. They had her picture leaning against a heavy brass urn—filled with her ashes, I suppose. I don't know about the child—our child. Nobody would say."

"What did you do?"

"Christ, it really got to me, Cartright. I guess I must have cared for her more than I realized. I blubbered and sobbed and maybe even tore my own hair and scratched my face a little bit. I must have, because that's the way I found myself when I woke the next day. But I don't remember that. I do remember wandering around and around in a daze, trying to get some answers from all those silent people. There were dozens and dozens of them, all dressed in somber white, every one of them staring at me.

"This was at some sort of a meeting hall over on Lincoln Avenue. They'd rented the place, which was owned by somebody like Knights of Columbus. There were flowers everywhere and a big table loaded with food. Nobody was eating, but there was nothing else to do and I was nervous as a cat, so I went over and put a few things on a plate. That's when I saw—"

Parker stopped talking and bent over, hunching in on himself again as if he was enduring some terrible pain.

"Saw what, Parker?" I asked. "What did you see that was so extraordinary that it makes your face wrinkle up just to remember it?"

He looked at me with a haunted expression. "An old man. An old, old man. God, he must have been a hundred and ten. No joke, he was so old his wrinkles had wrinkles, and he was bent and frail, with a long, white wispy beard and moustache. He couldn't even walk without one of those aluminum walkers, and he shuffled that thing toward me, taking three minutes to get across the room. Everybody in the room turned and silently watched the two of us, me standing there with the plate of untouched food in my hands, and this ancient fellow crabbing his way toward me. I don't know how I knew, but I felt something really bad was up. I just wanted to get out of there, to be anywhere else but there, but it was like my feet were bolted to the floor. You know, did you ever have that feeling, I want to be any place else in the world but here, but you can't move a muscle in your body?"

I said that I had. "It is a normal guilt reaction. You know, it wasn't completely your fault, Robert. Perhaps once you get over your—"

"Oh, can it, Doc. That kind of talk doesn't apply."

More of his crap personality spilling over on our session. It was too much. "Look, Parker, you asked me to help. I'm the doctor here, and you're the patient."

He gave me a long stare filled with what I took for a strange blend of hopelessness and pity. Pity for me. Just try to imagine that! I couldn't for the life of me begin to unravel just why.

"I'm sorry," he said finally. "Do you want me to go on or not?"

"Well, yes, of course. This old man came up to you at the ceremony. Go on."

"As I remember, his rheumy yellow eyes had a wild light, and he glared like the curse of death itself, and as he got closer he began to chant in Vietnamese. After he got right in my face, he went on for maybe three minutes, his voice rising and falling in this rushing waterfall of sounds, a mixture of guttural moans and bird chirps. His teeth were broken and black. His gums were runny with something awful. His breath smelled like rot from the grave. It had been too many years since I left Southeast Asia; I could pick out a word here and there from what he was saying, but I couldn't really understand. Then he spoke in English, saying four words that sounded stiff and broken, like he'd

197

memorized them by rote. 'All of you go,' he said. 'All of you go. All of you go.' He shot those words at me like black arrows from that broken-tooth black hole of a mouth of his. I'll never forget it."

That didn't sound accurate, and I raised a hand to question Parker further on this. "Whatever did he mean by that? Are you sure that is precisely what he said?"

"Of course I'm sure, Cartright. Four words. 'All of you go.' He kept saying it over and over, like a litany."

sighed and shook my head, rolling the bowling ball a little back and forth on the floor with my left foot as I spoke. "And this has you nervous, of course, because, considering the circumstances, you think he may have been putting some sort of hex on you."

Parker gave me a bleak stare and turned toward the small back room. "I made some tea for us," he said over his shoulder. "Would you like some?"

He'd already gone behind a curtain.

"Yes, that would be pleasant," I said to the empty room.

I stood and stretched, taking another look at the incredible rubble of fake riches scattered around me. Antiques and old stock certificates and the fake golden doubloons and a small handful of ruby-glass spilling out of a rotten leather pouch. Oh, I could go on and on, but after about thirty seconds the bell on the front door tingled and one of the most beautiful women I'd ever seen in my life stood half in and half out of the office. She was wearing a short, tight dress, and easy to observe little else as the sunlight was backlighting her curves.

"Bobby in?" she purred.

"Yes, if by that you mean Robert Parker," I replied. "He is in back, making tea."

"You're having a meeting?"

"Yes, sort of," I replied stiffly, not accustomed to being interrogated by strangers off the street.

"You a friend of his?" she asked.

"Yes, sort of," I replied, thrown off my game by her long and gorgeous legs. "And who are you?"

"Tammy. A friend of a friend, not necessarily, of Bobby's. Tell him I'll be back this afternoon."

That was certainly strange syntax, had I taken the time to think about her reply. But she was incredibly beautiful, and for the moment, I must admit, I wasn't my normal professional personage. She had a smile like a Mozart concerto, and I just knew I didn't want her to go away at that very moment. Or ever, to be completely truthful.

"Wait!" I called after her. "Don't you want to tell him yourself?"

But she didn't stop. One last incredibly delicious smile and she was outside. A few swings of her inviting hips and she was on down the street and out of sight.

I sighed as I wandered around the office. Some of the books scattered nearest his desk were collector's items: early novels and travel books and big quartos with hand-colored plates of illustrations. Others, equally as old and musty, were mythologies, ancient beasts and Oriental superstitions and the like, sea serpents with dragon heads fighting brave

199

sailors in little dinghies, ornate signs and symbols, demonic writing and so on. Some were in languages I couldn't begin to understand, and were stuffed with torn bits of paper bearing translations in English or in French.

When Parker returned, I was leafing through an 18th century tome on animism.

He looked worriedly at his candles, which flickered in the usual healthy way. He frowned and asked, "Did I hear the door?"

"Yes. Some absolutely gorgeous female named Tammy. She said she'd come back later." I gave him an accusing stare, "You have a more complicated and involved story than you're telling me, Robert Parker."

He shrugged and stood there with a teacup and saucer in his hand, as if her appearance proved something.

"I don't know her, you see," he said.

"No, I don't see. Parker, she called you 'Bobby'."

He shrugged again. "I honestly don't know her. I can guarantee, I'll swear on the Bible or my mother's grave—I never saw her before in my life."

In an obvious attempt to change the subject, he gave me his tortured, lip-twisting bitter-sweet smile and indicated the book in my hands. "I see you've got one of the key volumes. I think it's interesting how parallel our cultures are, East and West. You could change a few words in there and we could be talking about the back-to-nature bunch in Europe, you know, the Pantheists."

200

That gave me pause. Parker was a little deeper than I'd given him credit for. Behind that limited vocabulary and shrill, broken texture was a man who had at least read and maybe even comprehended some basic rudiments of the links between man and nature.

"Soooo?" I said in my most coaxing tone.

I set the book down and he handed me an exquisite cup of bone china. It was of an extraordinarily rare pattern I thought I'd recognized from one of Alice's art books.

"I hope you like Oolong," he said.

"Why—I believe this cup is very rare."

"Yeah, priceless. I read somewhere that means beyond value, when you're talking about money. I found it in a third-rate antique shop over on Wilshire. Guy sold it to me for two bucks. Happens to me all the time, now that it doesn't matter anymore."

I smiled sadly, watching the glow of the light from one of his candles through the thin rim of the cup. "What do you mean, Parker, *Doesn't matter anymore?* More of your riddles?"

"No riddle, Doc." He flipped a hand toward the door through which the gorgeous Tammy had recently departed. "Beautiful women are everywhere. Money—I won $26,000 last week, a California Quik-Pik at a 7-11 Store. Do you know what I am?"

I took a sip of tea and fell back into my role, "No, Mr. Robert Parker, what are you?"

"I'm the true, for-real fatted calf."

"Whatever are you talking about?"

"I'll show you."

He took a faded picture from under his arm. I hadn't noticed it before, but he must have brought it from the back room with the tea. It was an old black-and-white photograph, blown up to an 8x10 size and framed behind dusty glass in one of those cheap wooden frames one can purchase at K-mart or almost any place else, for that matter.

"Here's what's left of my crew—you know, the old Saigon intelligence bunch I told you about the other day."

After staring at the picture for some moments, he handed it across to me. It was pretty ordinary; I mean, if you didn't know them personally they were just three clean cut Americans in army fatigues. They were standing in front of an old, corrugated metal aircraft hangar. The background looked like the flat delta land. I could almost smell the dank mustiness of the place; almost feel the muggy tropical heat. The G.I.s didn't seem to care. Mad Dogs, Englishmen and army kids, out in the noonday sun. They were smiling, arms linked, nonchalant in their youthful innocence, their body language saying, we will most certainly live forever.

"Huh. Three on a match," I said. "You mustn't have been into the local customs back then."

He didn't say anything, and I took a closer look at the old photo. It was easy to make out the younger Parker, just as thin back then as he was today, but without the lines of age or the lime-wry screwed up smile.

"There you are," I remarked in my most conversational manner, hoping once and for all to get to the bottom of this. "And these are two of your buddies?"

Of course they were; I ask you, who else could it be? And yet Parker's face darkened and he snapped angrily at me, "You still don't get it, do you, Doc? You're not very bright, or you haven't been paying attention to me, not one little bit."

"No need to personally attack me, old boy."

"I told you, I had six in my little unit. There are supposed to be seven in this picture, me and the six guys who worked under me!"

Maybe you'll think I'm a little slow at this sort of thing, but you have to admit this was somewhat of an unusual client. Truth was, I didn't know whether to laugh or be angry. At first, I *was* angry. The unconnected thought passed through my mind that the picture was actually double-cursed, first with odd man out (if, as Parker insisted, there had been seven), and then, when four of the originals disappeared, with three on a match. But then I saw the ridiculousness of the entire situation. I'd been had, pure and simple, by that plump little penguin Turvie, and, indeed, had all the way.

"Gone?" I replied when I had my wits back about me. "Utterly gone from the picture? Parker, oh Robert Parker if that is even your real name, you clever devil, it's taken me this long, but I've finally caught up with your scheme!" I rattled on now that I was confident I completely knew the score. "This is such an elaborate way to pull my leg. Of course, it has to be! That chubby, tubby little Turvell put you up to this! God-in-his-holy-heaven-damn!

Good old Clarence! I never thought he had it in him!"

I had to laugh, and out loud, to boot. I'm normally a humorless person, ask anyone who knows me, but I'd been so completely, so utterly had, that this was ridiculous.

Parker must have been under specific instructions, because he couldn't let go the gag even after I'd uncovered his magnificent deception. In the next moment, he smashed his precious old picture on the floor in front of me, crying, "Wrong, Doctor! Wrong!"

"There's no need to shout, Robert. I know when I've been taken for the fool. I admit it. You fellows have got me, absolutely."

Parker stood before me, the absolute picture of rage, his thin face twisted into some grotesque mask and every vein on his neck bulging. It was one of those moments when I actually wished I'd gone ahead and gotten that license to carry a pistol. I remained seated, there being really nothing else I could do. My hands, I must confess, were shaking, and in the next moment the forgotten china cup slipped from the saucer and crashed with a splatter on the floor.

Ignoring the cup disaster, Parker glared down at me, his red face filled with menace. "My picture had seven people in it!" he shouted. "I want them back!"

He was probably upset because I'd found him out. Probably wasn't going to get as big a paycheck from Clarence as he had hoped for. Crazy actors—I have met quite a few of them in my trade, actually.

I had to do something, or the next thing he was going to throw around was me.

On the other hand, I've been a psychiatrist for a long time, and I'm fairly competent at it; words are my weapons, you know. Even after his game had been uncovered, Robert apparently had to play out his game, and that meant, so too did I. And why not? What could it hurt?

"Calm down, Robert," I said. "You can't be serious. I mean, it's been a long, long time. Perhaps you remember the photograph as having all the members of your old army crew in it, when it is actually some other picture taken from the same roll, probably tucked away in an old photo album somewhere."

With that, the iron seemed to drain out of him. He retreated behind his desk and slumped into his swivel chair.

"I remember it because that's the way it was," he said finally in a weak voice.

"No sense arguing about it," I soothed in my most professional manner. "Your mind saw it that way. No one else knows the photograph, I presume. Why worry about it? Remember, past is past—we all have to strive to live in the present, Robert."

"That's not all," he said. His voice sounded hollow, like it was coming from a dark and empty cave.

"What else, Robert?"

"Since that old man—disappeared me, I've been invited to four funerals."

That did it for me. That Clarence really was a topper. I never was one to play pranks, but I was going to go out of my way to get him for this one.

"No, no," I said, shaking my head and waving Parker-the-Dick to silence before he could continue. "As your practicing psychiatrist, please allow me to guess. Trumpet intro, Ta Daaa! It was the four friends from your photograph!"

"Exactly." His voice was very quiet, always a warning trigger to be very, very careful. Perhaps Turvell hadn't told this actor when enough was to be enough. Or maybe, God only knows, Parker was one of that rare breed who got stuck in a part and couldn't get out. Whatever, the tone of his voice made me edgy enough to want to continue to play along, at least until I could make a half-way civilized run for the door.

I had another six or seven minutes to go. I tell you any shrink worth his couch could get through that.

"Allll-rightie," I soothed. "Ahh, what do we do now?"

He looked at me, and a ray of hope seemed to glimmer somewhere deep inside the dark clouds of his despair. "Maybe—maybe you could talk to them for me?"

"And tell them—what?"

"Well, I think tell them that it's all a mistake. I didn't mean to get her pregnant, didn't mean for her to die. And I'd like to at least see my kid sometime. I don't even know if it's a boy or girl."

My one o'clock had cancelled that morning, Mrs. Buzby choosing to have her silver locks blued rather than her brains aired out, so I had an open hour and nothing to lose. The nub of it was, I agreed to go with Parker.

To me, it felt a bit like being part of a play and knowing you were in the show and still not knowing how it was all going to turn out, maybe like some murder mystery on a train, only without the train, if you know what I mean. I got my coat from its place next to the top hat and the ostrich boa on the coatrack while Robert replaced two of the shortest candles from the group around his gold flaked statue of the fat holy man, and then he locked up his shop and I accompanied him across the street to the Hai Cua restaurant. The trip was uneventful, except that he made a big show of finding a $100 bill. I don't mean he did it up grand; in fact, he didn't seem to be enjoying the part. But he did make sure I saw that he had found the money.

Once inside the Hai Cua, a middle-aged Oriental woman greeted us. Her smile was pleasant if not genuine - who can tell with an Oriental - and she led us back to a table in a surprisingly large dining room muted with sea-green colors on the walls.

"It's her. She's the mother," Parker whispered as we followed her into the room. We sat across from each other at a table for four, and a fellow in a high-collared silk jacket brought us a thick china pot, turned over our thick china service and poured us each a cup of steaming green tea.

"I'm sorry about that rare cup I broke back at your place," I said. "However, it really was your fault, over-acting like that."

"It doesn't matter, Doc," Parker replied with his nasty little gasp of a laugh. "Talk to Mamma San for me."

She stood at our side, ready to take our order. No time like the present, I thought. Admittedly, it's not what a psychiatrist usually does, involving him or herself in the life of a patient, but I had by this time stopped thinking of Robert Parker as my patient. He was an actor in a game, a trick being played on me by some rather inconsiderate Yalies and former associates. If he still insisted on playing the game, then I would roll the dice and see where it went. Nobody would ever call me a bad sport!

I pointed to my companion and said to the woman, "Mr. Parker here tells me he dated your daughter, then got her pregnant and then she died, and now there's some type of a disappearing curse on him."

The woman gave me her smile, which on closer inspection seemed thin as a knife edge.

"That all true," she said. "What is your question?"

She smiled again, and this time the smile seemed blander, perhaps even less pleasant, if that could be possible. We generally assume a stranger's smile to be something nice or kind, but one never knows. Or maybe it was simply that her expression looked a little forced because now I knew it was all a game.

I clapped my hands, pretending to be delighted. "Ohh, I see now. You guys are all in on it!"

Her smile broadened and she eyed me with an expression that might have been mistaken for pleasant, were it not for the sharpness in her eyes.

"You are friend of Mr. Parker?" she asked.

"No!" Parker threw out a hand and tried to interrupt. "For God's sake, man—say no!"

I reached across the table and patted his forearm in my most professional manner, and then smiled reassuringly at the old woman. "I thought I was his psychiatrist, but now I think I'm a friend of a friend."

She thought it over. "A friend of a friend is same-same like a friend, no?"

"Yes, in a way, I guess it is. Are the egg rolls good here?"

"Egg rolls here top Number One in L.A." she said.

We ordered, and I must say, I was pleasantly surprised. Everything was delicious. I don't remember ordering exactly what we had, but the meal they brought out was a feast. I remember thinking it must all have been part of Turvell's gag. I could almost see the chubby fellow down in Newport, sniggering in his gin-and-tonic. As if that wasn't enough, on the way back to Parker's office, I found my own $100 bill, just where they'd somehow managed to hide it, the green tip of one corner of the bill revealed under the back wheel of a grey Taurus.

When we got back to his office, Parker practically begged me to come the next day. I said of course I would. If old Clarence was going to spend this kind of money on me, the joke was going to be on him.

You can pretty much guess how the rest of the week went. When I came back on Wednesday, Parker had slipped the next old photo in the broken frame, and now there was only one G.I. in the picture with him. No more three on a match. I wondered how he did that, maybe by masking the photo at one of those developing shops. Maybe he still had some intelligence friends who were clever with negatives like that. Of course, I didn't say anything like that. By that time, we were too deep into the game for petty accusations. And then Thursday, there he was all alone in the picture, standing in front of the rusty old hangar with his arms folded across his chest.

All things considered, I thought Parker was holding up rather well enough, until the mailman opened his front door. The little copper bell tingled and a sudden gust of wind blew out all the candles on his makeshift Buddhist altar. That sent my client into a shrieking tailspin. As my dear old stage-struck mother would have said, *Such acting like you've never seen.*

I managed to calm him down, I'm not really sure how. I made him sit in the awful little Oriental chair, and then I struck one of his long barbeque matches and lit all the candles again. You'd think he would have been grateful, but he simply muttered, "It's too late. It's all over for me now."

He wouldn't say another word, so after the requisite 50 minutes passed in silence, I stood to go.

"Do you want me to come back tomorrow?"

"Doesn't matter, Doc. Nothing matters now."

"Okay, if you feel that way. Then I won't." By then he'd more than used up the $1,750 advance, so I didn't feel I was walking out on him. But then, I don't know why, for some reason I changed my mind. But when I showed up at the usual time on Friday, Robert Parker, Private Investigator wasn't there at all. The door was locked. I strained to look in through the dirt-stained windows, but from what I saw it was completely empty. No rubble of books. No Buddhist altar. No bowling ball, fake gold doubloons, no Robert Parker. The vacant sign on the inside of the front door looked like it had been there forever. I shrugged and went back to my car. I figured I'd done my part.

That evening I gave Turvell a call at home, but some lisping little twerp answered and peevishly informed me I had the wrong number, as if it was my fault. Clarence Turvell, where are you? I tried the next day at his office, but received a disconnect. Long Distance information didn't have his number. I knew it was silly, but that weekend I had nothing better to do, so I took a spin down to Orange County to look the bloody fellow up. More foolishness! Chubby Turvell's beach condo was occupied by a couple from Chicago who said they'd lived there for two years. They had no idea who had lived there before, having bought it from an agent. That all could have been, although I thought I might have attended Clarence's Christmas party two years ago. Perhaps it was more than two years, as they say, time flies when you're having fun, but I didn't remember Turvie saying anything about moving.

I was starting to head back to L.A. when I remembered his office building. I had been there any number of times, of course, in the old days when we were Turvell & Cartright. It was one of those bright and modern new buildings on Jamboree Boulevard south of the John Wayne Airport, a jumbled attempt at some vague Californian architectural statement sticking awkwardly out of the rolling tan seaside hills of what had once been the old Irvine Ranch in those earlier eras when cows still roamed the land.

Anyway, it was a Sunday and the place was nearly deserted. I walked through the granite-and-marble lobby and took the elevator up to the ninth floor. And Clarence's office was not there. It had been replaced by an accounting firm.

I don't know—I've always been a solid-as-a-rock person, but this particular gag had gone on way too long and I was getting to the point where I was feeling a little frayed around the edges. I wish the game had stopped right there. I wanted it to stop; by then I would have done anything to have it stop. But it didn't.

There was nothing else I could do but believe Clarence was still out there, lurking in the bushes. Okay, the weekend passed and maybe I did drink a bit much, but Monday found me in the office, hung over and full of repentance when I got a call from some hee-haw who said he was from KLAC Country Western Radio and I'd won a shiny new red Porsche and a pair of matching red snakeskin Tony Lamas boots!

Although I found it reassuring that Clarence could be so predictable, he really was getting in a bit over his head, as there was no way in hells-ville that I was going to give that car back. On the other hand, if you split a cost like that with all my old Yalie acquaintances with all their deep old money and inheritances and current runs at the stock market, it wouldn't be so much. The blond who brought over the keys was incredible, and I guess her services went along with the gag.

The next day, Mrs. Buzby cancelled again, something about an attack of agoraphobia, and so, with no other plans, I made my way back over to Parker-the-Dick's office. When he was around, I actually couldn't stand the man, but now that he was among the missing, in a way I sort-of missed him. As I expected, his place was still blank and deserted as an idiot's brain. I walked across the street to the Hai Cua. Mamma San welcomed me with the same generic smile.

"You like be seated, sir?" she asked.

Ahh, no, thank you. Do you remember me? I came in here last week with a friend?"

"She nodded yes, the same blank and polite nod you get from foreigners who don't really understand what you are saying, and she said quite distinctly, "No, sir."

"You must remember him. Mr. Parker. You called him by name."

"No, sir. I not remember that."

"I was here with him! I was here!"

"No, sir. If you not order, sir, you must go. We very, very busy now."

"Wait a minute! You put some act on here last week! You knew Robert Parker! You knew about the curse! You said you knew about everything he was talking about!"

"No, not so," she said with a sing-song finality that I couldn't contest. And the next moment she had pushed past me and was smiling her bland smile at the couple behind me, as if I was no longer there.

You know, I never had what one might consider really close friends at Yale. Part of that was my tender age, of course. And maybe—well, I was always the brilliant, acid-tongued loner. But there had been Buckridge and Horvath, and a few of the others from the honors club—and they must have been in on it, too! I knew this for sure because when I looked them up back East and called they pretended they couldn't even remember old Clarence. Bastards! I'd forgotten how much I hated the whole pack of snobby super-rich bastards that they were! Absolute rotten bastards to play this sort of kid's prank on me. I fumed about it for days. Finally, in a full fury, I stormed around my office, much as I'd seen Parker do a short time before in his own place. Without thinking twice, I took my old class photo off the wall to fling it in the garbage can. To think I'd been looking at those insensitive rich bastard monkeys for almost two decades with, well, at least some mild sort of affection!

That's when I made an arresting—even stunning—observation. Turvell wasn't in the picture anymore. No. No more Turvell. Or

Buckridge. Or Horvath. And when I called the latter two back on the phone, they weren't there, either.

I don't think I have the time to go into the sordid details of my breakdown. Suffice it to say, I was out of it for some time, and my life is quite different now. The one thing I thought I'd never do, that even good old Alice said I'd never do—I've given up my practice. Nothing seems to matter anymore, and, echoes of Parker-the-Dick's luck, I don't need the money. Lord, I'm rolling in money from all the things I've found, or won, or been given in trust by people I didn't even know. I'm actually as rich as all those pricks I met at Yale, not that it matters anymore.

I think you've gotten the idea by now. I've always been a fairly anti-social fellow, not at all uncommon in a psychiatrist. I never did have a lot of acquaintances, and I've always kept my list of Holiday greeting cards down to the bare, absolute minimum. So with a little careful planning, I've managed to avoid them all, even Alice, though that effort took the last scrap of my humanity, if, indeed, I ever had any.

Life does go by outside the door of my condo. Inside, I've stockpiled food and paid the bills for the rest of the month. I've disconnected the phone so people don't bother me with all the things I've won. I've got my altar and my golden Buddha, and I light candles and set out offerings of fruit and flowers, though I'm not exactly sure why, not ever having discussed it with Parker.

If you're listening to this, then perhaps you can visualize me sitting here on the floor in the middle of the soft glow from the candles, looking out to the dark ocean and the approaching fog. For some time now I've thought of almost nothing but my eminent demise. I've wondered about all the ways—does it come with a rush? Will the old Vietnamese man appear—hair wild like a vile devil's halo and waving his accusing hands as he shuffles toward me with his walker, the terrible words tumbling at me from the black orifice of his mouth. Will it hurt very much, the terrible twisting, racking pain of my soul crushed to nothingness? And, most of all, I've wondered how it can be that a bit of suggestive evil, like a germ or a virus, can be passed from human flesh to human flesh with such deadly consequence.

But I won't have to wonder about any of these things much longer, for I've just dropped my tiny palm-sized recorder. I can't hold it anymore. Odd, I can see right through my hand, not through the skin to the muscle and bone inside, but through everything like I'm seeing through a faded old transparency. I'm going bit by bit, dissolving slowly into thin air like the last wisps of fog on a sunny California beach morning. Actually, it doesn't seem to hurt a bit, but things being what they are, if you find this recording, destroy it and never let on that you listened to it. I know I shouldn't have made it, it's utterly selfish, but every man needs some sort of tombstone. Still, if anybody says my name, Richard Cartright, and asks you about any of this, just say you never heard of me. You don't know me even if I carried you bloody through a land mine field in Nam, rescued your wife from a frothing mad pit bull and gave your kid the bone marrow transplant that saved his life. And for God's and your own sake, don't ever, ever say you were my friend.

SEE MOUSE FLY

The wires on his tough little high performance catamaran throbbed and screamed in the wind, and Brandon Newberry felt the skin of the ocean under him as the wave flung him back in towards the land at over forty miles an hour. There was a fine line between joy and disaster, and Brandon relished that cutting edge. A little too slow and he'd flip over backwards; a little too fast and he'd run into the trough beneath him like a truck hitting a concrete overpass. *So what? Life was short; take the joy, 'cause soon enough the train wreck comes.*

He was nearly ten miles out, directly west of Marina Del Rey. Brandon's white teeth flashed in a grin that was mostly grimace. It was his thing, running a big roller like that, disaster a few feet in either direction, and he loved it. He played the way he worked, tough and hard. Brandon felt it was a man's job to be proactive, to take a stand, to put your fist down. People who never knew or said what they wanted? *Well, they didn't get what they wanted, they got something else.* Life had to be pounded, shaped and channeled into the fine metal, into the precise thing that you wanted. That was his philosophy. You stamped the grapes to get the wine, and you stamped them really good to get the really good wine.

Brandon Newberry was a hyphenate. In the olden days, when his dad was floundering around Hollywood, they had called a person like him a filmmaker. But the money people didn't like putting all their eggs in one basket. You could be a writer-producer, a writer-director, or even a writer/producer/director. Just don't call yourself a filmmaker, for God's sake. Brandon had watched his father hopelessly tossed from studio to studio…just another loser, a wanna-be, and then finally a has-been. The son had learned the lessons the father ignored. Brandon played the game and took their money and that was all part of the hammering that went down in his world. Just call him *hammer-man*.

Brandon Newberry wasn't his real name either. He wasn't going to hang on to a loser name. Now, *new berry,* that was something. New, sweet, delicious, ripe for success. Newberry said it just right. It was just another part of the game, what you did to succeed in show biz. And he was a success— he had three pix in the can with his name over the title, A Brandon Newberry Film. True, they were low budget cops-and-killers slammers and they hadn't made anybody a dime except the sleazy overseas distribution people who raped everybody, anyway. But rights eventually reverted, and Brandon still owned what was left of the pictures. He had a master plan. It was going to take some time, but it was tried and true. MGM and Universal weren't built in a day, either.

It took half a day to tack this far out; it would take just over an hour to race back in. Of course, Brandon hadn't spent all that time wrestling the wind, he'd had Rory (not his real name, either), his assistant producer, jockey the P-Cat out this far and then he'd persuaded Mouse to fly him out in her

219

Mousemobile (as he liked to call it), drop him off, and pick up Rory.

It was a tickle to scream at Mouse and shout her down close enough to the wave-tops so they could drop a ladder tied to the skids. It took a lot of bullying, but, of course, he'd had enough practice. If he couldn't push her buttons, nobody could. Once she inched close enough, he would scoot down and clip into the harness, and Rory would flail around for a bit until he grabbed the wildly flipping, flopping end of the ladder and was able to pull himself up. Not the way the Coast Guard did it, maybe, but it worked just fine.

Mouse was Brandon's Godsend, his own special little reward for being tough and smart and a number one all-around good guy. He'd met her in Hawaii, while shooting a commercial for a new pineapple-flavored pancake mix. She was an ex-army helicopter pilot ferrying vacationers around Kauai in that little Eurocopter of hers. Gutless wonder that she was, he couldn't figure out how she survived the Gulf War, or what business she had flying a helicopter in the first place.

Of course, she had her uses and her good points. It was four years later and half an ocean away, and she still had that damn little six-seater of hers; Mouse was frugal as her name, and she refused to sell it, even though he had explained the cash would fund the demo reel for his next production—a reel he desperately needed if he was to have any success with advance sales at AFM or Milan. Her stubborn refusal really pissed him off, but he wasn't surprised. Mouse even rolled scraps of string on a ball and she had a spaghetti sauce jar full of old nails. *Bizarre!* He'd had to pull out drawers and open closets to show people who didn't believe it. Show biz people—actors and directors and finance people he brought over to the house— they never believed it when he just said it. He had to show them. *Maybe in the Great Depression, sure, but who saved string anymore!?*

Mouse had started her one-helicopter airline with an inheritance from her Great-aunt Matilda. Once he'd seen what a little goldmine she was, Brandon had married her and convinced her to move her business to Marina Del Rey, and then to rent the house in Palos Verdes. Her fortunes, now nearly depleted, had funded the last two of his trio of blood-and-bullets movies. He was going to have to move on pretty soon. He could see it coming, and he knew she did, too. *God, he hated this part!* The way they turned all weepy and needy! Not real people anymore; certainly not the sturdy and independent gal he'd met and swept off her feet. He wanted to take her by the shoulders and shake her.

"Come on, Mouse, snap out of it!" he'd tell her. "This is real life! Real life sucks! This is the way it is!"

But he knew he wouldn't say those things. He would likely just pack his things and sneak away in the night, that is, once he got a few things straightened out. There really were fifty ways to leave your lover, even if you were married, which had all been a mistake in the first place. She wasn't nearly the bottomless pit of wealth and funding that he had calculated.

221

Still, you had to look at the good; when he'd met her, he already had Loose Caboose in the can. She had financed Sunny Day Shocker, and most of Righteous Anger, and she still had her little helicopter, barely staying in the black enough to pay their household expenses.

He adjusted the angle on the P-Cat, cutting the wave slightly higher. He was really barreling along, the sail rigid as a silicone breast, the little cat nearly climaxing with the strain. The late afternoon breeze was even stronger than before; he saw it was lifting little whitecaps off the tops of the waves. The salt water was in his face, the sun at his back, the wind whipping through his auburn hair. God was in his place and everything was right in the world.

He'd set up her appointment at the abortion clinic for next Thursday. She was going to keep that appointment, too. He'd see to that, even though she'd tried to pull that old familiar bruised look on him when he'd laid down the law.

"You said we were going to talk about it," she'd said.

"We are," he said. "We're talking about it now. Your appointment is for 3:30. I'm going to drive you. I'll be there, waiting in the lobby. I'll come in the fricking operating room, if you want. See, I'm there for you when you need me."

"I don't want you there."

"Oh, I'll be there," he'd said.

So that was settled. Still, there were a lot of details…he wondered how he actually was going to say goodbye. He would need the good car, and of course that had to be in her name, so he'd have to get tough about it. She could keep his beat up old SUV, which was better for carrying around old parts and her passengers' luggage, anyway. And she could stay in the house. There was no other way with that one. After all, how could he expect her to keep on paying for it after he'd kicked her out? He'd siphoned off money from the daily expenses on Righteous Anger…he had maybe enough for two or three months' rent on one of the high-rise condos in the Marina. He already had a lock on Sylvia Monroe, an ageing wanna-be actress with millions from her now-dead husband. Sylvia had married Sy Monroe when she was in her 30's and he was nearly 80. Still, he'd lasted ten years. Word on the street was, she'd gotten impatient there at the end, had held his nose underwater or maybe slipped a few powdered Viagras in his vodka…or maybe both.

Mouse hadn't believed him when he passed on the news that her gal pal was most likely a cold-blooded murderess. He loved the irony in that.

"You don't know she did those horrible things," Mouse had said, sticking up for Sylvia even though she suspected her friend had become a number with her husband. Rightfully suspected, he added in his mind.

"I know enough about it to make a good guess," he'd grinned, wrinkling his nose and the dimples on his cheeks standing out. He was a handsome guy, and he knew it. Leading man material, except that he froze up behind the camera. He'd never found the right director, the one that could bring out his true persona. He shrugged it off. Some people were better behind the scenes

"People aren't that way," she'd said, still talking about Sylvia the Killer. Mouse could be stubborn that way, talking about stuff long after the conversation was over.

"You don't know anything, Mouse," he'd told her, the old words springing from his lips for the thousandth time.

"Even Sylvia isn't that mean," she had said. The kick was, Sylvia had been Mouse's pal, not his. She was a real estate lady. She'd even found them their place in Palos Verdes. She claimed to be Mouse's friend, but she had been pretty transparent in her attempts to reel in her friend's hot young movie producer husband.

"Mouse, do I have to teach you everything?" Brandon had hooted. "That's the way of the world. The strong take from the weak. That's how life goes on."

She hadn't said anything to that, just giving him her sullen, defeated look. He'd wanted to smack her in the face, but she'd turned away before he could say anything.

It was a perfect day out on the high seas! Every now and then Brandon caught a glimpse of the sharks, just a fin or slick gray back surfacing behind him. There were three that he had counted, and probably a couple more. It was shark season, but he didn't care, he actually enjoyed their company. Like the film business, he told himself, sharks everywhere. There wasn't any danger. He was on his P-Cat, creaming along, and they were back there in his wake, struggling to catch up. Just like the rest

224

of Hollywood, struggling to catch up with the Newberry Juggernaut.

Of course, Sylvia was going to be a colossal pain in the ass. He would have to find roles for her, secondary roles but still big enough to keep her happy. His new pic was an underground disaster flick. He'd picked it up for next to nothing from a writer who needed a few hundred to score some dope. Still, it was a great idea. These picnic people go into a deserted mine on a lark. There is an old legend, see, the mine is haunted. But coincidentally, there actually is an old Spanish treasure hidden there by Indians a couple hundred years ago. Plenty of doomed souls in that cast, Sylvia could practically take her pick, so long as it wasn't the female lead. She could be the older sister, maybe. Or the tainted and doomed other lover. Brandon knew enough not to suggest anything like mother or maiden aunt.

Nothing but the glorious sun and the wind! *How great it was to be young and hard-bodied and in control!* His mind drifted and he found himself thinking about Lulu, his new find. Talk about hard bodies! He'd met her in a strip club on Magnolia Street in the Valley. Perfect, but like his P-Cat, high strung and definitely high maintenance. With Lulu in the lead, Mine Trap would be sure-fire, a boffo hit at the box office. And if he could just keep Lulu away from some sleaze-ball agent who would fill her empty head with all sorts of nonsense, the sky could be the limit for her. Brandon was already seeing her on a regular basis, when he could get away from Mouse and Sylvia.

That was the thing, he already had his next picture in pre-production, but Mouse was holding out on him, at least he was pretty sure she was. It was all he could do to squeeze the money out of her to pay for the completion bond and build a little escrow account to hold the actors. *What ever happened to mine is yours and yours is mine?* He thought they were going down the road of life together. He thought she shared his dreams. Their last big argument, he'd laid down the law—you get yourself un-pregnant and you fund my new picture. That had been two months ago. When he said it like that, she'd given him her burning look…but then she'd kicked in the little pile of money, saying it was all she had. He might have been grateful, but he knew she hadn't even bothered to tap any of her other rich goddamn useless relatives, and she was looking like she'd put on two inches around the waist. Christ, it wasn't any time to have a baby, what with his big dreams and plans at stake. He wasn't even sure it was his kid, though if he ever caught Mouse fooling around, he'd kill her.

He'd finally come to figure out she wasn't very bright in the first place. They'd talk and talk and talk and she just didn't get it. He found himself breaking things down into simple sentences, like an old Dick & Jane Reader.

"Mouse was a careless little girl," he told her. "Mouse went and got herself pregnant. Mouse wasn't supposed to get pregnant. Now see Mouse get an abortion."

She didn't have much to add to the conversation after that.

Anyway, so much for that sharing the dream crap. She really just didn't care about his tough times or where he was going. AFM was in a week. He needed somebody to make sure his pants were pressed and he had the right shirts. Next week a few snips at the clinic, and then he'd give her the old adios right after AFM, before he had to start making his plans for the European show.

A clear mind and a glorious day! Angled perfectly on the slope of the endless 15 food wave, Brandon found his thoughts swinging back to Mouse. He'd given her that nickname, because of her soft brown hair and her soft brown eyes. Once she'd claimed to be so proud and independent— *what a laugh!* All any woman needed was a good man to show her where her place was. Once she was in the harness, she'd been dependable enough, he supposed. A little bit like a taxi driver. That's what he always told her, *You're my taxi gal in the sky.*

And, perhaps because he was thinking about helicopters, one appeared like a dot on the horizon. *Great, the whole fucking ocean to fly over and they have to pick my little corner of the world!* It was probably the Coast Guard. It was too far away to make out any details. There wasn't one chance in a million the chopper would come anywhere near him, certainly not near enough to disrupt the delicate balance between his high strung craft, the huge roller he rode and the ever-stiffening wind. He wasn't really worried about it, but it bothered him. He supposed they had to be about their business, but this was his ocean, his perfect day, his harmony with the sun, the wind and the sea!

He wasn't going to think about it anymore. If he started to let it get to him, it would drive him crazy. He pushed the chopper out of his mind and thought of possible log lines for his new movie. They were on a picnic—from hell! *No, too banal.* A frolic in a mineshaft turns deadly! *No, mineshaft wasn't right, too mechanical.* Lust for love, lust for gold, lost forever! *Maybe that would work.* Deep underground no one can hear you scream! *Somebody had used that already. Damn, somebody had already used all the good lines.* Underground no one can feel your pain! *That was better. Fresher. But it didn't mean much. You're underground and you're hurting...not a very good reason to go see a movie.* He wanted something with more sex, more tits in it. Hot bodies and cold gold! *That was more like it!*

Brandon fine-tuned his angle on the clear wave running under him. He glanced at the sky. He could see the helicopter more clearly now. It looked a little like Mouse's chopper, but he knew that couldn't be. Mouse had lost her nerve for flying over water. His brave little mouse, a coastline hugger! By now she would have dropped off Rory at the Marina and would be driving back to their house in the battered SUV. Brandon had recently copped the keys for the Jag, and he didn't think he would be giving them back.

Of course, he had teased Mouse about her reluctance to fly over water, just like he teased her about everything else. She lived in a world of flowers and sweetness, a bowery little place where everybody was nice to everybody. Sometimes he couldn't stand her.

"It's a tough world, Mouse," he'd told her once when she started crying. A crippled baby bird had fallen out of a tree in their back yard, and he'd stepped on it, an act of kindness to put the thing out of its misery.

"Noooo!," she'd wailed, but it was already too late.

"He was going to die anyway. You touch him and the mother never will," he told her. "There is no patron saint of hopeless causes."

"I don't like your world," she had sobbed bitterly.

"Well, I didn't make it," he'd snapped back. And then he'd given her his litany, the way he always did, "Life is details, thousands of details. I'm a success because I take care of every detail. You have to follow the details; you can't listen to your heart."

"Well, I do that with my helicopter."

He dismissed the thought, "You have a mechanic for that."

This was just about the time they'd started arguing about the money and the baby she was going to have to get rid of. Maybe it was the idea of impending motherhood that had turned her soft and stupid. He didn't know, and he didn't really care. Another week and it wasn't going to be a problem.

He was a little deeper in the trough, or maybe the waves were larger, and the approaching helicopter was riding not more than ten or twenty feet over the water. He didn't see it again until it was practically on top of him, two hundred feet away and on course for a direct hit. *Jesus H. Christ, didn't the pilot see him?*

He waved frantically, shaking his fist and gesturing violently. The helicopter had to veer away. Committed as he was to his angle on the wave slope, sails taut as drums and careening along at max, the P-Cat had no room for any variables. But still the chopper darted towards him like a kingfisher or a crazed hummingbird.

Damn it, it was Mouse, flying back out here alone! Balls in an uproar! What emergency had brought her out here? Had one of her stupid old relatives died? Couldn't she take care of anything on her own?

He thought for a moment she was going to hit the mast, but she cleared it by a foot or two. Still, in spite his desperate attempts to wave her off, the helicopter roared directly overhead, and it was more than enough to destroy him. The down-draft from its main rotor ripped his sail and bent his metal alloy mast like Uri Geller with a fork. Out of control, the sleek hull of the P-Cat lost its angle of momentum and dove into the wall of wave that loomed up in front of him. Brandon hit the water so hard he was nearly knocked unconscious.

He wasn't a fool. He had on his wetsuit and was still tied by his lifeline to the crushed and half sunken hull of the P-Cat. He would be okay, and after she picked him up he would make the stupid bitch pay, and pay dearly. He dizzily reeled himself in and began to pull himself up the nylon webbing toward the one good pontoon that remained. And he almost made it, but he lost his grip and slipped back in. It took some churning around in the icy water to free his safety line because it had wrapped itself dangerously around his neck. Details. One step at a time. He managed to untangle the rope. He lost his concentration for a moment while he involuntarily vomited and gagged on some of water he'd swallowed. *One-step-at-a-time!* he sternly reminded himself. He took a firm grip on the lifeline and began to hand-over-hand, pulling himself steadily back to the pontoon. And just as he reached it, the first of the sharks took a chunk the size of a loaf of bread out of his left buttock. He couldn't believe it. His left buttock, he actually saw it, a lump of raw meat in the shark's mouth! A sense of outrage swept over him. *His own perfect ass!*

He clawed to pull himself up the webbing, but something had his leg, pulling him back. He looked up and saw the Mousemobile heading away, still straight as an arrow as if she hadn't even seen him.

"Mouse!" he called, uttering her name in recognition rather than with any hope that she might actually hear the sound of his voice. The helicopter didn't veer an inch. She wasn't turning around. She wasn't going to come back for him.

"Mouse…" he said again in a voice that was reduced to a whisper or a prayer.

He tore his gaze away from the sky. His bright-red blood painted an irregular splotch in the water around him. Something sharp cut at one of his ankles, and then his right foot was gone. He saw his own ragged flesh at the stump end of his leg, and his shinbone flashed white for a moment in the churning water. *No. Some mistake, the wrong script! This wasn't Mouse. He knew Mouse—she wasn't capable of this, she was a good person, she didn't have it in her! No!* But in another second he was pinned against the black nylon webbing, alone except for the sharks thrashing about in the crimson colored water. No. No. No. Overwhelmed by fear and panic, he was only dimly aware of the eggbeater sound of the helicopter, now steadily retreating in the distance.

THE ADVENTURES OF JACK CHEESE

Chapter 1

What I'm about to tell you didn't really happen. It couldn't have; I mean, it's just too horrible. I was dreaming, and this was my dream: We were back in Southeast Asia, in Tay Ninh province. It is very much a jungle like in the movies out there, with coconut trees and green killer snakes and spiders big as pie plates.

I'm Jack Cheese. No, that's my actual, honest, real name, I guess I had a mom with a sense of humor. Don't know that for sure, she left when I was still in diapers. My pals called me *Cheeser.* We were – scratch that – *in my dream we were* torturuing a poor gook we'd picked up along the trail. I saw a lot of things in the war, but this never, ever happened in real life. If you want me to continue, you've got to believe me. Okay? Okay.

Anyway, the guys in my unit were torturing this gook like mean kids with an alley cat. I mean, in my dream, I was doing it, too, and it was awful.

Pulled tight like that around his neck, the piano wire cut right in and popped an artery, and before we could think to move out of the way the skinny little dude pumped a spray of bright red all over the three of us. It was so unexpected, on the broad green palm leaves, on the rotten tree trunk where we'd tied him, glittery in the tall saw grass, and even moiling down the little muddy brook at our feet like tomato juice in warm chocolate. Yecht! I coughed and sputtered, having taken a spurt up my nose, and in my dream I gave him a bash across his slumped over face. I guess it was our fault; we didn't have any experience with wire, it was just something I won from a Lurp in a poker game. See, that was the real part; I'd actually won such a thing, though it gave me the creeps and I refused to even touch it. Anyway, in my dream, Arnie said shit and ducked behind a tree. Don grimaced and wiped his face, dripping like a butcher.

I felt meat-hacker slide from his oily sheath and become a solid weight in my hand. "Come to papa", I said, wading back in and sawing off the guy's left ear.

"Just one, Cheeser?" Arnie asked.

"Yeah," I said with a grin. "Conventions of war. A single isn't really maiming, it's a trophy."

"Why don't cha just mount the whole head?"

But that's when the dead gook's eyes popped open, staring around like dim little penlight flashlights and finally fixing on his ear which was still dripping in my hand.

"Oh, oh," Arnie said. "I think he wants it back."

Then the little gook ghoul shifted his attention from his ear to me. He smiled, not a pleasant smile. I'm no fool; I backed off right away. A quick glance over my shoulder confirmed that Arnie and Don were gone, nowhere around, shriveled away like balloons with untied ends. It was just me, all alone with the freak show. I managed to get a little more distance between us while the gook carefully took the wire from his neck. *What the hell did he need to be careful for?!* Panic mounted in my throat, and I reached for my M-16 and gave him a long burst, the bullets dancing a frothy spray against his chest. He smiled more broadly. His eyes glowed a sickly greenish-yellow. He shuffled toward me; arms outstretched with the piano wire in the killing position. I managed to scream, "NOoooooooooo!"

And woke with Elaine shaking me, saying over and over, "Jack, Jack, take it easy, man, take it easy." I was sweating in spite of the heavy-duty Los Angeles air conditioning, the sopping sheets a tangled, chilly mess around me. She's something else, that Elaine. She wasn't even pissed off, just shaken a little bit. She got up and put on the water for tea, strong green stuff the way I learned to drink it over there, and we sat on her balcony overlooking the yellow and orange streetlights of the West Valley, sipping the tea and not saying anything.

The mind plays funny tricks.... the skin on my forearms, where they used to stick out from the sleeves of my fatigues, was red and bumpy with nettles, just like they used to get in the bush. I didn't mention it to Elaine.

235

Chapter 2

This nightmare stuff was the oddest damn thing in the world for me. Sure, I did some stuff in the Nam, we all did. But I wasn't a standout. Yes, I'd lope an ear off a dead guy, hear and there just to keep the bad-asses in the tribe off my case, but it always made me sick, you know, like when you try to catch z's after hunting nightcrawlers only you can't because your stomach's turning over and the images in your mind are all wiggly and slimy. Beyond that, the gooks did us plenty, too. They had a tradition, centuries of horror, they had torture in their genes. I mean, I've seen G.I.s cut so bad— well, you don't want to know.

Funny thing is, here I am having these comic book horror nightmares when I never, ever used to dream, not even when I was a know-nothing ten-year old kid scrambling to make a living in the muddy banana-peel streets of Antigua. Yeah, Guatemala. My folks were hippy crossers out to save the world for Christianity. They believed in Jesus Cures rather than penicillin, and they both died of yellow fever in 1955, leaving me $200 dollars, an American passport and a stack of Bibles they hadn't gotten around to passing out to the newly anointed. *What, me worry? No way! I'm Jack Cheese, born to scramble and scratch my way in a mean, mean world.*

In Central America, the good folks wail to a crazy blend of voo-doo and Western religion, and in two months I was selling individual pages from those *miraculoso* Bibles to cure love-sickness, to put the hex, to remove genital warts. Inside of a year I was kick-back with my own apartment and a string of girls who worked the bars. Believe me, I will survive. If there's a way, I'll find it.

I never should have migrated back to the States, but hey, nobody's perfect. Here's what happened to me: grandpa died and left my dead folks 360 acres in Oklahoma. I found out about it in a sorry-but-congratulations Christmas card, sent by that Okie farmer's bank to my already planted parents. I was sole surviving heir, and we're talking about land ownership in America—I went for it like every poor sucker who ever heard of the Statue of Liberty. That's when things started curdling for me. I was seventeen and farming wasn't my style. I worked hard enough at it, but the locals said they never saw anything like it. *Hard Luck Jack,* they called me. I caught bugs, drought, floods and even a prairie fire in just over two seasons. Then the bank came in like the worst plague of all and picked everything clean. I managed to sneak away and join the army. I wasn't exactly broke. I had a few thousand in a Florida bank account that nobody knew about, and a little hand-carved wooden toy I found in my grandfather's barn a few months before it burned down. The toy was a black, pop-up demon in a box, and it was probably over a hundred years old. I found it in a corner of the barn along with a lot of other useless junk, and it caught my eye. It was a plain wooden box, a cube about four inches to the side. There was a little button in front, and you

237

pushed it, and the wooden lid came up and the demon popped out. He was crudely drawn with a grimace rather than a smile, and he was missing one horn, to boot. I guess in the old days, the rurals didn't have much to do with their long winter evenings, though I never could figure out why they didn't just put a clown in the box. Anyway, it was my lucky little devil, and I dragged that damn box halfway around the world and back, for the sentimental value, I guess you'd say.

Since then, I've been up and down and here and there, but somehow I've always been tough and smart enough to see things through. *Street-wary*, you know? And, yeah, everywhere that Jack goes, his lucky little devil is sure to follow. Sentimental? Not a chance. Superstitious? Right on, brother. We're talking about the little demon that brought Cheeser through *the mud and the blood,* as they say.

But back to these dreams. I mean, now when everything else was so sweet, I was starting to fall apart for no reason at all. The real question was How much longer was Elaine going to put up with me? Not too much longer, I didn't think. We were a number, and she was always saying how much she needed me, but face it, I'm just somebody she picked up at a Vons supermarket ten months ago.

How did all that happen? Believe me, it was almost like a dream. But a sweet dream, not one of my new nightmares. Back then, I was baked brown as a lizard and running lean as a Zuni dog, flitting through parking lots, mostly pulling the old *wash'yer windows* scam—you know, where you scare the good citizens into giving you a buck or two to go away? Money-wise, I was doing okay, concentrating on a slow but steady increase in my high four-figure bank account, itching to see the nine turn over into a zero to bring up that big one in the fifth column. I was definitely low-overhead, me and the little demon-in-a-box sleeping in a culvert buried in a patch of scrub-brush pepper trees on the south side of the Ventura Freeway, a couple of hundred yards west of the Canoga off-ramp. *South of Ventura Boulevard, the best real estate in the valley.* It's a joke, get it?

Elaine was an attorney, and when she met me she'd just been passed over again at Benhoffer & Meyers, her big-shot law place in downtown L.A. that specialized in representing white collar fraud. She was in a surly mood.

"Hey, Lady, wash yer windows?" I said.

"*Beat* it, *bum,*" she said.

Elaine could really be nasty. They teach you that at law school, but I do believe she came by some of it naturally.

"I ain't no bum, lady. I'm an *itinerant laborer.*"

I didn't know anything about her back then, so I gave her *the threatening scowl*, just enough to set her on her teeth and then I started wetting down her window as I went into my monologue. It's like a lot of the scams; what you really do is sell guilt, of course, not window washes, and the experience was a lot more frightening when I talked to myself. You can be as whacked-out as you want when you play the muttering crazy man *shtick*.

"Oh, sure," I grumbled, talking to passers-by, "*insult* a Nam vet. *Everybody* does it, why

239

shouldn't she? I've seen worse shit than this bitch can dish. I survived Tet, I breezed through the invasion of Hue. I've seen the worse crap in the world. I'll do her goddamn yuppie window *free!"*

"Get away from my car, you creep!", she yelled. She raised her half-open fist karate-style like she was going to back-hand me.

Just my luck to run into a kung fu nut! I may put on the weird act from time to time, but I'm not really wacko; I backed off fast, the Cheeser Number One Rule being *Fly away, fly away, live to fight another day.* And that's when I tripped over my own goddamn window-wash pail.

Today Elaine jokes me, at least sometimes when we're getting on okay, that I scammed my way into her life—but that one time, I swear, it really was an accident. Anyway, I wheeled over backwards on my ass and the back of my head slammed hard on a car fender as I fell. I didn't go all the way down for the count; as I wobbled to my feet two old ladies were yelling at Elaine and telling anybody who would listen that they had seen the whole sorry thing and it was a clear case of assault on this here poor man. They actually scribbled on the back of a flyer and pressed their phone number in my hands and said they'd be glad to testify. I tell you, dress in clean rags and it brings out the sympathy in everyone. Look, just *do* it—wear worn and tattered jeans, and find a wool shirt on its last legs in the last-legs bin in some Salvation Army store. But make sure they're *clean*, and always scrape your face with the old Gillette, even if it cuts you. You've got to look like you're really *trying*

your best, man, but since The Nam, man, after all
what you seen, man, life is just too damn much.

I don't know the deep inner meanings of why I do what I do, but what the frick-frack, I bet you don't either. Life flows by, who thinks about it? You just go with the flow. Take this nutty moment for example; I got the broad dead to rights, but instead of grabbing up the scrap of paper with the phone number, which is what any decent scammer in his right mind would have done, I calmed the old ladies down and plucked Elaine off the hook, fibbing she was my sister and we were just having a family spat over who was going to be lucky enough to take care of our dear old sainted mom. In a way that was a mistake, because the two old ladies started to pitch *their* rest home which was only a block away and had all the modern conveniences for getting old, and didn't we want to come right over and take a look? I somehow made it through all that, and even started to walk away before I got dizzy and had to sit down. No scam, the real thing. As it was, I flopped down and a pick-up truck nearly ran over my legs.

Chapter 3

Sis figured she'd better get me out of the parking lot before I put myself on life-support with her toting the tab, so she piled me in her dented and dusty yellow Toyota. She headed west, her sputtery car climbing the winding road over Topanga Pass. I could tell she was trying to descretely smell if I had a bath or not.

"If you can't tell, I'm clean."

"Why's that?" she said, eyeing me warily.

"A real bum, you'd have to roll the windows down."

"You're a real bum."

"Suit yourself," I shrugged. "The reality is only perceptible to the purified soul. Plato said that." That was back before Elaine knew it was better not to question my quotes. I never even finished high school, but I read a lot and it sticks like shit on a tabula rasa. Plato was one of my favorites for his questioning the ature of evil. *May we render evil for evil?* And, even more comforting, *Is evil always to be deemed evil?*

"Plato never said that." My new lawyer acquaintance brought me back to reality. Her lip curled with her remark.

I quoted, "'The senses are untrustworthy guides; they mislead the soul in the search for truth.'"

"Pure crap. Where does he say that?"

"In the Phaedo Dialogue."

Some of that lawyerly smugness of hers seemed to replace itself with uncertainty. Or maybe I just imagined it. Anyway, she drove us up over the pass and down into the oak tree cluttered canyon where she bought me dinner at an outdoor cafe. Soon we were sitting on the redwood deck under the gnarly oaks, drinking the house red and listening to the bugs chirp and the idle chatter from the tables around me. Nobody paid any attention to my shabby outfit. In Topanga Canyon lots of people dressed like me, holdovers from the hippies, all of them still squatting back there in the hills, dipping their own wax candles, building bee hives, fertilizing their pot with their own squat, sipping their herb teas and yearning for the good old days, the golden time of free-love madness before AIDS socked everybody in the crotch.

The next table over, a middle-aged film cutter with a sprinkle of snow on his mousy, whisk-broom moustache was cheating on his wife with a fresh, young cupcake in crotch-revealing hot pants. The waiter was a fine example of what weightlifting can do for your pecs, along with a twist of the gay life; I managed simple disinterest without turning him mean, no little trick in this day and age. An old lady with silver-tip hair and trembly frog-lips hobbled in, huddled over an aluminum walker and escorted by a 29 year old wearing weary eyes and tight beach cut-offs. Two frowsy sweethearts who looked like May Company salesgirls tried to hold hands without attracting any attention.

Hey, I had no complaints. The world was at my door and I was being entertained. I'd already

243

made my nut for the day, dinner was on the lady, and chances were, my sleeping bag, carefully stowed behind a dumpster in back of Vons, would go undetected for a couple of hours. Supermarket dumpsters are wonderful providers for guys like me; things get real bad, there's food and lodging under the same tin roof.

The waiter came by, ignoring Elaine like she had the plague. "The *sea* bass," he said to me, "is *really* worth *taking a look.* An *mmmm, so buttery* lemon sauce, with just the *tiniest touch* of tarragon."

"Why not?" I said.

"Bravo. *My* kind of man."

"Make that two," Elaine said.

"Why not," he said tolerantly, twitching one eyebrow at me. I rubbed my chin and sighed, reflecting. *Life is not so simple.* He tossed his hair and danced away.

"That guy really likes you," Elaine said.

"His problem."

"It doesn't bother you?"

"Modern living."

I gave her a little salute with the wine glass. I'd learned more than I ever imagined about yin and yang in Saigon, *pearl of the orient,* where sex came cheap, easy and in endless variations. It was enough to widen my eyes, and I'd thought I'd seen everything in my youthful days as a purveyor of biblical lore and sex for hire in Central America.

Elaine was maybe seven or eight years younger than I was, say thirty-two or thirty-three, with a strong, handsome face softened by one of those teased curl-cuts that cost a small fortune at those chi-chi little grooming boutiques which replaced places like Jimmy's Foreign Car Repair, Orange Julius and Ted's House of Pool Supplies all up and down the now-trendy Ventura Boulevard. Elaine looked good, and what's more, she had *attitude*. Plain print-out, I fell all over myself for her right from the start.

"Tell me about these kinds of stunts you do in parking lots for money." She looked professionally interested, which was good; she wasn't making any judgments, she just wanted to know how I pulled it off. I had nothing to lose, and so I told her. And really, that was how everything started.

Chapter 4

I poured us another glass of merlot from the carafe and shrugged, "It's easy. It's a nice profit for very little effort. You're out in the sun, you meet a lot of people." I gave her the classic, loopy Cheeser smile, which drifted up one side of my face while the other half remained flat and skeptical, "The downside, you've got to think on your feet."

"Always ready to run, huh?"

"You got that one right."

The lady was picking up the tab, so I told her about my personal nemesis, Officer Ramsey.

"You mean, he shakes you down?"

"Don't be so lily-white. You're a lawyer; for Bub's sake, look the part."

"I know. It just seems so—I don't know, out in the open, I guess. By the way, who's 'Bub'?"

"Doesn't everybody say that? *Holy Bub. What the Bub's going on? Here but for the grace of Bub.*"

"Nobody says that. What's he look like?"

"Who?"

"Ramsey. Your crooked cop."

"He's a big, pasty faced Mick. He belongs in Boston or the Bronx. I guess he got misplaced somewhere." I was seeing that beet red face, the eyes hidden behind the curve of his blue blockers, his greying hair straight up and spiky. I'd been sleeping in my favorite culvert when there was a sudden glare in my face and the sudden impact of

246

rough hands slapping me around. There were two of them, actually. His partner held one of those heavy, black flashlights while Ramsey slapped me around like a rag doll. They were going to haul me in until they found my bank passbook. After that, it was all business. We settled on a weekly business license fee, and Ramsey even dusted me off with a few heavy slaps from his big, meaty hands."

"You made a business deal?"

I could see it was a whole new frontier for Elaine. "Sure. No choice. Look, sweets—there's dirty cops and bum-bashers and goody-doers like those two old ladies—but it's not really very dangerous if you know your marks and keep your wits. Stay light on your feet; always ready to drift, that's *the Cheeser Way*."

"Hmmm. Very interesting." She looked at me over the rim of her glass.

"Specifically, what's your interest, m'lady?"

Her eyes were brown and her gaze was steady. There was something intense and at the same time tremendously inviting about her. At least, I thought so, and I still do. If I had to explain this thing I have about Elaine, I'd say we were two of a kind.

"I like to know everything," she said. "Just like you." So over the next few months, I taught her, and, in turn, she taught me.

Chapter 5

It was an even exchange of ideas and techniques. I was a genius at fringe living for fun and profit, a world record-holder in continuous scamming, a prophet of the pitchin' pinch, *how to suck the buck on the edge*—but Elaine showed me *how to manage.*

Only a few lessons and I started to think I had a flare for it. I picked up the basic concept right away, and after a few weeks of intense recruiting at the down-town Greyhound station, we stationed 22 freeway off-ramps in the West Valley with our own "I WILL WORK FOR FOOD - GOD BLESS" soldiers. On top of that, we trained about a dozen scammers to play the parking lots on a rotating basis, about all the West Valley could handle without getting the city council on our asses. We added out-of-gas and dead battery pleas to the wash-yer-windows trick, and put on a thin as a stick woman from Kansas who featured a raggedy little daughter with a wan smile who did a brave tap dance in floppy workman's boots about five sizes too big for her.

When Elaine and I took over, we did have to to shoe-horn out a few regulars, but since my tour of duty in the wet, green killing place, I've never shied away from leg-breaking. In a little less than a month we had our operation down smooth, the whole rag-tag bag bringing in over $1,000 a day, 365 days a year, and every bit of it tax-free, clean, and clear except for the normal payouts to cops like Ramsey and to a few city fathers, which were running at about 20% of the take. Cost of business, Elaine called it.

After what seemed like a very short while, Elaine and I had dozens of imported beer can cartons slid under her big, heart-shaped mattress or thrown overhead in the stoop-over attic above her condo ceiling. They were stuffed with mostly singles which we ironed flat and rubber-banded into packs of 100, and we were going nuts looking for ways to get those greenbacks back into the economy without having to declare them to Uncle Uncle. Another month or two of prosperity and we would need storage rental space, our own little money room.

Never *the fool for romance,* I was bleeding 10 to 20% of our take, so *bravo!,* my private little account at the Topanga branch of Wells Fargo was moving up, as they say, *rather crisply* through the low five figures, and I even opened an interest-bearing money market account at the Great Western down the street.

Before you turn bleeding hearts on me, I should point out our new arrangement changed Elaine's life, too. She paid cash under-the-table for a grey-import Jag convertible (that's not a color of car, it's a way of getting expensive foreign wheels into California without paying for all the anti-smog add-ons). She was wearing designer suits and tinted glasses with little diamonds discretely imbedded in the curved glass, and this time if she didn't get her promotion, she had something already lined up with the law firm that happened to be Benhoffer & Meyers' biggest rival.

See, all any of us ever need is a little confidence. I was born smooth as the devil's son, and as soon as I understood her problem was *simple lack of gumption*, I was able to bring her around. Pretty soon she was figuring she could pull enough business away from B&M to double her salary in the first year. So things were looking up all around.

Meanwhile, Elaine & Cheeser Enterprises was moving out so fast it was scarey—we were dickering to front a low-budget cops-and-killers movie, to buy a string of taco trucks or hot-dog carts, or maybe do a rock concert. You get the picture; we were feeling up the kind of businesses where a lot of money floats around, and a paper loss isn't necessarily a dive at all.

That's when I started meeting all these crazy Los Angelino types. Seems like all you do is coat your ass with honey and the Hollywood slime oozes out of the woodwork. It was worse than prime bug-time in Nam. Elaine and I let it be known that we could come up with a couple hundred grand, and in no time we were fighting off more sleazy producers, directors, actors, song-writers and other assorted quasi-personalities and Hollywood Henrys than I had ever imagined existed.

We never entertained at Elaine's place—us both being a little paranoid about somebody taking a carnal hump on our bed and finding over a hundred grand in little ones a few feet under the festivities—but with all the parties and private affairs we were invited to, it was a load and a half to stay solid with our primary business, which had always been the street scams since the day we met. We'd had a few arguments about it; I thought we were moving a bit too fast. Odd, for me. . . but then, I'd never had so much go right before, not even in the good old days in Bananaland with the Babes n' Bible biz. Like I told you, the farm was a bust, and then I had to leave my stash in South East Asia. You try carrying fifty pounds of gold bars when you're running through the streets of Saigon to save your nuts. Life was sweet right now, and I just wanted to hang on for a while, fatten the old bank accounts, and maybe get into mutual funds and bonds and paper which said right on it "payable to the bearer." That was about the time I met the Manhatdu Radi. In a way, he changed my life. One must not be afraid of change, Eric Hoffer, the dockworker-philosopher once said. Perhaps Eric's life experience has been different from mine.

Chapter 6

Radi was one of those moist-eyed, globe-hopping saviors with his own sophisticated bag of inner-mind tricks, and he always seemed fresh in from a successful Tokyo or London tour, where he'd once again made a killing sprucing up the human spirit. I guess Hollywood party-throwers usually invite somebody like Radi in case one of the guests has a spiritual seizure, or somebody needs a channeler to take a call from Attila the Hun or the court of Louis XIV. Once I met a wispy blond mystic with the *blue sense* who helped police track down serial killers. I didn't like her. She said there was something funny about me. Not 'ha ha' funny, but she just couldn't quite figure it. I told her not to bust a tube over it and when her agent gave me a hard time I cracked his dentures. There was a lot of strangeness floating around the town. I also ran into the 'Hipster Hypnotist', the purple crystal lady, the wizard of speed and time, and a man who talked to pine trees. I didn't consider the Manhatdu Radi to be more or less spectacular than any of them.

Radi wore swaddling clothes and his dark hair long like Jesus. The good life had plumped him out like a mango or an avocado, moving him across the prophet scales from the lean, aesthetic Gandhi types toward the jolly fat men like Laughing Buddha, Santa Claus and the Chinese god of fertility. His presence commanded a sort of respect, but when he wasn't around, everybody joked and called him

Buddha-butt. It seems like, since all those TV evangelists took the dive for lust, fornication and money-changing, there's no respect any more for the *men of the cloth*. All it takes is a moldy wafer or two to spoil the whole communion, and maybe that's not right, but who am I to say?

Elaine knew Radi, and I had the feeling they maybe once had been a deal, nothing big, maybe just a quick roll out behind the assembly tent. I'd seen Radi a time or two since I met Elaine, at a beach party in Santa Monica and an entrepreneur's week-ender in Malibu. He was always hanging around, giving her that moist-eyed look, but I'd never paid him much mind. I mean, don't get me wrong, I've got tremendous admiration for those who work the Fear-Of-Death game. They've got the greatest line going, *Hey, friend, there's one last insurance policy you may not have thought of.* It's clean work, nice hours, first-class travel, gourmet food and prime nookie, and, generally speaking, you leave people feeling better than before they met you. You give them a sense of hope, you know? The big-time grand grifters have it knocked, and even a minor key number like Buddha-butt, whose game was tuning in on the old psyche-waves, could play the cash register for weeks on end and never put a callous on his plump little hands.

On the other hand, I also believe to the bottom of my hard little heart that anybody—even the most harmless little spitual twit-mouse—who dabbles in the mystic arts can be dangerous; you're sitting on the entrails of the unknown, and you never know what warts you'll grow. According to Uncle Walt,

253

even Mickey Mouse conjured up the wicked spirits in <u>The Sorcerer's Apprentice</u>. You really never know exactly what's out there. So it pays to be a little careful. Anyway, one evening Buddha-Butt came right up to me at a party. "'Lainie tells me you are not with the sleeping well. . . ", he said, cutting to the chase without bothering with the opening reel. I guess that's okay. When you are a Manhatdu you can take all sorts of social short cuts. Did the one, true Christ ever make it much with the small talk? I don't think so. *How's the weather, Jeezer? Oh, pretty good, thanks; the humidity's just right for walking on water.*

I didn't know whether I was more pissed at Elaine for making my problems public chewing fat or at the Manhatdu for his superior attitude. We were at one of those bashes where people who barely knew and hated each other hugged and fetched drinks and sniffed from the same straw. We were supposed to be celebrating a Finnish producer's cartoon feature film, but the party was more like a solicitation for funds; the word on the street was the *new animated classic from the Northlands* was little more than an endless series of story boards and script revisions and had yet to go into serious production.

It was a stupid waste of money, if you ask me. Everywhere you looked, grownups were acting like silly kids; a bunch was dropping acid in the dining room like they didn't know the 60's were thirty years ago. Another snickery little group was snorting themselves delirious in one of the bedrooms. They had laughing gas in the living room and cookies in the kitchen and Elaine was off getting herself stoked, smoked, laid or powdered, I couldn't be sure which, but until Buddha-Butt interrupted, I was on my way to find her, and I was even a little worried about it. *What, the utterly cool Cheeser, care about anybody? Naw, man.* Elaine was an investment, and you don't let the goodie what laid the golden egg out to play in traffic.

Radi looked a little lost, like always, so I shrugged and gestured toward a chair.

"To sleep, to sleep, perchance to dream. . .", I said, more to fill the air than to make any sense.

It didn't matter. Nobody ever really listened at these parties, anyway. They all wanted to talk about *their work, their latest role, their new screenplay, their superbly reconditioned Austin-Healy, their greatest piece of ass.*

"Ahh, the Great Bard," Radi replied, standing behind the chair like he didn't know what to do with it. "MacBeth, was it not? 'Out, out, damned spot!' You, yourself, have the red stain upon your palms, then?"

Without thinking about it, I slipped my hands in my pockets, like maybe Radi really could read something in them.

"Okay, Manhatdu—you've been everywhere and done everything—what's your cure for the common insomnia? Belladonna? Maui Wowie? Two belts of Old Crow? Rat poison?"

Radi took me super-seriously. "I do not advocate the chemical aides," he said. "My way is the spiritual road, the way of the enlightened warrior. And then, we do not know if your affliction is *common* or something entirely else."

The modulated tones of his Indian English made everything sound like a polite question, and I didn't know whether it was my turn to ask or answer. I decided on the non-committal approach.

"Oh. Yeah. Well, we all could use a little enlightenment."

He waved his hands dramatically in the air, "Yes, you are right, Jack Cheese. It is true. We all could." His fingers wiggled, his hands fluttering and drifting dramatically downward, "Our bodies, filled with the heavy phlegm, the noxious vapors of our past, become too corrupted. We want to reach heavenward, but we are crushed by the heavy weight of our recollections, the gravity of our past."

"I'm sure you're right; just don't know enough about all that, pal."

He adjusted the sarong-like robe-thing he wore for clothes, "It is obvious that you do not."

What a sanctimonious little prick! But at the time I figured he wasn't really a bad guy. I figured I could see pretty well through his line of fog, us having been in similar businesses and all. Still, I probably would have snapped out something that I'd have regretted later if Elaine hadn't come back just then. She sat next to me on the sofa and took a sip from my scotch-and-water.

Chapter 7

"President Nixon hired Radi during the Watergate Scandal," Elaine said. "Old Tricky Dick told Pat that was the only way he got through those grim days."

"And Pat told—?" I asked.

"A good friend of mine in real estate who sold their compound down in Orange County, who told me."

Obviously pleased, Radi cocked his head at me, a sparrow eyeing a juicy worm, and flapped his fat beak, "Would you like it for me to be of some help to you?"

I shrugged and gave him the little nod that means *you're on, buddy*. I'd become very good at that sort of thing in the past few weeks. At these parties, if you couldn't prove you personally were a dealmaker yourself, it was important to show you knew the ways and gestures, all the nudges, twists, flicks and winks. Ahh, show business. "Okay," I said, "but nothing long-term. How much for a quick fix?"

He gave me a similar shrug in return, the one that intimated my friendship was immeasurably more valuable than mere crass money. He had to know it was a weak gesture; after all, I hardly knew the guy. But, like I said, we all were into these mannerisms as much for the form as the content.

"Who knows?" he said. "I will charge you everything. Or nothing. How about *whatever our psychic connection becomes worth?*"

"I decide?"

"Yes. You decide."

"That's certainly fair. How can I lose?"

Radi's dark eyes took on a great depth and mystery, the sort of thing you can get by making them go out of focus and looking over your subject's shoulder, and I could see why he was a source of inspiration to the wayward souls of our lost generation.

"You can only win," he said.

"Oh, goodie. When do we start?"

"Start by staying sitting there," he said. "I think the best way for you is to get outside of your body, itself." Elaine moved over to make room for him, and he sat between us.

Elaine took his arm, "Radi, maybe some other time. . ."

He patted her hand and pushed her gently away, "'Laine, nothing of danger will occur here. It is all in the mind. I can assure you, I have a flawless record, I have never lost a patient through meditation."

I thought I saw him wink at her. I didn't like the implications of what I suspected was an old, shared closeness. Maybe it was more than just a little roll around the old tent. *Who do you trust in the whole wide world, Cheezer—who do you trust?*

I didn't say anything; Radi took that for assent, and started up in a voice warm as farmyard butter on an August afternoon. He went on and on, telling me that same old crap guys like him always use about just relaxing to tune in to the mystical secrets passed down from the ancients, etcetera and so on and so forth. He got up once and actually lifted one end of the sofa while I was still sitting in it so I lined up with the earth's electro-magnetic power lines. And then he instructed me to be awake while I was asleep so I could *control the drama of the dream.*

I hadn't realized what a dull geek he was or what a boring voice he had. My eyelids felt heavy as bags of sand. In twenty more seconds the party was just a dull bee-buzz fading away in my ears and the last thing I remembered was the Manhatdu murmuring, "You must face your fears."

And then I was back in Soc Trang province on what was just another normal, muggy summer day in the countryside.

Chapter 8

Prick-Captain Bailey was red-faced and yelling and waving his .45 caliber pistol in the air, and still nobody wanted to get in the hole, so the shit was flying both ways, words like *frag* from the enlisted side and *court martial* from the stars-and-bars crowd. I had the certain heavy feeling that at least a couple of our Viet Cong buddies were down there, so I didn't want to go. Nobody would give in, so in the end the squad figured it out by the crazymaker game, you know, *Scissors cuts paper, Rock smashes scissors, Paper covers rock*. After what seemed like endless rounds of stupidity, somebodies rock smashed my scissors and before I knew it I was being pushed toward a square hole in the thick tangle of potato plants on top of a small, fifteen foot high man-made ridge separating two rice paddies. I knew there was a good chance gooks were in that hole because we'd stumbled on this tunnel by accident, one of the guys tripping over the potato plant vines growing from the cover and setting it just enough ajar so the next guy, doing his best to step in the exact same footprints and so avoid annihilation by land mine, sent one foot crashing through and went in up to his hips.

Bailey wouldn't let me dump a grenade, because he said he wanted a live one to interrogate—you can translate that, *torture until dead*—and so they held my feet and lowered me head-first, my big Browning 9 millimeter automatic in one hand and my heavy black flashlight in the other with the guys giggling about what a big prick I was as they pushed me down the hole. I hadn't quite reached the bottom when they ran out of leg and let go. I tried to do a tuck and roll, but only managed to break the fall a little with my hands and to crash heavily on my shoulders with my neck twisted and my head jammed against the mucky dirt floor. There was a gale of laughter from up above, and a voice yelling, "Hey, Cheeser, you okay down there?" The fact that I could have shot myself or broke my neck was lost on those shit-faces. I fished around and found my flashlight, and then my pistol.

The smell of rotting flesh was like raw pus in my face, but I couldn't climb right back out like I wanted. Captain Bailey, who somehow in my mind had become confused with the plump Manhatdu, had ordered me to go forward. *Sure, this was a dream, but I'd never before been down here, in this particular tunnel. Never before in my life.* I tied my handkerchief around my nose, turned on my flash and moved deeper into the tunnel, which was just high enough for me to crab along if I stooped over. Thirty feet in I spotted the first trip-wire, tied to a grenade lodged in a tin can buried in the side of the wall and hidden by a small pile of loose dirt and a thin scrabble of dirt across the floor. I remembered that I carried a small tin snips just for this reason; I snipped the wire close to the grenade, stepped over the wire and continued.

The floor sloped gently downward, and in another ten steps I was ankle deep in mud and scummy water. *What if I snagged a trip-wire under the water?* I took baby-steps, trying to lift my feet straight up and down. That's how I found the pit, my left boot hesitating over a drop that I couldn't figure. I didn't have to feel it all the way down. I knew there would be three or four feet of water with sharp punji stakes at the bottom aimed to spear me as I stumbled and fell. I fished around underwater with my foot and found a wooden ledge on the left hand side. After two steps, supporting myself with both hands against the sides of the tunnel, the ledge switched to the right hand side. I crossed my feet over to that side, knowing I was a potted pigeon if a gook spotted me just then, and went on like that for another ten feet, until the tunnel sloped up again and I was on solid ground.

Here the smell of the dead was so dense that I could only take in air in small, sucking breaths. I rounded a corner and was in a low, timber-reinforced burial chamber, a ten-by-ten room stacked with naked bodies. It was so low my head brushed the ceiling, and there must have been three dozen corpses, although their state of decay increased from top to bottom until the bottom-most were decomposed into what looked to me like half-earth slime-creatures. They were all natives, mostly men of military age (which in Nam was anything from 16 to 60), and they looked like they'd all died of gunshot wounds to the back of the head. *A burial ground for VC executions.* Let me explain; these rural peasants, too outspoken and loyal to the government for VC tastes, had simply disappeared. It happened all the time, all over South Vietnam, to tens of thousands of civilians. *Don't want to join the VC? Good—BOOM! Don't want your kids to attend the VC school? BOOM! Too bad you had your shots at the government hospital. BOOM!* And then the bodies disappeared, never to be seen again. But the VC had to put them somewhere.

I thought I heard a noise, and swung my flash around the room. It was just rats. Big Vietnamese rats, their eyes shining like red beads. *Time to go,* the voice went off in my head. *Cheeser, get out of here, NOW!*

And then a dead gook on the top of the pile stirred, flexed his rotting arms and sat up. He turned his frozen death grin in my direction, and said in his sing-song native tongue, "*Nguoi My!*", which means *Mister American!*

263

Chapter 9

I had nothing to say to a dead man. I started hyperventilating right away, and turned tail to run when I remembered Radi's advice. *Face your fear. The illusion will go away.*

Ahh, it was only an illusion! I gritted my teeth and turned back to the gook. "*Nguoi Nam*", I said, spitting the words out with all the contempt I could muster for these people, remembering their weird curses, their reverence for their ancestors, ancient, moldy green cemetaries dotting the landscape, and their belief in the living dead and everything else I'd always hated about their backwards, god-forsaken country.

He slowly stood up and came toward me, arms outstretched like some jerky parody of an old Frankenstein movie..

"*We believed in you, Nguoi My. You said you would protect us. Have you come to protect us?*" It took some superhuman effort to stand my ground, let me tell you! I felt the bony fingers of one of his cold hands wrap themselves around my throat. I was gagging when I panicked and pulled off six or seven rounds from the pistol. I felt him shudder, but the shots did little more than whistle through him.

His grin broadened. "*Khong chet, toi chet roi!*", he sang triumphantly. "You can't kill me, I'm already dead!"

His fingers tightened on my throat. He was incredibly strong, he only needed one hand to shut off my windpipe. Desperate, I clawed his hand away and croaked, "These are *silver* bullets!" That seemed to work. *Interesting game: It's silver if I say it's silver.* The pistol bucked in my hand and he was flung back in a spray of blackish-green sludge. In a moment he had shriveled away to a smoking skeleton.

"*Nguoi My*," voices behind me sang softly. *"How many silver bullets do you have? Surely not enough for all of us?"* I turned slowly to see the rest of the naked corpses coming to life. All of them were lurching to their feet and shuffling toward me, except for five or six of the most decayed, who were oozing out of the ground and hitching forward on their elbows like lepers.

Chapter 10

I screamed in terror and woke to see I'd brought down the Hollywood party, having knocked over a lamp and crashed headfirst through a glass coffee table, splintering it into shards. What a scene! There must have been fifty people staring at me, and the Finnish producer's nasty blond girlfriend was right in my face, screaming at the top of her lungs about her irreplaceable coffee table that was etched by Franklin Moses or somebody, while I was just lucky enough to be alive with the jagged edges of glass all around my neck like a deadly collar.

Radi was no help at all. He was staring at me with his mouth open, sure that I was going to die. It was Elaine who got me out of it.

"Don't move, Cheeser," she yelled.

She slugged the nasty bitch, and shoved her backwards over a sofa. Then, working bare-handed, she removed the pieces of glass, one by one. Radi nearly killed me trying to help, but she barked at him and he retreated a few stepsl and let her do the work herself. Once I was free of the dangerous splinters, Elaine got me up and took me by the arm, leading me to the bathroom where she picked the glistening bits out of my face and arms and cleaned off most of the blood. The damage was nothing serious, particularly compared to what it could have been. I had a few bruises and plenty of superficial cuts.

Elaine got us out of there, and fast. Radi stayed behind, I suppose to explain the powers of suggestion and that I, Jack Cheese had piles and piles of dough (he'd seen us counting and ironing it) and would pay for everything. And he would probably want to hand out his business cards advertising private consultations to those who could pay the heavy-duty freight. At least, that's what I would have done if our situations were reversed.

Chapter 11

It was the next morning, back at Elaine's, and I was shaving when I got my first good look at the bruises on my neck; they were starting to turn a deep purple-yellow. *That's where the gook grabbed me*, I whispered to myself. Of course, that was impossible. I must have hit my neck on some piece of furniture when I was thrashing around.

The doorbell rang and who should Elaine usher in but good old Buddha-butt, all smooth apologies and concern for my well-being. Elaine looked troubled and not all that happy to see him, but he just smoothied his way on in. Once you've got the visionary scam going for you, you've got everybody so worried looking for foxes, they forget you are the fox. Radi sat next to Elaine, comforting her by holding her hand and patting her shoulder while he began his diagnosis of my spiritual malady. The psychic ramifications, the troubled spheres, yadda, yadda hoo hoo hooie. I half-listened to Radi prattle while I managed to down a bowl of Nutri-Grain with blueberries and no-fat milk. Eat right, you know. When facing the mystical unknown, your health is everything.

Radi really was in a high babble. "You were on a trance-like plane of existance induced from the *Para* state of meditation," he said.

"Ahh, crap. How do you know?"

"Friend Cheeser, I followed your being down, down, down to the very fundaments of your reality. That is how I know."

"Followed me all the way, huh?" A dribble of milk ran down my chin. My mother always said I ate too fast.

"Well, what then?," I asked.

"Then," he said dramatically, "I spotted the very center of your troubles!"

"Which is?—or, which are?—whichever is correct."

"Oh, poor Jack Cheese, you must be serious, here. Unfortunately to relate, there is a crack in your psychic universe. Through it, evil spills directly like hot black lava, pouring out to boil in your very soul."

"I guess that explains the heartburn."

He put his arm around Elaine, "Oh, no, Sweet-cake-pie, Cheeser should not make joking matters of this. These dreams he experiences are radiations of evil, reaching out to destroy whatever they can of humanity. I am having the feeling he personally is in very great danger, as well as all those around you."

I wished he'd take his hands off Elaine, but she didn't seem to mind. Maybe everybody hugs and pets once they attain some higher level of spirituality than I've gotten to. I threw my arms up, jumped up from the table and started pacing the room.

"Okay, okay. Tell me about the evil crack."

"Well. . . I went very close to have a look." Radi cast his gaze down at his plump hands. He didn't look very happy, maybe guilty like the little boy caught with grape jam on his fingers. "It was very unstable. I was walking my way carefully through a jumble of volcanic rock. The sulphurous shootings of steam and the wicked smell of brimstone were all about my head like a wreath. I could not see well, oh Cheeser. And then I lost my balance for a moment and reached out for support—and I'm afraid I pulled down the wrong rock."

Radi gave me a soft look of wonder, just a slight widening of the eyes that did more to raise a feeling of alarm in me than any shouting, buzzing of alarms or ringing of bells could have done. He stopped me in my tracks.

"You did what? What do you mean?" I asked.

"An entire shelf of rock peeled off. I heard a mocking laughter of pure evil. And I saw—"

"Saw? You saw *what?*"

"A blacker black than I ever imagined it to be possible in this world."

I gave Elaine an exasperated glare. She shrugged and looked out the window. It was obviously my ballgame. *Why had she done this to me? Was she trying to get rid of me?*

I had a sudden flash of anger. I poked Radi in the shoulder, "Let me see if I got this right, my dear Manhatdu. You went bumbling around in my spirituality. You found a little opening leading to evil. *And you widened it?!*"

Radi flinched as if I'd hit him with a cattle prod. Then he sniffed and straightened his narrow shoulders.

"Yes," he said. "That is the essence of it."

Chapter 12

"I am sorry, Jack Cheese," Radi said. "What we do is not an exact science."

"What you do isn't a science at all, Radi. Look at these claw marks on my neck!"

I tried to calm myself. This wasn't getting me anywhere.

"Okay, Manhatdu, what's your advice? Should I continue to *face my fears* like you suggested yesterday?"

The sarcasm seemed to miss him entirely.

"Ahhh, noo," he replied smoothly. "That would not be a good thing. I have rethought our position on that point."

"*Our* position. I didn't know *we* had one."

He stiffened again, ever the professional. "You *did* hire me. This means the essence of our auric spheres overlaps." He continued, seeing I wasn't at all clear on this explanation. "What we, you and I, have developed is a special para-normal connection," he said. "You must allow me to continue to deepen the channels of understanding between us, so that-"

"*Para-normal connection?!*", I yelped. "Your advice almost got me killed!"

Elaine put her hand on mine, "Shhhh, Jack. Radi is just trying to help."

Buddha-butt was scratching Elaine's back and looking at me like I was some sort of insect on a pin. I could see he was already set for the next

271

experiment. Maybe I was being too hard-assed, but the way I had it figured, guys like him are always fishing around in the unknown, and yet, they're never the ones who get hurt. *Still, what to do, what to do?* I mean, I did have this horror-movie dream problem, and maybe it wasn't the kind of thing the simple Filipino priest over at St. Mel's could exorcise with a random sprinkle of good old holy water. Or, who knows, maybe it was. But the good priest was—*all* the good priests were somewhere else, while the magnificent Radi was right here in all his cosmic wonder and incredibleness, ready to fix me good as new. *The mighty Manhatdu: Have vibrations, will travel.*

So, I ask you, why not? *Go with the flow, Cheeser. Go with the flow.* I assured Radi I would be willing to continue with him, but first, I had more important stuff to attend. I needed a few hours for business. That's the thing about big-time street scamming, it's like a chicken farm, a 7-day a week job, they're always making eggs and I had to get out there and do the collections. I passed around my excuses and slammed the door on my way out. Nobody argued at all that I should stay. In fact, they seemed relieved. I walked down the hall humming that old Paul Simon tune *Fifty Ways To Leave Your Lover.* I wasn't being cool, believe me—Elaine had me plenty worried.

Chapter 13

Six long hours dragged by. Not counting my upset and jumbled emotions, it was pretty much my normal day; a hundred transactions going down, including a fist-fight with a rangy tobacco-spitter from Tennessee who needed his nose broken with the short pipe I carry in my old army vest before he coughed up *his whole due*.

Just when I thought my gig was in the box, I was lifted off my feet and slammed into the side mirror of a big red-and-white Ford Bronco. For a moment I thought my back was broken. My legs felt wobbly and a big shiny leather belt and a holstered .38 went up past my eyes as I slid to the butt-down position.

"Officer Ramsey," I said. "I was just coming to see you guys."

"We missed you, Cheeser. And we missed you yesterday, also. The boys and I don't like to eat donuts alone."

"But I—we just *missed*—"

He slapped me three or four times across the face, *left-right, left-right*, before I could get excuses or the envelopes out. There's good heat and bad heat. Ramsey was the worst. Even after he had the money he couldn't resist rattling my teeth a few more times. He just liked to hit people. I gave him an extra forty and he finally went away. I got up and leaned against the Bronco, trying to crack my back the good way. The sun was blinding and there

273

was a coppery taste in my mouth. People were looking at me so I used the key I'd had made from a soap impression and ducked into the EXXON bathroom on Canoga Avenue. There was blood oozing from the gums around some of my teeth, and I had a split lip. I guess it could have been worse.

Chapter 14

It was mid-afternoon before I got back to Elaine's place. I had a blistering headache and was in no mood to hear any more about the spirit world. Radi was motionless on the balcony, sitting in the lotus position looking out at the blanket of smog covering all the little houses of all his little sheep in the big valley spread out before him, probably hoping the devil would come and tempt him, *Hey, Buddha-butt, all this you see before you is yours if you'll just let me give you a blow job*. But Buddha-butt didn't need a blow job. Elaine was humming around the kitchen, a rarity in itself. I headed for the bedroom, pulling wads of cash from my pockets as I went. The bed was mussed up more than it had been when I left. I notice things like that; I didn't say anything, but Elaine came in at that moment and saw me looking at the bed. She didn't open her mouth either, but her look said it all for the both of us. *We were two alley cats, what the hell did I expect?*

I turned away from her and went to the bathroom, where I took a long shower, first hot, then hotter and hotter until I could hardly stand it, and then jerking the handles and forcing myself to stand under the icy cold spray. Mind over matter. You learn that in Nam. I could put up with anything.

After toweling down, I changed to some soft sweats and reached in the fridge for a Beck's beer.

It hurt, even though I never really believed Elaine and I were a permanent photo on the wall of life. You know, people get attached automatically, like clams, no matter what you do, and did you ever see a clam that could just detach itself and float away on its shell like a little boat, *hey, nothin' bothering me here?*

After a while Buddha-butt came in from his meditations and we ordered Thai carry-outs from the Little Orchids Restaurant. The three of us sat quietly on the floor around Elaine's coffee table, chop-sticking down the thick garlic noodles, shrimp-in-lobster-sauce, pea-nutty Phat Thai and pork-stuffed Thai chicken wings. Everybody was buried in their own thoughts, nobody wanting to say much. I wasn't surprised to see the Mahatdu was a real plate cleaner. Elaine just picked at her food, but Buddha-butt choked his down like it was his last meal. I went back for another Beck's while he vacuumed up the few remaining noodles, and when I came back I was ready to talk to Elaine.

"I think I should leave," I said.

She gave me a wary look, surprise and pain flashing in her eyes. "Just like that?" she said in a low, flat voice.

"The rolling stone," I said.

"I think this is the talking of nonsense," Radi chimed in with that mid-eastern modulation of his which allowed the most peculiar string of words to come out and actually make a sort of sense.

"Shut up, Radi," I said. "Nobody's talking to you." I stood, ready to leave at that moment, "Never fun, the role of the cuckold."

"We never –" Elaine started to protest.

The Manhatdu held up his hand and looked at Elaine. "Materialistic things," he said, raising one finger philosophically. "You must never tell a lie in the face of eternal verities."

Elaine's face went red, then white with anger, plainly feeling the great guru had sold her down the river.

"'Laine," he said in that softly imploring way of his, "what does the casual linking of two corporal bodies have to do with the presence of the eternal oneness?" That may not have been the approach I'd recommend under the circumstances, but it was original; I had to give the plump little swami credit, he may not have known much about women, but he had *guts*. Or maybe he was just dumb.

Whatever, she was about to tear into him when I held up my own hand. "Look, pals—this is getting a little off the track. Elaine, I don't know what you see in Fatso, here, but I'm not in a commune sort of mood."

"Jack," she said. "He can kill you with a thought. With a look. With one little twitch."

Well, hit me over the head with a Chinese gong—now she was saying she was doing it all for me! How long do you think it took me, Ace Scamster, to fall for that one?

"Stick to the point, Elaine." By this time, I was shouting.

"What is the point, Jack?" It was Radi, looking at me with those radiant, soft black peepers of his.

I directed my words at Elaine, ignoring him for the sack of crap he was, "We're all adults here.

277

You've tumbled over plump-boy, here. Okay. We can work this out like mature, grown people." I heard my voice tremble a little as I spoke, "I'll get out. I'll leave tonight. We'll split the money, Elaine. I trust you to divide it fair and square, and I'll pick up my half in the morning. You keep the business. I've been scouting the territory north of here, on the Simi Freeway. I'll recruit my own soldiers and move over there. It was a good thing while it lasted. For me, anyway. Thanks."

I moved to the door before she could say anything to change my mind. I paused with my hand on the doorknob, "Just one thing, Radi. This morning you said you'd rethought my nightmare thing."

He blinked. Maybe his mind was having trouble shifting gears. I guess under all that mental blubber swamis are about like everybody else, with the same basic human desires and emotions. Still, he wasn't too fast on his feet. A casual meditational screw was one thing, but I doubted the poor guy was going to last more than a week with Elaine. She was a piece of work, and even a scammer like me had just barely been able to stay even. I prodded him, "You know, Manhatdu Radi—Come on, where do we find a little Dutch boy to stick his thumb in the leaking evil?"

"Ahhh. . . the dreams." He stared at me, looking bug-eyed like one of those strange oriental carps, and then cleared his throat, "It is a decision in my thinking that the dark creatures are loose."

"The ones *you* let out??!"

He shrugged, raising his eyebrows, "Who is responsible is no longer the question. For now, you must fly away; you must make your grand escape to the cosmic oneness."

"You mean *die?* You'd like that, wouldn't you?"

"No. I am meaning you must meditate high thoughts and--"

"You've probably sicked some kind of curse on me, some little voodoo trick to get me out of the way!"

He fluttered his hands up like his inner gyroscope had gone off-kilter, and his voice was loud with angry denial, "No! I am having no idea of whatever you are talking about now!"

"Tsk," I clucked, "All this shouting. Unbecoming of you, Radi." But I was getting angry myself, my voice rising and rising still higher as the pent-up rage and humiliation came spilling out, "It couldn't be *guilt* that you screwed my lady, or the *shame* you're feeling that I've discovered you don't know what the hell you're talking about!"

He stood and came toward me, and there were red spots on his cheeks and his eyes were wide and strange, "Cheezer. I take your woman. The strong always takes from the weak. But I tell you, beyond your momentary loss for your cravings and your lust, there IS something I have found, something not associated with the ordinary and the hum-drum!"

"Why are you telling me this?"

"For karma, for the cosmic oneness. I have taken, but I give."

"Oh, sure—you decide what to take and what to give!

"You must listen to me, Cheeser! Because of your past, you are well known to-those of darkness!"

I had to hand it to him. Here was a guy that could cogitate under pressure. So far I hadn't paid him a dime, and he was proving worth every penny. "Hey, real deep, pal," I said. "Everybody knows I was an evil, baby-killing monster in Nam."

"No, no, no, no - NO, my dear Cheeser! *More* than that. There were many who killed in Vietnam, as in every war. But it is the very essence of unspeakable evil of which I speak. You will perhaps not believe when I say so, but I have read the proper passages in your name, and meditated long on this, again in your behalf. The very *feelings* are abnormal. There is, in your case, I am very, very afraid, a direct path to the heart of the blackness."

"And?"

"And I now think it best for you to avoid your dreams altogether."

"And how do I do that, Oh Great One?"

"I suggest a heavy prescription sedative."

"Oh, fine. The great guru reverts to Kool-Aid and sleeping pills. Where's the purist of yesterday?"

He shrugged, "An *unspeakable* evil. . . "

"You really believe that?"

"Yes, I do."

"Well, Radi, now that we're *psychically connected*, as you claim, *you're* the one who should be afraid, not me!"

"Not me, Cheeser. You."

He was a smug prick, I'll say that for him. I tried to it off with a sardonic laugh as I drove Elaine's old Corolla toward the Vons parking lot. *What was Elaine so afraid of? How could a guy like that take me out in the first place?*

The waist-high drainpipe was still there, but there'd been a dog or something using it, and it took a half-hour before I got it cleaned out. I went back to Elaine's car for my sleeping bag and hiked a little detour to the Thrifty Drugstore at the other end of the parking lot to pick up a flat pint of Wild Turkey. By the time I crawled into my culvert, the fog was pouring over the pass from Topanga Canyon and the ocean beyond. There was a cool breeze up, but I was snug inside the down bag. *Back where I belonged.*

I'd take a little nip at the bottle every once in a while, but mostly I'd just lie there, thinking it over. I knew in my bones that fat little creep had something over on Elaine. Hey, I was her meal ticket; she wouldn't have let me go without a real fight. That meant she was afraid of him.

It must have been midnight before the Manhatdu's monsters, or whatever they were, came shuffling through the heavy brush along the fence which separated the freeway right-of-way from the parking lot. I guess I was expecting them. It had been that kind of day. There was a little one and a medium one and a big one, like the three bears only

281

bigger and smoldering, and they were orientals—
you could tell that much by their eyes, or maybe,
when faced with the *awful impossible* the mind just
sees what it thinks is right and translates it into
something a mortal can bear without dying of horror
right there on the spot. They were huge and foul
and bloated, and they knew the culvert was blocked
behind me with a thick, rusty grill under the
freeway so I couldn't get out the other side. I'd left
my pistol in the car; all they had to do was wait
until I stuck a foot out or something, and they had
me.

The smallest one was so big that he could
barely manage to squeeze one clawed paw in the
hole, which he did almost at once. My back
probably looked like a waffle from trying to
squeeze through the iron grill. I was deep as I could
get in the culvert, but even so, he was just able to
scrape my right knee with the tip of one claw.
There was fire burning in the flesh and ligaments of
my knee. In the dim light from my flashlight the
wound looked moldy, like it was already infected.
Part of me said, *Wake up, wake up, it's only a
dream*, and the rest of me said *So what? Dream or
real, I'm not going to get out of this alive.* I know it
was irrational, but hopeless as things were, I started
to get angry. I guess it's all in how you want to die,
like that old joke, *Nobody wants to be run over by a
Volkswagen.* Was I going to let these guys play
<u>Squash the Tick</u> without fighting back a little?

That's when I started working over Buddha-
butt's words in my mind. *An unspeakable evil, he
had said.* What did Unspeakable Evils like for

lunch? MacDonald's burgers? Domino's pizza? Chicken fajitas from Taco Bell? The answer rang in my mind, clear as a church-bell. *Monsters ate sacrifices. Munch-a-bunch-a sacrifices, dudes!*

Did I have the courage to present what I, as a professional scammer of little wisdom and moderate experience, might call *my package*? *GO for it, Cheeser. Face your fear.*

"Stand back, I'm coming out!", I yelled. I pushed the clawed paws back with both hands and scrambled out of the culvert. They actually moved back a few feet to give me room, or more likely were just using the space to work out who should take the first bite. Scammer to the last, I raised one hand and said the famous words, "Gentlemen, let's make a deal." And no mighty fist came crashing down—they were listening! *Wonder of wonders, I had caught some live ones!*

I looked over these ugly, slimy creatures, still smoking in their own grease. They didn't wear any clothes in hell, and plain to see, they were all male. Ever see a genital wart as big as a potato? No wonder Rosemary screamed.

I put my hands on my hips, "Okay, guys, anybody going to give me his name?"

They shook their heads no. Of course not. It was an easy gambit. *If you know their names, you've got some power over them.* I shrugged, "Okay, left to right, I christen thee, Gladwrap, Slushee and Phud!" I sprinkled a little Wild Turkey, which evaporated the moment it hit their skin. They hissed and snarled, but it was still my play.

Gladwrap was the biggest one, a steaming hulk with wisps of smoke coming from his pointed ears and fangs the size of a prehistoric tiger.

"You, boy," I said, leveling a finger at his navel. "You gotta lotta nerve crawlin' through a crack into *my* world. What the heaven do you think the Big Guy is thinking about that right now?" I flipped a thumb skyward and did the rolling eyes bit. "Oh, yes. You guys screwed up bad! You didn't even think about it, did you?"

The littlest one stepped forward, "We did not make the crack in the universe!"

Gladwrap slapped him backward. Slushee raised one taloned hand, his nails like three samurai swords, "You not treat us like criminals!"

"Well, that's just what you are, isn't it?"

"You are the human! You have broken every one of the ten commandments, many, many times!"

"Slushee, babes—come on, put away the knives. What I do is none of your business, at least until I die. What do you think the three of you are, anyway, the Big Guy's little avengers? No, of course not. Nobody appointed you. You're on the other team. *The losers, remember?*" I moved forward, pushing both my hands against his hairy green stomach. My palms prickled like they'd touched poison ivy, and his long hairs were hot wires against my skin, but my hands were rough and calloused, and I didn't let on. "I may have broken the ten commandments, but you guys just broke *the big one.* THOU SHALT NOT TRESPASS. Remember? Or didn't Mikie and Gabe sling your ass out of here a few years ago?"

"There's things you don't know," Slushee grumbled, "They cheated a lot!"

I threw my arms out, "Hey. I wasn't there. I just read the book."

"The winners always write the history," he grunted unhappily.

Gladwrap put one arm on my shoulder. My sweater started to smolder, and I shrugged him off before he could do any real damage, "Hey, back off—that's real wool!" Gladwrap moved back a little but he was definitely getting twitchy. I had keep hammering them.

"You're not gonna smirk like that when the Big Guy hauls you in!" I shouted.

His smirk became a joyous snarl, and the three of them enclosed me in a tight circle, "What if we just haul you back, Cheeser—ass, soul and all, back in through the crack with us?"

I had to fight off the illusion. I was falling, falling, falling with the speed of a meteor toward a jagged line of blackness.

"Stop!", I shouted. "Do I have to do all the thinking for you smoking morons?" We came to such an abrupt halt I thought I was in a car crash. I looked up at them from the ground. Oddly enough, we were still in the parking lot. I rubbed my neck, "None of you guys ever hear of whiplash?" I got to my feet, "Seriously—what's the Big Guy gonna say fifty or sixty years from now when I don't show up on the rolls? You can seal the crack with your best brimstone, but he'll still find out. After all, a soul's a soul for all eternity."

285

Slushee waved a negligent hand, "Details. We work that stuff out at Armageddon."

"Uh-uh. No. Not with me." I shook my head. "I'm *aware* now, and I'll make a fuss. You'll have to drag me through that crack kicking and screaming. I'll be belting out the lost soul blues. Even the cherubs will hear me."

Phud sat on the asphalt, where he soon had the spots under his buttocks sizzling. He looked lost and helpless, while Slushee and Gladwrap walked around in small, smoking circles. "We must bring someone back. It's Lue's orders. You only get a crack in the universe once every millennium or so."

"Okay, but why *me*?"

Phud scratched his head, "We go for the worst we can find."

I saw the ray of light and went for it. "Okay," I said, "I accept the premise. But think a little more about what you're doing. Sure, I may have done some scurvy things and might grow into something really impressive, but I'm just getting started. Maybe I offed a few dozen innocents in the Nam, but I was scared, everybody scared me over there. Hell, those people don't even speak English, like you guys. And those other indiscretions, sins of the flesh and so on, who doesn't get their hand around it every once in a while? So far, I'm just your petty nickel-a-shot minor league sin-king. Give me a chance, guys. I have all these *wonderful* ideas. I want to get into movies and business and politics. Think about my *potential*! You take me now, you'll be harvesting the weed before it even blooms, much less grows the evil seed."

286

Slushee waved an angry hand in my face, his sweat leaving little boils across my cheek, "So what you suggest? We already got Hitler, Hedda Hopper and Sid Vicious." The three of them looked at me. I had their attention, all right.

"Well, don't be so single-minded. There are plenty of others, bad dudes who are right up there, far more worthy of your attention, and if you pull a quick sneak play, I'll bet you can nab a couple and scoot back down the crack before anybody notices. If the price is right, I may even be able to put you on to them."

"The *price* is your *soul.*"

"Ahh. . . I was afraid you were going to say that."

There were odds and ends, of course. Haggling, squeezing on both sides, just to see how good a deal we both could get. You know the ropes. I just wasn't going to give them Elaine; after all, she was my main squeeze. We had to go back and forth for almost an hour, but in the end I passed around the Wild Turkey and we all had a swig, though I must say, that's one bottle I was careful to wipe before I put my lips to it. Even at that, I burned my tongue. Monsters! They take almost as much getting used to as people.

After that, I crawled back in the sack where I slept like a log. It was nearly noon when I woke with the hangover of the century. I'd lost a lot of blood from my knee, and my entire leg was swollen and burning like it was on fire. I groaned and held my head and managed to crawl from the culvert without scraping off any more skin.

After a few minutes in the bright sunlight, I felt even worse, but the habits of a lifetime die hard, and business had to be done. I stuck my sunglasses in front of my face and got in the Corolla to give the line a quick spot-check. Surprise, no trouble and everybody was out and doing their job.

I sorted the cash and took an envelope over to the Winchell's Donut Shop near DeSoto, just in case I'd been dreaming, but Ramsey wasn't anywhere around. A couple of cops I didn't know were huddling around their steaming cups in the parking lot, so I limped over, "Officer Ramsey been by today?"

They looked at me like I was carved out of dried dog turd, "Naw. He ain't here. Beat it before we arrest you for something."

"I - I owe him a ten spot."

"Well, he ain't never gonna collect it. Now get out of here."

I nodded—half-bowed, really, edging back and then hobbling off as fast as I could go before they changed their collective little minds. By that time I was coming around; my leg was killing me, but I was hungry as the proverbial bear; I felt good enough to stop for lunch, crab salad at the Pommes Frites on Ventura. It was there I found out Ramsey had been hit by a gas truck. He went up—down, I guess—in flames. There was nothing left. It was in the Metro section of the Times, I read it over a fat guy's shoulder.

After that, I guess I didn't want to get back to Elaine's place too fast. You know, it's the same old advice that always seems to ring true—if you're going to be late, don't just be a little bit late. Stay away a while; better they should be worried than angry. Or maybe I was just afraid of what I would find. Anyway, I limped along Sherman Way in Canoga Park, stopping for a beer in the Gotham Bar and browsing in the funky antique shops; I bought an old red vase with gold plate trim for $50 dollars, not even bothering to haggle, and I stood for a long time with the newspaper-wrapped glass vase in my hands, staring at the posters outside the Pussy Cat theater until the assistant manager came out and shooed me off. With one thing and another, I didn't get back to Elaine's until four in the afternoon.

The rest of the place was okay, but the bedroom was a mess, what with scorched blood all over the walls and a hole burned right through one side of the mattress like something had been crisped to a cinder there. Elaine was in shock, still in her cream-colored silk nightie, crouched on the floor in one corner of the bathroom. I got her cleaned up and dressed, and I tried to be nice to her, but I could see it was going to be a long haul.

It actually took about a month before she started to come out of it, to get back to worrying about her promotion and stuff like that. I knew she was finally on the mend when she came to me wondering how come, if the Simi Freeway was such a hot deal, we didn't expand up there? You got to hand it to them; for all their wailing and screaming, women are really resilient.

It's been two years now, and I've started to feel like maybe the two of us are going to make it after all. We did expand up to Simi for a while, but we're not into the freeway offramp scams any more—we sold out to a young couple from Little Rock, Arkansas. Not a bad deal; low six figures and 10% off the top for the next three years.

We're moving into *show biz*, the movie distribution game being the next scam up the ladder. We didn't *directly* do any business with that Finnish guy or his bitchy girlfriend, though we did pick up the rights and finally complete his feature. Seems they were filming volcanics in Hawaii and the lip-edge where they were standing broke off and they fell right into the molten red soup. That was our first "big break", as they say, though since then I seem to have developed a sixth sense for picking winners, usually horror movies, and if you look at the numbers you'll see that's no joke, pal.

Something else—believe it or not, night after night, I've been sleeping like a baby. Honestly, my head hits that old goose-feather slab and my mind goes blank as a baby's. I haven't had a single bad dream, not once. Isn't that the dinger?!

It did take a long time for my knee to scar over, and you know, sometimes when I'm reviewing our deal and looking for loopholes that's the one thing that comes to mind. The three smoldering bumblers really did try to take my leg. I hired a lot of docs, and they stitched it and poured in every antibiotic known to man, but nothing seemed to help. For months it just got worse and worse, opening back up with the green stuff running down my leg into an uncomfortable little puddle in my shoe. I refused to let the docs chop me at the knee, even when it got so bad it looked like the whole leg was about to *putrefy*. That made me furious. You can correct me if you think I'm wrong, but I thought the deal was, *Buddha-butt and the others for me—<u>all</u> of me, not just a part.* But you know how scammers are, always holding out that last little bit, and I guess the Unspeakables are just like anybody else when it comes to that. One Sunday morning I'd finally had enough. *Who in Buddha-Butt's name did they think they were dealing with, anyway? I'm the guy who sold curses straight out of the Bible before I was old enough to jack off, almost.* I pulled on my favorite hooded sweatshirt and a pair of runner's shorts and went down to St. Mels. I waited at the front door until nobody was looking and then moved as fast as I could drag myself over to the little brass fount bolted to the wall. The second I got there, I scooped right in and tossed a big handful of holy water on my knee. That water bubbled and burned like acid, but I tell you, new skin started to form that very night. Although, to tell the truth, in spite of the thick, rope-like scar, I don't think it's ever really healed inside. We don't talk about it, but Elaine has that feeling, too. I know she does, the way she sometimes looks at me.

THE END

ABOUT THE AUTHOR

John Klawitter has been a writer, director and filmmaker in Chicago, Detroit, New York, San Francisco and mostly Hollywood for over 40 years. As a documentary filmmaker he won an EMMY for "Scene: Politic". Many of his books, both fiction and non-fiction have won awards. Credits lists of his work are available at www.amazon.com/author/johnklawitter, www.imdb.com, www.ascap.com and www.dga.com.

www.ingramcontent.com/pod-product-compliance
Lightning Source LLC
Chambersburg PA
CBHW051245260626
47162CB00002B/615